Out of Office

Mark Piggott

Legend ▮ Press

Independent Book Publisher

Legend Press Ltd, 2 London Wall Buildings,
London EC2M 5UU
info@legend-paperbooks.co.uk
www.legendpress.co.uk

British Library Cataloguing in Publication Data available.

ISBN 978-1-9065581-3-0

Set in Times
Printed by JF Print Ltd., Sparkford.

Cover designed by Gudrun Jobst
www.yotedesign.com

Legend Press

Independent Book Publisher

Also by Mark Liam Piggott:

Fire Horses

Reading Fire Horses is like riding pillion on a
motorbike driven by a poet.
Jonathan Trigell

Passionate, powerful, poetic a fine debut
from an original talent.
John King

(published by Legend Press 2008)

www.legendpress.co.uk

This book is dedicated to my wife, Lynda, and children, Emma and Sean; to my mother, Sandra, and my father, Michael; to auntie Tim and uncle Kate Down Under; to Tom at Legend, for his continued support and courage; to Pat and Dee, with apologies; and to Hilda and Des, for giving me some invaluable time and space – R.I.P.

'Where did you go, when did I lose you?
Was it all my fault, did I fail to amuse you?
Whatever happened to all the love we shared?
When was it love, when you decided not to care?'
– Ben Marron, **Chronology**

'Sun and moon, sun and moon, time goes'
– John Updike, *Rabbit, Run*

Hook's had this recurring dream – or is it fantasy? – almost ten years, since rescuing Monica from America. He's a stewardess on a 737 into JFK, tottering along in way too high heels, uniform too short, balls swinging low, Sharon and Arafat sneaking a peek as he demonstrates the life jacket. He's serving drinks, pushing a trolley down the aisle, the passengers a motley crew of Rabbis and Mullahs, the Reverend Jim Jones playing poker with the Dalai Lama while Ian Paisley sets light to the Pope's Y-fronts singing "goodness gracious great balls of fire".

When he gets a call up to the cabin, Hook pushes open the door and sees the pilot, Osama bin Laden, and co-pilot Mohammed Atta, grinning childishly as they steer toward the Twin Towers. He pleads with them to change their minds but they won't. So, decapitating them with pallet-knives, he takes up the controls, turns the plane on its side so it passes between the two buildings and, because this is a dream/fantasy, moments later he's over DC.

Down on the White House lawn he sees the Bushes having their barbecue, Blair in shorts turning the sausages, Thatcher bronzing herself in a leopard-skin bikini, venerable guests including Jerry Falwell and Jimmy Swaggart, shade-wearing CIA men paddling in the duck pond with rolled-up trousers.

Sometimes at this point he has a long, impassioned debate with the head of Atta about theology, politics and nihilism; sometimes Atta's corpse hands him a cluster of children's balloons in the shape of animals so he can float away. He *never does – he must stay on course, see this one through.*

Hearing the incoming thunder Blair looks up into the clear blue sky, fork in hand, to see the plane coming right for him. It's not too late to pull out of the dive, Hook has full control, but this is what he wants. None of these people have ever spoken for him and never will. Even as he sees the whites of Blair's eyes and Hook screams with exhilaration and terror, he knows he's doing something good for the first and last time in his lousy life.

Monday 21st June

Just as the plane hurtles into the White House, Hook is shanked awake by a sharp pain in the abdomen and opens his eyes on a world of fire. Orange sprites dance on the ceiling and pins of sweat puncture his forehead. He lies on his back dazed and spread-eagled as if nailed to the mattress by his own inertia.

Hook shivers. When he'd given up waiting for Monica it was too hot for sheets, but at some point overnight the building's mediaeval aircon had ground into action and now he feels exposed, naked and gleaming like a beached fish on a pebble strand. Fiery ripples wash over the ceiling like water on glass.

Throwing his left leg out of bed Hook steps on an upturned plug. With a yelp he hops naked to the window and pulls up the blind with trembling fingers. The room is dark; he has no reflection. Pushing the panes apart and sucking in the fetid summer air he looks out on the patchwork lights of London.

Beyond Canary Wharf and the Olympic stadium to the east, an ethereal glow flares brighter than all the streetlamps and milky stars in the light-tainted sky. Hook looks at the LED clock beside the bed, beneath the wedding photo on the wall – Hook and Monica smiling outside a country church, the words digitally imposed: *THE HONEYMOON NEVER ENDS*.

Too early for the sun: must be another bomb.

Impossible to say whether it's the liver-pains or the familiar *crump* that jerked Hook out of his dream. From his eyrie the damage seems limited: a faulty car bomb or a quarantined suicide bomber, the latest in a line of hopefuls failing their audition.

Whenever Hook hears about suicide bombers he feels mildly vexed until he reminds himself of phosphorous sprinkled on Fallujah, bulldozers flattening Gaza. He feels sadness for the irrational, desperate act and for those left behind but he quickly moves on. Yet this morning he's hopeful this latest bomber has succeeded in his task of shutting down the city, shorting all the circuits, because then Hook won't need to go to work.

He rolls over towards Monica but there isn't even a warm hollow in the mattress to wallow in. So, ducking beneath the meringue duvet, he closes his eyes and the converging sirens and flashing lights of the various public services are sucked down into the languid vortex of his dreams. If Monica was here maybe they'd spoon sleepily as the sun rose, but she's out and about and, for all he knows, screaming in agony in some gutter as stray dogs fight over her entrails.

He's almost returned to his own secret place when Hook feels himself ripped back into the world by a sordid revelation. Monica's fucking someone else and there's nothing he can say or do to stop her guiding this faceless stranger deep inside. The images gain colour, setting, plausible plotline; he watches Monica unzip her own skirt and unbutton her blouse, hold someone else's cock, take it in her mouth and dribble seed down her chin.

He tries to refocus. Another side-effect of Hook's coerced sobriety has been an insomnia that seems to get worse the longer the heatwave sucks all the moisture out of the city. As Hook lies on his back listening to the slumbering giant rouse, he imagines the planet's a gigantic bowling-ball tumbling down a celestial avenue of stars; pre-PC Cherokees have ripped off his eyelids and he's strapped to this turning world unwillingly ogling the orange haze on the horizon, praying it's a bomb but knowing it's the sun.

Hook calculates the number of spins behind him and those still ahead. He's survived 13,601 turns of the earth on its axis and 37 orbits of the earth around the sun, and (assuming he makes three score and ten) has 11,966 days and 33 orbits left.

The sirens fade like the end of a song, like the end of something good, leaving only that dawning silence into which Hook imagines omens. Maybe the sound that woke him wasn't a bomb? But of course it was: what other unnatural force sends orange flares and deadbeat crumps across the sleeping miles?

Now Hook finds himself fervently desiring explosions; then perhaps something will give, the storm will break. Why does it never rain? A few nights ago a great black cloud settled almost on the balcony, its smoky fingers prying open the windows, and there was cacophonous thunder. Yet not one drop fell against the dirty glass.

His alarm pips metronomically and now fatigue harasses him, like a guest Hook hoped would come to the party but only turns up as he's off to bed. Pulling on his gown he pads to the cold white kitchen, yawns, weighs and flicks the kettle. Hook has his finger on the radio button but then he notices Shelley's door is closed. He can't let his daughter see him like this, frazzled, missing, distracted by her absent mother, so he twirls the volume to a notch above zero.

The voices on Radio 4 discuss the failed bomber; he was driving a stolen gas tanker and exploded dismally and prematurely on an industrial estate – singularly inept even by recent standards. This is the latest in a series of incidents in which only the bomber has died: cue the mocking columns, the jokes on *Mock the Week*. Hook wishes the plot had worked, sucked a few commuters into its commotion, just to wipe the smile off their smug English faces.

'...*plans for a multi-denominational prayer of peace, which will take place at the Olympic Hall next week, seen by many as a symbolic and neutral venue where people can come together whatever their...*'

Hook tweaks to zero. As he waits for the digital whistle, Hook inspects the two goldfish in the tank on the breakfast bar, christened Ken and Deirdre by Shelley: twins that fuck. He taps the tank lid and they rise blindly to the surface, mouths frantically popping. To Hook there's something depressing about captive fish, the way they swim around in their own slime all day, waiting for the hand of god.

His hibernating laptop sits next to the fish tank, the pixelated fish of its aquarium screen-saver keeping Ken and Deirdre shallow company as it re-charges. As a teabag stains the boiled water, Hook logs on and, apart from the usual cries for help, sees a new message from Karen flagged red:

Chris has your pass arrived yet? Let me know if not URGENT.

His stomach rumbles, but the toaster remains unfixed and as there's no gas he can't make toast. Hook curses the bomber for spoiling his breakfast. He's late for work and the longer he dawdles the greater his chances of bumping into Shelley – or Monica. He doesn't need that: his cheating wife's averted eyes and laddered stockings she no longer wears for him, bleeding someone else's semen or, worse, fresh from someone else's shower.

At least with sobriety, mornings are bearable. He likes the apartment at this hour, the rising sun sieving through the curtains to his left, the great blank screen straight ahead, and on the right-hand wall the Van Gogh self-portrait above the computer desk. Drinking black tea, brain blank, Hook looks up and Van Gogh's haunted eyes stare back.

In the empty bedroom Hook dresses quickly in a white shirt

and dark trousers and decides to risk a shave. There's no hot water in the tiny en-suite so he carries the kettle through and fills up the sink. As he lathers his face Hook inspects himself sadly.

The stranger in the mirror has mileage: 13,601 turns on the clock. This time-traveller is tall, skinny, lips as thin as a rubber band. His hair's dark, shoulder-length, and unkempt, chin peppered with old stubble, his cuckolded eyes are bottle green and no longer shine.

Too bored to shave he washes off grey suds, threads a blue polyester tie beneath his collar and pushes the knot up to his apple, the tie hard with baked sweat, collars off-white. Grabbing the Librium bottle from the cabinet he returns to the kitchen and swallows two tablets with cold tea.

Slipping into his jacket and grabbing his essentials Hook walks to the front door, raps his knuckles on Shelley's portal.

"Shelley? I'm off. Time to stir, sweetie."

He hears a body or maybe two shift on a mattress, sheets rustling, but no answer: nary a groan. Hook spots a real letter amid the pile at his feet, a reminder from the mortgage company in solemn red. Stuffing it in his jacket Hook slams the door, sees the lift down the corridor is cordoned off and walks tentatively down the echoing back stairs. He's always been bad with staircases and escalators: some minor vision problem that confuses his addled head.

As he exits Liddle Towers and walks through the drab gardens an urgent sensation makes Hook look up. A lump of concrete is falling towards him out of a clear blue sky and he dives out of the way as it explodes with a great boom on the pavement, inches from his cowering body.

Breathless, heart speeding, Hook backs away and squints up the tall building, but sees no-one lurking on balconies, no sniggering kids with time to kill. Left hand clutching his chest and taking deep breaths, he sits on the bench in the gardens that skirts the twenty-storey block. The apartments are a few years old and already showing signs of neglect, but he's never heard of anything like this.

Maybe the residents' committee are taking revenge for his voting to admit refugees to the block. Or maybe this message hasn't come from the Towers, but from the heavens: he without sin, all that malarkey...

Holding up his left hand, weighted down by his heavy wedding ring, Hook sees he's shaking. On trembling legs he walks over to the point of impact. Concrete has spread in all directions like a Damien Hirst spin-painting, the block practically vaporised, and there's a strangely inconsequential dent in the pavement.

Hook glances over at a CCTV camera above the main entrance but it's still broken. Uncertain what to do, determined to do something, he pulls his BlackBerry from his jacket and takes a photograph; a fly lands on the lens. His heart still cutting his ribs, he shakes his head again and exits the shade of the gardens for the burning street, shivering with shock yet sweltering in his jacket.

Tasting blood, Hook hurries up the car-jammed high road selling international phone cards, newspapers, fast fried food. The heat makes the thin material of his trousers stick to the hairs on his legs. Hook's halfway to the tube before realising he's forgotten to thread a belt through his trousers; his arse sags with gravity as if gravity has nothing better to do than drag him down.

The secondary school across the gang-banged high street is half-term silent. There's something desolate about an empty playground, Hook decides – a no-man's land where warring postcodes meet to powwow. Shelley never speaks to the glowering hoods who loiter beneath the stairs of the main block but it doesn't keep her safe: nothing does, apart from her father's money, the same magnet that draws them close.

'Taxing', the hoods call it: reparation for injustices inflicted upon their ancestors by Shelley's privileged bloodline. Hook has always found this notion shocking but now feels indignant; when are the Algerians paying up for our Cornish lassies, where should he post the invoice?

Between his building and the tube there are two pubs, two wine bars, three dedicated offies and a constantly-changing number of supermarkets, newsagents, kebab shops and cafes which sell alcohol. Hook counts them as he does every day, but for some reason he doesn't feel the usual virtuous pride: he feels a deep shame that he's given up.

Outside the derelict Woolies, cops have erected knife arches like the ones in airports. From this angle it seems that if he steps through one he might enter another dimension. Hook walks towards the barrier and a cop waves him through. But when he gets to the other side and opens his eyes he's still in north London.

As he crosses at the lights he fishes in his pockets for change for the garrulous kid with *Big Issues*. For as long as he can recall Hook has given the kid two pounds for a one-fifty magazine that's worthless and which he leaves on the tube unopened. Somewhere along the way the kid's smile of appreciation became a surly nod; he suspects if he now handed over the cover price the kid might get angry.

Hook's so busy feeling in his pocket for the right coinage that he slips in some dog shit and twists his ankle. This is the moment all the minor irritations of his life combine to become something deeper, more substantial; at this revelatory point the sum of all his miseries and frustrations are concentrated in his throbbing joint. Hook feels something must give.

The boy holds out an upturned palm.

Hook gives.

Swiping his Oyster, Hook joins the headlong rush underground. The lift's out of action so he teeters down metal spiral steps with yellow edging, a day-glo constrictor corkscrewing its way into the planet. Hook descends cautiously, one hand on the rail, as grumbling commuters fall past and warnings, announcements and regulations tumble from loudspeakers above.

The walls are decorated, dogmatic proclamations in vivid colours. Halfway down someone has scrawled, in large red marker: *Boycott Hotel Ukraine!!* Beneath, in thoughtful blue biro, Hook's added: *To be honest it doesn't sound like the sort of establishment I'd wish to frequent on a regular basis anyway*. He's beginning to think it would have been funnier just to write *OK*.

Near the bottom, tube-noise echoing, ankle throbbing, Hook sees something that makes him smile: a banking advert has recently been removed as another lost cause; the brickwork exposed for the first time in decades and there's a symbol, a cross between a CND sign and the sign symbol for 'anarchy', all sharp edges and arrows; and beneath it a teenage punk has scrawled:

Hook.

In the thirty seconds or so it's taken him to descend from street level at least three messages have been broadcast from the PA: don't smoke, forgotten bags will be vaporised, have a nice day... Hook's oblivious to it all; he's thinking about the spiky child he once was, before he was jemmied into suits, followed orders from above.

When he finally squeezes into a train Hook notes men in plain clothes with bulging trousers looking for someone to shoot. An Asian boy makes the mistake of wearing a rucksack in a public place; the seats either side of him remain empty despite the crush so Hook sits down. The kid isn't grateful, maybe he prefers having his space. Hook can relate to that. At

Moorgate everyone raises their paper as the kid's pulled off the train.

The DLR is closed due to a security alert. It's a relief for Hook to emerge into hard sunlight at the centre of the whirlwind that is the City. In the shade of a building resembling a root vegetable he swipes at the flies landing on his nose and turns on his BlackBerry, but there are no messages to say work's cancelled. A line of buses avail themselves; Hook boards the most relevant and drowses on the top deck. When he resurfaces he's floating on his invisible ship through the crystal canyons of Canary Wharf, like Hook sober and on the twelve-step programme after decades of extravagance.

When the bus stops at a temporary light Hook watches a young, business-like couple walk along the pavement beneath a monumental glass building; in its reflection he sees an escalator inside the foyer and his bus on the street, Hook gazing into space with a blank, urban expression. Then the woman ascends the escalator, the man walks along the street. Hook decides to get his eyes tested.

While he's at it, he vows to get the full MOT offered by the private family health insurance Monica took out against his will – or, as he'd put it, over his dead body. Hook's teeth feel tender and loose, his hair damp and itchy and his ears buzz with tinnitus, his liver panel-beaten by some demented mechanic. It's a bad sign he can feel his liver at all, squatting under his ribs like a troll beneath a bridge.

One morning last autumn Hook was standing in his line manager's office shaking uncontrollably, sick on his breath and guilt on his conscience.

Karen sighed and smiled. "I had a dream last night. I dreamed you were dying."

He'd dismissed it as wishful thinking and they laughed nervously before moving on to important business like how to promote equalities among binmen. But since then the pains inside have increased in frequency and intensity; today it feels as if it's caught between an anvil and a cheese-grater, dispensing melancholy flames and squawks, and though Hook's daytime side laughs it off as psycho-schematic his night-time aspect, the side he listens to, knows Karen's right.

Hook checks his BlackBerry again: seventeen new messages, none from his wife. He's tempted to read the Trojans and trackers with clean, innocuous names like *C-lop* and *xxxsearch*, anonymous death threats from suburban warriors, spam add-ons and Nigerian Laureates: at least they show someone cares.

Monica went to a meeting at her newspaper yesterday morning, Hook's protests about it being a Sunday unheeded. She then text to say she was on a story and not to wait up. He'd gone to bed before Shelley came home from teenager land. He's gone almost a spin of the planet without speaking.

As the bus crosses the moat into East London proper and the drawbridge raises behind him Hook grabs one of the free papers that clog up the city's tubes. The heading reads: *What does your screensaver say about you?* Rather than find out Hook gets off the bus and limps to work.

The council block towers above an identikit high road: cloned charity shops, sports bars, pickpocket delis. Gangs of men hang round street corners in indigenous groups bellowing bellicose epigrams. Outside the boarded-up bank, yobs cluster round a prone body and push each other around, ululating harshly, creating more mess.

Hook looks upward, contemplating the vast building in which he's worked for over a decade. He's startled to find that the block has had its windows tinted: he's never even noticed the scaffolding, the workmen, the darkening interiors. The security door's propped open by a swivel chair but there are still barriers to the lift. The shaven-headed security guard in a black polo shirt raises his huge, bushy eyebrows, and Hook has to fish the Oyster holder from his pocket and go through the ancient ritual of swiping his biometric ID.

The barriers beeps and won't part. Hook curses. It astonishes him that anyone would go to the bother of breaking into an office, but then he's never been so desperate that the motherboard of a PC could change his life.

He walks towards the lift lobby, but the security guard, a Canning Townie who regards people from North London like they're from another planet, shakes his head and holds up his hand, shutting him out.

As he places a huge hairy hand firmly on Hook's chest (Hook closing his eyes a microsecond, relishing human contact), the guard utters one word that tells him all he needs to know about his day:

"No."

From the security guard's terse verbal report (his eyebrows providing additional emphasis) Hook gathers the town hall is closed due to the terrorist incident. He'd been anticipating his brie sandwich from the trolley. Some sadsack who can't get a girlfriend has deprived him of his breakfast not once but twice: his feelings towards the bombers undergo a paradigm shift.

There's no point arguing with the guard. He'll still get paid next month and today's pay-day for months gone by. All he has to do is fill the hours of freedom ahead. On the bus Hook removes his tie and breathes easily. Then his BlackBerry pings and he reads a message:

From: Jack
Subject: meet
Message: Fancy meeting in town tonight?

As if for the benefit of unseen observers Hook frowns. This

in itself is nothing odd; he and his brother meet every six months or so *sans* better halves, somewhere private where they can talk about the old days and swear good-naturedly. But it's only a fortnight since their last drink (if that's the word, as Hook's on the wagon and Jack rarely drinks to excess) – and that was so dull he'd almost taken his own life in the toilets. But right now he's yearning for a conversation with anyone who'll listen, even though Hook has nothing to say. He texts back:

Make it lunchtime?

As the bus sails regally through Canary Wharf, parlous now, devoid of that cocksure confidence, Hook checks his watch: not even ten – hours to kill. He could swim the Thames; take in a gallery or museum; money in his pocket and London with so much to offer a broad-minded adult weighed down with urbanity. Hook doesn't want any of it: he just wants a cluster of balloons to lift him Pooh-like into the blue.

When he finally reaches the West End he withdraws a hundred pound from an ATM, which also advises him to shop a benefit cheat. With no balloons on the horizon his options are limited. He could take in a bistro or brothel, get a tattoo or gonorrhea; but nothing offers him the oblivion he seeks, so in the end he finds a gloryhole cinema off wheezing Leicester Square and watches Meryl Streep in *Mamma Mia!*

Leaving the cinema a good deal more depressed than when he entered Hook checks his watch, curses. London's gasping, the heat and insects sending people crazy, invading orifices, sapping souls: the great freeze of a few months ago just a melting dream. Entering the Coach and Horses he sits at the bar with a juice, remembering the argument he had with the aggressive barman, Norman Something; Monica explained he was *paid* to be rude.

Due to an incident in Uxbridge or somewhere similar, out

on Romilly Street an army check-point has been set up on the cobbles; a soldier peeks into the bar, gun at the ready. Hook emails Jack to bring forward the meeting and gets a quick reply. His brother doesn't mind: what else does he have to do except sit in his big house all day counting money?

Before leaving the Coach Hook turns on his 'out of office assistant' and feels much better. When he arrives Jack's sat at a small round table with his half of bitter and a book in his usual get-up of blazer, shirt, jeans and brogues: more *Top Gear* than *Top Gun*. His trimmed blonde beard's wet at the edges, his eyes nauseatingly merry with faith and the newfound joys of heterosexual love.

Hook and Jack's childhood was messy, fun and a little insecure. Home was a chaotic terrace off Holloway Road with their father, Frank, a wiry builder from some bumpkin hamlet in the Fens, who was both too young and too old-fashioned for his mother, Vanessa – a London-born grammar-school girl, liberal, wild and erratic.

Frank and Van, an odd couple who met at a Vietnam demo, were told they'd never conceive. Jack was their little miracle; then five years later, along came Hook. He sometimes has the feeling he's gate crashed this miraculous party, made it less special in a way none of them can define.

After the blazing day the pub's dark, quiet and as cool as autumn woodland. Hook cocks his hand in a drinking gesture and raises his eyebrows: smugly Jack shakes his head. He never drinks to get drunk and considers this a virtue. Hook limps to the bar, annoyed, and orders the juice of some fruit from the blank-eyed barmaid.

Carrying his pap to the table Hook perches on a tiny stool. Clearing his throat with bitter, his brother speaks in that deep, posh, confident voice: the accent their parents bought for

Hook, only to have it thrown back in their faces.

"I have Mum's Will."

"Oh."

Hook sips sour juice and winces. The business of the Will has dragged on for years: there's been the sale of their parents' house, delayed by a naive idea the market might improve; solicitor setbacks; attorney arse-aches; finally, at a vital moment in the labyrinthine proceedings, the executor, some pedantic uncle on their mother's side, inconveniently died.

Pulling a bulky envelope from his jacket pocket Jack wafts Hook's nose. The hairs on his beard shimmer corn-like and the entrance to his mouth is like seaweed, like wet heather. Men, women and in-betweeners are always throwing themselves at him, literally, yet Jack has eyes only for Maya, the medic who nursed their mother until the end while weaning Jack off boys.

Hook takes the envelope in both hands and, noting it's been opened in haste, pulls out the top sheet, so full of legalise jargon it might as well be written in Welsh. Shrugging, he passes it back to Jack, who he now sees has been reading Naomi Klein; her told-you-so face stares seriously from the book's back cover.

"What does it all mean?"

Jack grins through his beard, hazel eyes shining with amusement. In them Hook sees himself squatting on his stool, knees touching the table, waiting for scraps. To his brother's credit, his voice when he speaks is serious, any hint of mirth, of victory, well concealed.

"It's... as we thought. Mum left me everything. I'm sorry Chris."

"Ah well." An elderly queen at the next table slurps on Guinness, creamy and black. Hook's hungry and doesn't feel like eating. His stomach roars; his ears whistle new songs.

"Not that it matters," says Jack, smiling broadly. "I'm giving you half. That should sort out your mortgage. Maybe you could take that cruise you were on about, some quality time with Monica."

Hook looks round the pub then back at his pontificating brother, set up for life even without the new money: out of the banking world before the crash, savings invested in gold, frankincense and Maya. Jack takes a sip of bitter and smiles again, a hint of authority in his eyes, that awful confidence.

"...And maybe you could do something for Byron: give poor Karen a rest, get him into a proper home. You do realise he turns twenty-one this year? I read about this place in Kent where they use some new therapy that seems to work – to a certain extent. Expensive, but hey, who's counting bruv?"

Hook nods wearily, puts down his juice and sticks out his hand. When smiling Jack goes to shake it, he smiles too, wider, broader, deeper, and raises his middle finger.

"Fuck you, Jack."

Standing so abruptly the queen splutters on his Guinness, Hook goes to the bar, smiles at the unsmiling barmaid.

"Double whiskey."

The sparkling glass levitates beneath the tap and amber fluid splashes round the bowl, then floats to his hand and to his mouth. Hook takes a deep breath and swallows the measure whole, gasping with pleasure as blood rushes to his cheeks. He counts out some coins, leaves his brother sitting there with his nursed half and that same stupid smile like he knows everything, before pushing open the door and plunging into the sun.

Hook can't go home and as he's had one what the hell so he limps through Soho looking for trouble. Entering the Pillars of Hercules he takes a swift pint then takes another at the Blue Posts on Berwick Street; his liver nudges him so he nudges right back.

Back on the street he looks north and sees the post office tower, its restaurant back in business and spinning slowly, so diners can look down as they nibble on blow-torched otter. Hook spits at the building, falls short. Holding up his hands he sees his fingers shaking and he puts them in his ears as if to dig out the ringing noise, then walks toward another swinging sign.

Outside a tattoo parlour Hook leans his forehead against the glass and looks at the dreamy drawings of large-breasted women and snakes, crosses and lightning. As his eyes adjust he becomes aware of a middle-aged rocker looking out, frowning through his beard. The man raises his eyebrows: Hook shakes his head and in the Magpie's cool cellar takes three pints of cider in quick succession to shut out the sun.

Why has he never had a tattoo? Never wild enough, he supposes: even as a fourteen-year old scrote on the Holloway streets he was too afraid to permanently mark his own skin, to do anything that might leave an indelible reminder of childhood.

Darkness is falling but many of the streetlights stay off. Some of the shops are brightly lit but some have metal shutters over the entrance so that it isn't clear if they're even in business. It's rare that Hook comes to Soho now. He's always felt safe in this neighbourhood but today he's shocked by the menacing figures lurking in doorways, the expletive-riddled shouts and angry conversations, the prostitutes. A young woman in a mini and fishnets stands outside a shop smoking; as he limps by a smile passes over her lips like a cloud over fields. Hook stops; if he had a titfer he'd tip it.

"How much?"

The woman's face is transformed; Hook has never seen such loathing, such utter hatred. He backs away, almost tumbling over a pile of rotting vegetables.

"I'm so sorry, I –"

The woman screams. Hook runs painfully, certain he's being followed by Albanians or vampires through the narrow, bustling streets. After several corners he slows, his ankle a knot of pain, and catches his breath. Hook wipes his brow and his eyes and leans against a wall, trying to gather his wits as midges congregate on his forehead.

After a final drink in Molly Moggs Hook feels he's had enough. At Leicester Square he descends into the bowels, liver spiking and weeping. When the northbound tube thrusts through, Hook hops into the quiet first carriage and pulls out the fold-down by the driver's door. Newspaper headlines fill the empty seats but his eyes water too much to read so he stares down the carriage, chest heaving, one hand ensuring the BlackBerry is still in his jacket.

As the tube accelerates out of the station he watches all the light, noise and dark being sucked out of him like a long intestine. The past isn't a foreign country, decides Hook, it's another world, where people don't just do things differently but become their own guilt-edged ancestors.

As Hook emerges from the tube he sees the gang of youths outside the kebab shop and knows he must pass them or look weak. He tries to push by but the men murmur angrily and one pushes him in the back. Hook ignores him and walks on, hearing scuffling steps. Instinct tells him to turn round but instead he strides quicker, footsteps close behind. The street is eerily empty, Liddle Towers a beacon of false hope in the dusk.

Hook turns at last to find six or eight of the men walking quickly behind him, hands in hoodie pockets, scowling. Hook runs. Opening the gate he jogs as swiftly as he can through the scorched-earth gardens, not even seeing the mark where the block almost killed him. At the block entrance, as he pulls a mattress away from the doors, he glances back fearfully but the yobs have stopped at the road where they cluster laughing, swapping high-fives.

The foyer of the apartment block is dark, ghastly: in order to make the building more environmentally sound the communal lighting has been dimmed. As he waits for the lift Hi-NRG mozzies blitz his ears like atomic engines; Hook hears distant screams, breaking glass, and shivers in the sultry night.

Liddle Towers was erected at the peak of the boom and they'd paid peak prices to escape from the Georgian terrace off the Cally. This is meant to be their safe nest from which to look down on a city that has at some point become strange to them.

The day after Hook had put down a substantial deposit on the flat, Monica warned him blocks like these would one day be high-rise slums. Back then it had a concierge, potted plants in the corridors, and the lift smelled of scented water. Despite these enticing amenities, only two-thirds of the apartments (Hook can never bring himself to say 'flats') have ever been occupied. As a result there were soon calls by people who didn't live there to move in families from the council's bulging waiting list. Monica campaigned against the proposals; Hook secretly voted in favour. He won. At least the concierge hung around for a while; the perfumed water dried up after a week.

As Hook exits the lift and walks to the front door, holding his key out like a torch, he hears noises within. For a moment he stops, leans his forehead against the cool metal, listens to the sounds of mother and daughter relaxing, existing and coping without any trace of Hook, the man of the house, the provider.

Twisting his key Hook pushes open the door of the cramped apartment. Shelley's door to his immediate left is ajar, her room in darkness. The voices seep from one of those ghastly radio plays Hook can never listen to without wanting to run amok with axes, with swords...

His wife's in the galley kitchen cooking something vegan and waves brightly enough when he enters. Monica's still lithe with the flawless skin and perfect teeth American dollars can buy. Her long, auburn hair's tied back, exposing a high, intelligent and easily-furrowed forehead; her pale blue eyes look tired and troubled lately. But she looks good in her tight black skirt and thin purple blouse, padding about in her tights. Hook stoops and they kiss; her mouth tastes of garlic and he doesn't linger. Frowning, she wrinkles her nose like a child.

"Chris, have you been *drinking*?"

Her soft Boston accent stretches out the last word like silk and he shrugs, too drunk to feel shame.

"I had a couple."

Monica turns back to the dinner; her hair looks concerned, somehow.

"I thought you were... taking it easy for a while."

Hook drops his bits on the breakfast bar and gulps at Ken and Deirdre. It's not sorrow he feels, contempt, even sympathy; it's hatred, of their dependency, their supplication, their stupid gaping mouths. Sometimes he over-feeds the fish, knowing that's just as cruel, but it doesn't seem it.

"I haven't had a drink for months Monica, give me a break."

"But didn't the doctor say –"

"Fuck the doctor."

Hook expels the words forcefully and Monica winces. To ease the mood he glances sideways into the open-plan living room, which is empty, the vast plasma screen a black hole in the wall, a frame without a painting. The curtains are drawn: why does she do that, all the way up here? Who'd want to spy on *them*? As if in answer Monica goes over to the curtain and whips them back. Hook is confronted by a wall of cardboard and yellow tape.

"What the fuck?"

"The end of the balcony gave way this morning. You must have gone out. Shelley came home and went out there and damn near fell off."

"Shit."

"The place is falling apart, Chris. The surveyor said we can't go out there till it's all been repaired."

"How long will that take?"

"Who knows? Weeks."

Hook is about to mention that morning's incident but something stops him. Instead he nods at Shelley's open door.

"Where's Shelley?"

That damned hypocrite Monica pours herself a glass of wine from a bottle he notes is two-thirds empty. The first stirrings of an erection trouble him and Hook tries to cast aside his snap reaction to Jack's offer. He's in need of affection and understands that turning down a hundred thousand or thereabouts isn't the way to find any.

Reaching up into a cupboard on tip-toe Monica holds out a clean glass with a resigned air. Hook has difficulty working out her reaction: she hates him drunk but more so sober; at least drunk he doesn't care. He takes the glass, concentrating on his shaking fingers. Monica's eyes examine him then she shrugs, returning to the simpler business of dinner.

"Shel's stopping with a friend."

When he sucks on the wine he winces. It's good but combined with all the other tastes of the day it makes Hook's stomach turn. Grabbing the bottle he backs away towards the safety of the blank HDTV, but his arse meets a high stool and he's stranded. Unchecked words babbled forth.

"What – again? Who is this 'friend'?"

When she turns from her chopping he sees now there's flour

on Monica's cheek and trails like she's been crying. In web talk she'd be a MILF, but Hook finds that hard to accept because that makes him a middle-aged dad and he's not ready for slippers and the Telegraph yet.

"Katie, from the drama school. She's fine. I've met her parents, they're people like us."

Hook bites his tongue, and the wine filling his mouth tastes of blood. Monica knows he hates her snobbery; the only time her decadent airs turn him on is in bed. She returns to her chopping, mashing, blending: all that energy to create a woodburger. Why does he eat this tofu, this *bean*?

Monica addresses him through her sheeny hair. "Anyway, how did it go?"

Hook takes off his jacket and hangs it over the desk chair. Van Gogh scowls through his ginger beard, hair swept back like a greaser.

"How did *what* go?"

"With Jack."

Hook frowns at his wife's bobbing behind. When does a quickie turn to rape? What are the signs? Is she too drunk to consent? Is he too sober to fuck?

"How did you know I went to see Jack?"

Monica looks over her shoulder, cheek pinking. "You sent me a text, remember?"

He doesn't. Hook sips his wine before risking a reply. "I thought you didn't have your phone?"

Monica stops chopping and looks back at him with increasing exasperation. Why not move round the table? What's she *hiding*?

"What is this? I'm just asking, okay? Still no news about the Will?"

Hook watches her behind as she bends to the oven. No, no signs. Yet he's her husband – what sign does she need to send out, what pheromone telegram? Should he just take her now, right there on the floor, or would that be crossing some line? According to an American professor he's read, women sometimes orgasm when they're raped: it's down to evolution. Women who don't get wet get hurt. Do rapists kiss their victims? That seems worst of all, somehow, that self-deceit...

"Not yet," says Hook, acclimatising to the wine.

Now Monica practically has her whole head in the oven. What with her accent and her tights it's like chatting to Sylvia Plath. What does that make *him*?

"Why so long?" Her voice echoes metallically. "It's been months. Doesn't he have any idea about timescales?"

"I think he does, yes."

Walking backwards from memory Hook slumps on the sofa and sees the standby light on beneath the TV screen. Kicking off his shoes he stretches out, looks up and examines the spreading brown patch on the ceiling. Monica comes over, stands in front of the TV and looks at him earnestly, pushing a straggly fringe out of her eyes with one hand, raising her glass with the other, multi-tasking.

"The money would come in useful, Chris. We could pay off the mortgage and sell up."

Hook was always being harangued by his mother for being sexist when she was alive and he'd always agreed. Now he feels like a row.

"With no fucking balcony? What the hell would we sell up for now?"

"I was talking to Gonzales on the City Desk; he said the market's still plummeting. We should get out while we can. This place is going downhill. Did you see that mattress beside the garbage chute?"

"No," lies Hook. Two lies in two minutes: one for luck. He nods towards the little building site on the kitchen table.

"No dinner for me, I've eaten."

Monica stops dead, glass almost to her lip as if playing

statues; any remaining music leaves the conversation and she rushes to the en-suite. Hook zaps the remote and looks through his window on the world.

The main news is all about the failed suicide bomber, a recent convert to Islam. Hook smiles at the idea of this rabid fanatic, unable to wait, prematurely ejaculating into barren space. How disappointing, to wire yourself into your bodybag basque with trembling fingers, go in search of company, swarming with impotent fury. Then to appreciate at that final moment you're going out all alone, your intestines will splash onto empty concrete and brick, no *kafir* will make the journey with you to that honey-trap heaven you were promised by old men in safe houses.

Monica takes a pointed bath. Hook decides to get a beer. Pulling open the safe-sized fridge door he curses: nothing. When he slams the door it exhales an asthmatic groan. Now Hook's confronted by the calendar and curses again. Written in red ink on tomorrow's box he's written *INTERVIEW*.

Getting on his hands and knees on the sticky lino Hook roots through the recycling box and finds last week's edition of the council rag. Slapping it on the floury table he leafs through page after page of smiling councillors and long-serving traffic wardens. Near the back he finds an irresistible trailer:

Next week: as part of his series on community cohesion our man Hook goes behind the scenes at the Olympic stadium!

Sighing, Hook looks up at the patch on the ceiling; he'd forgotten about the story till now. There's wine left so he takes a few deep draughts. Monica emerges from the bedroom with a spare duvet, before going back in and and shutting the door. Hook decides he's drunk enough to read the letter from the mortgage company. Pulling the envelope from his jacket pocket he rips off the top and inspects it, wincing. Thinking about money his addled brain boggles and, unsure what to do, he calls Jack. Jack doesn't return his call: nobody ever does. He's disappearing and no-one's noticed; he's becoming the invisible man.

He doesn't like checking his inbox last thing because his messages are becoming more frequent, more ominous: the virtual threat of beheading, stoning and numerous other threats from people he's never even met. But something compels Hook to log on and a bold message catches his eye:

From: Ulrike Nechayev

Subject: victimisation

Message: Hello, I have a story for you.

In some desperation Hook presses 'reply' and writes:

Tell me more.

Tuesday 22nd June

By the time Hook, in boxers and t-shirt, emerges from the sofa with the hangover sticking close like an old friend, Monica has left for work. She hasn't even drawn the curtains to let in the morning. Hook does and instead of a view of the rising sun he's confronted by hoardings.

Hook squints through a gap in the temporary wall. The morning has dawned as hot and cloudless as all the others, a caravan of identical days, nose to tail and no end in sight: a Punxsutawney holiday. Blearily he looks along the hall to Shelley's room and the door's open; the room too light for teenage sleepers. Hook weighs, flicks the kettle.

Ken and Deirdre gulp in their tank; squashing his nose on the glass Hook gulps back. The fish food is in the same cupboard as the cups. When Hook reaches up to search for his *'world's greatest dad'* mug – bought by Monica, he now suspects, rather than Shelley – both fish swim upwards in expectation. Unable to find his special mug he takes down a cup, sure he can read disappointed looks in their little fishy faces.

Apparently it's not true, about goldfish's memories – even if he hasn't fed them for a week, when he opens the lid they slide to the surface.

According to *Wikipedia* they grow to love their owners, miss them deeply when they go away. Hook finds this information appalling.

The aircon's off and mucky sweat coats his body, but there's no time to shower. Hook's jealous of the fish in their cool water. He taps on the greening glass, algae spreading like ecophagy. Monica says that tiny sound is enough to frighten them to death. Are they so precious, their wild world so timorous?

Last night Hook stayed up late watching *Fitma* and assorted nonsense while drinking corked wine and he regrets it now: his liver feels like a lead balloon. It's been another sweaty night, but the booze helped him sleep and at least no little bombers came to prick the night sky like bloated fire flies.

Turning on the radio Hook tweaks from 4 to 5: the gap between Monica and himself, from thoughts for the day and morality plays to talk, sport and phone-ins. The weather girl sounds delighted about the continuing heatwave; then the news presenter talks about empty reservoirs and hosepipe bans, crop failure in Cornwall, dustbowls in Dorset.

Afterwards, the main news: another propaganda-fest at the expense of drinkers. Why does the BBC never mention the revenue alcohol raises? Not that he even *wants* a drink. Hook's starting to suspect there's no such thing as alcoholism: it's all a myth perpetuated by the government, NHS, and Auntie. If he ever gets his fucking plane maybe he won't point it at the White House after all; he'll aim right at Broadcasting House.

In the bedroom Hook finds fresh trousers hanging over the ironing board and a clean shirt in the wardrobe. Flicking through his ties he decides not to bother. Nor will he shave. Instead he takes several Librium and returns to the kitchen, switches off the radio, which is talking about sea monsters for some reason, picks up his charging BlackBerry and sees a new message:

meet me anne boleyn pub gibbet st 12
ulrike x

East London is one enormous building site. Clouds of concrete dust and aphids invade orifices; the noise of metal on metal and drill-bits into pavement fill Hook's aching head beneath a hard helmet that's way too small. The inner support digs into his skull, cracking up with dehydration. The oversized orange bib makes him sweat and, although it's not yet ten, the searing heat compels Hook to memorise escape routes.

The site is to be a Building of Belief, part of the Olympic development. Hook finds it difficult to get worked up about the project. What was it Orwell said in *Homage to Catalonia* about blowing up all the churches?

The Bengali site supervisor showing him round the unfinished foundations is also wearing a hard hat; Hook tries to work out the squat, middle-aged man's religion. He's always taken pride in his tolerance, his understanding of complex issues – a few years back he won the regional award for Journalism that Promotes Racial Harmony (London East Region).

Yet now, Hook realises, he's forgotten much of what he wrote: the difference between Sunni and Shia, the origins of Ramadan, why it is Muslims pray to Mecca five times daily. The thing that scares him most is his own ignorance. He's supposed to care, understand and empathise, when all he wants to do is run away.

The Bengali shouts in his ear but as they're standing next to a pneumatic drill Hook can hardly hear him. Impatiently the man points a stubby finger up at an unfinished dome, closing like tulip petals against the white hot sky.

It occurs to Hook that he'd better pretend to take some notes for the article he drafted on the bus: mostly he writes from memory, but some people find that suspicious. Reaching into his jacket he extracts the notebook and pen Shelley bought him last Christmas, pages virginal.

His drafted feature extols the virtues of diversity and tolerance; Hook's written a million similar pieces on how the mosque provides a sense of belonging and the caring sharing *Tablighi Jamaat* instill discipline in the young. Maybe they do – Friday prayer beats sniffing glue in bus shelters.

The walk over uneven ground makes his ankle throb and a tiny insect swims in his eye. The site supervisor shouts something that sounds like "I was born on a bus", and Hook dutifully writes it down; he'll worry about the quote later. When he sends the feature to the management committee of the mosque it'll be amended to requirements. That'll keep the councillors happy, and that means Karen's happy, which seems more important after yesterday's snap reaction.

Hook's throat is dry from dust and hangovers, and despite a rash promise he vaguely remembers making to Monica he longs to be in a pub – any pub. Flashbacks from the day before keep popping up: running through Soho; that woman's disgusted face; giving Jack the finger instead of shaking his hand.

When he shakes hands with the Bengali the guy seems put out, which hits a nerve: it's Hook who had to wait on site for half an hour because the prick lost his pass. Hook walks towards the lift to the underground car park and exit, waving his arms ineffectually – neither waving nor drowning.

It's cool and dark under the stadium and he walks slowly, glad to be out of the hammering sun. The council's staff are among the lucky few whose passes allow access into the subterranean space: a car catacomb built on a plague pit, arches holding up the fractious sky. For some reason there are an abundance of large green boxes everywhere. Hook has never quite determined what they're for but decides he isn't in the mood for large, green things at all.

Painfully Hook limps up a shallow ramp, dodging huge trucks full of aggregate and steel, through a security gate and along a dusty road with buildings rising on both sides, practically as he walks. A shadow's falling over him, a tsunami of shade that seems to hang on his shoulder but makes no impact on the flies or the heat.

Hook limps between brand spanking new apartment blocks in random clusters, mostly empty, the supermarkets beneath them full of wares no-one wants. He purchases a bottle of water from a shop-keeper with the bewildered look of a man on a promise but turned down.

There isn't much shade round the stadium but plenty of water: canals, rivers, overflows, weirs, rivulets, ponds, lakes, reservoirs, linked by rickety lattices of foot-bridges and warped pipes. Steam, smoke and dust rise from ruptured outlets, while planes from London City split the sky where police helicopters hover like Afghan drones.

Trains for faraway Richmond thunder over ancient brick bridges, beneath which derelict pubs and nests of shambling terraces rub alongside warehouses of modern goods: bathroom fittings, car supplies, organic mush. Lost Russian builders wander in packs wearing orange jackets and hard helmets, puzzled newcomers waiting for vans that never show up, dwarfed by overhanging tower blocks and mountains of gravel.

As Hook rounds a corner he spies the pub in the middle of a busy roundabout, or rather an island with a dual carriageway that wraps round it like a river round a rock. The sign above the door portrays a pretty girl in sixteenth-century dress and bears the name 'Anne Boleyn'.

Hook looks round at the uninspiring environs: the row of shops opposite are closed, the factory next door boarded up and semi-demolished, and the DLR weaving across the distant skyline seems like it has come from another planet and is in a rush to get back.

He looks at his watch: almost twelve. He can have lunch in the pub and ask Ulrike a few questions before going back to the office to check his quotes. Except he guesses the pub won't sell food – let alone vegetarian options – and doubts it specialises in soft drinks.

When he plunges over the car-jammed road and enters the solemn space of brown wood and glass Hook is confronted by an old, mournful, Jewish-looking guy with shaggy white hair polishing a dirty glass. He wears a dirty grey shirt with rolled-up sleeves and faded black trousers and seems surprised, or maybe scared. The sudden silence embraces Hook like a friend; he nods at the taps.

"Guinness please."

Hook sits on a tall stool and looks up at the TV suspended above his head, where men in shorts hit balls into nets. Hook's liver pokes his rib and he stifles a grunt. The barman raises his eyebrows.

"Chilled or normal?"

"Chilled."

The barman frowns in concentration as he pours. Removing his jacket and hanging it on a bar-peg that jabs his knee Hook swallows in anticipation, tasting the dust and dirt of the building site. To his dismay the barman leaves the pint standing and goes to polish a chipped old table by the door. Hook looks at his drink then at the barman.

"Hot today."

The barman doesn't look up. "Yus."

"Yus": the old London way, memories of Arthur Mallard. The barman keeps polishing the old wood table as if searching for himself in its depths.

"Quiet?"

"Quiet every fucking day."

"I suppose the Olympics will change all that."

The barman laughs humourlessly as he gives up on the table and, flinging the cloth over his shoulder, goes behind the bar and tops off Hook's pint. He shakes his head and grins ruefully but his eyes are dark, deep orbs of woe. "Yeah, right."

"You don't think so?"

"I'll be amazed if I'm still here when the Olympics start. Three-twenty."

Hook takes a sip to make sure the pint's good, hands over the money.

"Why's that?"

Taking the money without counting the barman looks around furtively, as if to make sure they're still alone, then leans over the bar. His breath smells of something Hook can't identify but turns his stomach.

"They want me out."

"Who do? The Olympics people?"

"Nah, mate. I wish, that way at least I'd make a few bob. The Muslims."

As he looks round the empty bar for Ulrike, Hook realises he hasn't explained who he is. It seems easier sometimes just to talk. That's the thing with journalism: some people expect him to pull out a card, a Dictaphone or a notepad, where others tend to shut up, lie, or turn nasty – often all three. It's all about instinct, which always lets him down.

He takes another sip of the creamy cold liquid and closes his eyes. Why has he wasted so much time on sobriety? What's it done for *him* lately? Hook wipes white foam off his lips before speaking.

"What do you mean, 'the Muslims'?"

"They reckon there shouldn't be any pubs round here no more. They want the council to close me down."

"Who's 'they' exactly?"

"The mosque committee."

"Right."

Hook's story-sniffer closes down: the usual anti-Muslim rant. He'll finish his pint and get to work. There's a wine bar opposite the town hall. Maria, the owner, is in her forties, tall, Italian – during bleak points their flirtations keep him going. The barman turns those old sad eyes on him, reading his mind.

"You don't believe me."

"Sure I do. But I've heard it all before. They can't shut down pubs just because some in the community don't *like* them. There'd be uproar."

"You'd think so, wouldn't you?" The barman scowls. "But who's gonna care round here? There's hardly any pub folk left. I should open a halal burger bar, I'd be laughing."

Hook feels it would take more than halal burgers to make those eyes twinkle. He drains his creamy pint, feeling dizzy: still not twelve. His ears ring from all the drills and his bowels need unblocking but there's no way he's taking a dump in this place.

"Oh well, gotta go."

Hook stands and puts on his jacket, damp with old sweat. As he goes to leave the barman reaches out, grabs his arm with a surprisingly strong grip. Unsure what expression to pull Hook tries a cool smile, scared. The old man leans over the bar and whispers, "I know who you are."

"Do you now."

"You work on the local paper. Seen your face loads of times."

"Have you."

"Yeah."

"I would offer hearty congratulations, if you hadn't known I was coming."

The barman looks baffled. "Eh?"

"I got your email. Made it sound like you had the story of the century."

The hand lets go. Hook straightens his sleeve as the barman

backs away and leans chewing beneath a shimmery row of optics.

"Wasn't me, guv."

"You didn't send an email?"

"No mate. You sure you got your facts right?"

Hook looks at him: he doesn't look like an 'Ulrike', but who knows in cyberspace? Every time he chats to 'PVC Queen' or 'Busty Bertha' they turn out to be the same hirsute lorry-driver from Swindon. Hook swallows, unsure.

"I'm not sure, I – so you don't know an Ulrike?"

The barman frowns, his knotted forehead a zebra of shadows and contours. "Never heard of 'im. What's this message say?"

Hook tells him. The barman shrugs. "That must have been Susan."

"'Susan'?"

"My niece Susan. Fuck knows why she called herself that other thing. I don't get all this internet lark."

"Nor me," lies Hook.

The barman sighs, defeated. "Look. If I give you a scoop you could flog it to the nationals."

"I used to work for the nationals, not anymore."

"You saying if you went to them with a story and it was good they wouldn't listen?"

Hook shrugs, conjuring up a vision of his wife, the inquisitive feature writer, fingers in her ears, eyes closed, singing "*la-la-la*".

"Okay," says Hook, "I don't know if you sent this email or not. It mentioned something about a phone message."

"A phone message?"

"Yes."

The barman gives him a strange look, seems to remember something, disappears through a bead curtain and plods upstairs. Hook sighs, waits. Whichever way he looks at it his pint is empty. The barman returns with a mobile phone, anachronistic in those barky fingers, scrolls through clumsily and hands it over. Hook hears a crackly voice, ghetto London, heavy with menace.

"...out old man, fucking Yids, this Muslim town now..."

Hook looks up at the barman with mild interest. "What's this?"

The old man's anti-light eyes, lava-like wrinkles dictate their own story: sleeplessness, loneliness, ancient purges.

"They ring most nights. Susan said I should tape them. I told my copper mate and you know what he said?"

"What?"

"'Get out while you can'."

Handing back the mobile Hook snorts and shakes his head. "I find that... hard to believe."

The old man shrugs. "So are you going to follow this up?"

"I dunno. I mean, I haven't much to go on."

The barman holds up the mobile. "Maybe you could analyse the messages, voice technology whatever."

Hook laughs; the barman looks confused. The sunlight through the windows makes the optics sparkle, wood shine. They're in the middle of a motorway, yet it's so quiet Hook can hear the old man's laboured breathing.

"You telling me how to do my job?"

The barman holds up his hand. "No offence, mate."

"None taken. Okay, I'll take the phone. And oh – when you pour a cold Guinness, you don't need the interval." Hook puts the mobile in his jacket pocket.

The barman shrugs. "I wouldn't know mate, you're the first ponce that's asked for it."

"Yes, thanks. So, this Susan – is she around?" The barman shakes his head. "She due back?"

"Susan," smiles the barman, the expression strange on his face, "is a law unto herself. Shall I pass on a message?"

"Just say I popped by," says Hook. "Hopefully we'll catch up later."

The barman's eyes follow him to the door and it's a relief for Hook to see it close on that sad old face. As he does so, he sees something he hadn't spotted on the way in: a swastika in blue aerosol, its harsh angles reaching over the wood/glass of the door like a warped spider. Cautiously, as if it's corrosive, Hook touches the savage symbol and blue rubs off on his fingers – still wet.

Maria isn't in Da Vinci's so after a disappointing visit to a cubicle Hook nurses a pint of cider, takes out his notebook and tries to remember what the site supervisor said. Though he can recall nothing except that mournful old man's sad eyes. A dinosaur: soon there'll be none like him left.

'The city belongs to the young' – where did Hook read that, on a bog wall? This is a young man's town, cosmopolitan, a city state named flux. Soon the old man will die and the Anne Boleyn will become a block of flats or a curry house, something *relevant*.

According to the free news sheet he's picked up on the DLR the mayor's disputing the cost of the Olympics: she isn't the only one. Council taxes have gone through the roof but so far all they have to show for it is that great cement bowl in the middle of the East End. Hook wonders if the mosque being built is funded by the taxpayer. Does it matter? What the hell does *he* care if his taxes are used to perpetuate fairytales?

Hook looks around the empty chrome and neon lounge, dabbing at his forehead with a hankie. The walls are covered with images of old Italy, famous Italians and, in case customers still don't get the message, framed football shirts of legends like Baresi and Zoff.

Da Vinci's sits on an artificial island on an artificial canal protected from the East End by the town hall, a gated community for suits only. The sunlight slanting through the windows casts ripples on shining surfaces and gives Hook a powerful headache. He's always felt more at home in old pubs like the Anne Boleyn; shame if they all bite the dust in the name of progress.

Reaching in his jacket pocket Hook pulls out the barman's mobile phone and listens to the sad, despairing warning again, but his mind keeps drifting so draining his cider in one long breath he limps over to the bar with his glass, smeared with swastika blue. Maria appears from the kitchen: tall, forties, long black hair and a cruel mouth that smiles when she sees him.

"Christian!" Leaning over she kisses his cheek, and Hook catches a glimpse of her breasts in the low-cut peasant dress she wears for effect. "Long time no see; you been away?"

"Sort of," smiles Hook. "*Sidro* please, Maria."

Maria pours into a girly stem. They've flirted irregularly and without much enthusiasm for years, but just when he thought she was serious he was hurled on the wagon. Hook tries to recall who poured his first drink, fails. To break the silence he looks round the bar.

"Quiet."

"Not for long. There's a bankruptcy party coming in later."

"Bankruptcy party?"

"Some women from Canary Wharf been made redundant, coming here to celebrate. You should hang around."

"I might. I –"

He's interrupted by an unfamiliar mobile ring from his jacket pocket. The brick of a mobile suits that ancient ring tone: the phone was probably bought by the old man's daughter to make sure he was safe. A name, 'Susan', flashes up. Hook presses 'answer'.

"Hello Ulrike."

A pause at the other end: Hook smiles. Maria smiles too and he thinks he detects a wink, or is that a nervous twitch?

"Who's this?"

"It's OK. My name's Chris Hook, your uncle lent me his phone."

"Why did you call me 'Ulrike'?"

"It is you who sent the emails, isn't it? The 'exclusive story', as you put it."

"Oh yes, the Paki story."

Hook's heart falls to the polished floor and he sighs. Maria sits on a stool sipping red wine, pretending to do her books by hand.

"Actually," says Hook, "most East Enders originated from the state of Bangladesh. Pakistanis tend to congregate in Northern mill towns like –"

"I know that smart-arse, but the bloke who's been hassling me Uncle Sid is a Pashtun from Balochistan."

The distant voice sounds bright and young. Hook blinks, surprised. His liver – or some other, unnoticed intestine getting jealous – knifes his ribs and he expels a sharp breath before responding. "You seem very knowledgeable on the subject. I'm sorry."

"Sorry you thought I was just another racist chav?"

Hook takes in a deep breath to argue, catches a whiff of spagbol which makes him feel sick. "Yes."

"That's the trouble with your sort," says the voice of Susan, or Ulrike, or whatever she calls herself. "You think we're all just dying to burn down the mosques and put them on a leaky boat. I tell you – we're better at mixing that your lot. If it wasn't for your sort everyone would get along just fine."

Hook gulps cider, enjoying himself. It's nice talking to someone new.

"*My* sort?"

"The middle classes."

"How do you know I'm 'middle class'?"

"Well, aren't you?"

Hook thinks about it, but not for long. He's spent too many years at parties and in pubs discussing a subject he has little interest in.

"For the record, Susan, Ulrike, my dad was a builder."

"Oh. Right."

Hook can hardly bear to hear that disappointment. "However, for reasons best known to him, dad did plonk me in a minor public school for a while, so you're spot on. Well done."

"I knew it," says the girl, and Hook hears the relief in her voice. People don't like having their expectations confounded; why tell her that after that one disastrous year he was expelled back to the same North London comp that had almost done for Jack?

"So," says Ulrike, finally, "are you gonna help me out?"

Hook smiles. So does Maria, her lips red with wine. "Help you out?"

"Help me sort out my problem?"

"What makes you think I can help?"

"I just have this feeling we can help each other. Know what I mean?"

"I'm not sure I do."

"Look," says the girl, "do you want to meet to get this *straight*?"

"Yes," says Hook, hardening. "I think I'd like that."

"Me too. I'd like to get things straight with you."

"Would you?"

"Mmm."

Maria watches him, sipping Bardolino. For an ephemeral moment Hook thinks he sees the tip of her tongue poke out. He meets her gaze. "What would you like to get straight with me?"

"You tell *me*. Tell me what you want."

"What *do* you want?"

He's talking to the girl, but looking at Maria in her low-cut dress. The bar's still empty; he hears breathing at the end of the invisible line.

"I'd like you to get on top of things," says Susan.

"On top?"

"Yes. I need some help. I need you."

"Need me for what? What shall I get on top of?"

Maria parts her bare legs a fraction, her eyes boring into him. At that moment the door crashes open and a dozen or so women in city suits enter, laughing and talking loudly. Rolling her eyes Maria gets off her stool to serve and Hook concentrates on the voice.

"You know what I want you to get on top of."

"How old are you, may I ask?"

"I'm old enough, legally, for anything that's required."

Hook frowns; an odd phrase, especially in that accent.

"Anything?"

"Anything you like."

"Well, I'd be flattered if you knew what I look like."

"I've seen your photo on your column. Quite hunky for a posh boy."

Hook smiles. The women who enter are noisy and over-laughing to hide their anxieties. Maria kisses one on both cheeks. He closes his eyes.

"One thing. Would you rather I called you Susan or Ulrike?"

"Call me whatever you like, darling. *Anything*. I'll be in touch."

Hook's trying to think of a suitably flirtatious reply when he hears the line is dead.

Hook's replaying the conversation and watching the sacked city girls knock back champagne when he remembers his meeting with Karen. Waiting until his hard-on has macerated he leaves the bar and walks over a miniature bridge to the town hall. As he enters the lobby the shaven headed security guard stares coldly from beneath his great eyebrows so Hook puts down his eye, swipes his new ID, and when the barrier opens hurries to the lift.

The lift door is held by a tall, well-built woman in her thirties, a round, pretty face and eyes as green as his own: Karen. She wears a top that Hook can't tell is a blouse or a dress because she's wearing trousers; the top buttons are undone and a crucifix dangles between heavy breasts. The beer and lack of food make him feel vulnerable and he hesitates. But he can't back out so he nods and puts his eyes down.

Releasing the button Karen speaks. "All well, Chris?"

"Fine, you?"

Hook tries to direct his breath down towards her feet, but only his voice descends: bilious clouds of stale alcohol stream into her face. Karen makes a tiny but visible gesture of disgust and looks at the buttons.

"We're both good."

Hook winces; Karen continues smoothly. "How did your story go this morning?"

"Story?" For one horrified minute, Hook thinks Karen's onto him: using work time to chase his scoop. Then he remembers the man in the hat.

"Oh, that. I interviewed the site supervisor, seemed fine."

Karen frowns. "'Site supervisor'?"

"Yes, that guy whose number you gave me."

Karen's cheeks pink slightly with alarm, embarrassment or impatience. She's one of those middle class women who walk round with a little smile on their lips, and whose only show of anger is a slight rouging around the nose.

"Chris, *that* was Councillor Ahmed! I thought you met him at the AGM last month?"

"Oh. Right. No, we haven't been introduced."

Hook swallows. That explains the guy's bafflement when he asked for more details about the cantilever support structure. Karen drops her eyes, so does Hook, to the little golden man with the sad face.

"I do hope you got the relevant information, Chris. We need all the copy by the end of the week. That means getting it to the Leader by Thursday."

The lift stops on four: two large ladies step in and the lift rocks slightly. Hook and Karen squeeze closer, her large, soft breasts on his arm. He hasn't sucked them for twenty years: how would they taste?

"That's fine, Karen, I'll have everything ready."

The two fat ladies get out on seven and they're alone again, but there's another awkward moment; Hook's arm still touches Karen's breast. He sweats and wonders whether to back off. Karen looks into his watering eyes and he watches her lips move.

"I... was talking to Brian about these features actually."

"'Brian'?"

"Brian Harvey, the chief executive of the borough? We were just thinking the content seems very... *white*. Do you know what I mean, Chris?"

Hook clears his throat, bringing up sour cider. "'White'?"

"As in not many profiles of prominent local people? You know – councillors, businessmen, that sort of thing. I mean, this *is* supposed to be a series about 'community cohesion'."

"I tend to concentrate more on characters really," says Hook. "Local colour – pardon the pun. In the words of the comedian, 'I don't care if you're black, I don't care if you're Muslim, I don't care if you're gay. I don't care about *you*'."

Karen doesn't smile. The lift opens on nine and Hook steps out, but she pushes the 'open' button and looks him sourly up and down. Probably the beer on his breath but what's it to her anyway? Why can't everyone leave him alone?

Karen steps out onto his floor and for a moment their noses almost touch; Hook holds his breath, wondering if he should kiss her. He tries to think about something bland but all he can imagine is putting his hand down her lacy bra and suckling on those plump nipples. A hard-on swells and he holds his BlackBerry over his crotch.

Karen sighs, looks at her watch. "Look, we need to hammer this out. There's going to be national attention on this service and that means getting the right balance with our editorial. I'm on my way to a meeting. Could you pop by my office later? Say four?"

"Four. Sure."

Hook had planned to write up the mosque story then head back to Soho to find some trouble. Being told what to do is frankly over-rated. Karen takes her finger off the button and her judgemental face is replaced by Hook's own on the polished metal. He leans his hot heat against the doors and closes his eyes.

At his desk, marooned between coffee machine and toilet door, Hook sits on his swivel chair with a sigh, logs on and wades through emails. He hasn't eaten since yesterday afternoon; remembering Maria's hungry expression he pulls the chair closer to his desk.

Hook looks round: an open plan plateau where no-one can take a call or check their emails in privacy, separated in their half-cells by material-covered boards. A frizzy-haired woman who always sits in the next cubicle is on the phone and, unable to see her mouth, it's impossible to read her eyes: what's that emotion behind her huge glasses, scorn, hatred, lust?

Unable to concentrate on the barely legible notes he took this morning Hook scans the webpage of councillors for Iqbal Ahmed; up pops the site supervisor, *sans* helmet. Bored, using 'Paint', Hook adds a 'Bob the Builder' hat to Ahmed's head and writes his mobile number in his pad.

Looking furtively over his shoulder and seeing no-one's looking Hook types 'looner' into the search engine but ever-vigilant council censors are waiting for him: an exclamation mark appears on screen, the word 'scenarios'.

The more he thinks about it, and he's thinking about it far too often, the more convinced he is that Monica's having an affair. Too many late nights, too many coy looks, not enough proper sex. Handjobs, dirty words, the odd picture message... it all feels cold, distant. When they first met it was Monica who made all the moves...what happened?

Hook looks round the empty office then calls the councillor. To his annoyance Ahmed answers in dialect.

Hook speaks as clearly as he feels able.

"Councillor Ahmed?"

There's a slight pause; Ahmed is affronted. "...Speaking?"

"Chris Hook here, we met this morning."

"Ah yes, hello Chris. What is the matter, checking your shorthand?"

"Kind of."

Hook starts to doodle balloons on his pad. The tinted windows are encroaching from the extremities: in a week or two it'll be dusk all day. Marooned, far from any windows, through which he can see only suburban streets and clouds, the sepia mist of the city's edge, Hook has long stopped looking out; but the fact the sky will now be tainted by cheap chemicals smudged on the glass like Vaseline on a pornographer's lens dispirits him, makes him sore.

"Well Christian, what do you wish to know? As I explained

this morning I have no real knowledge of the intrinsic design of the building, but if you speak to the architects responsible, a firm named Osborne and Bush –"

Hook looks down at his notes, where he's written: *I was born on a bus??* Scrubbing out the words, yanking out the offending pages and ripping them into shreds, Hook continues, "Do you ever visit a pub, Mister Ahmed?"

"...I'm afraid not."

"So you don't know any of the pubs in the Gibbet Street area."

"I'm afraid I have no real knowledge of 'pubs', Christian. Why do you ask?"

Hook peers between the lines of desks and through a clear window at Da Vinci's. Closing his eyes tight he rubs them and sees the shadows of his eyeballs jiggling in their sockets.

"Chris is fine. I was talking to the landlord of a pub near the Olympic site this morning. He seems to think there's a campaign of hate being directed towards him by local youths."

"This is very sad news. What is this gentleman's name?"

Hook flips his pad, curses: he hasn't got the guy's name.

"I can't reveal my source. The thing is, Mr Ahmed, this landlord seems to believe the organisation behind the mosque is in some way responsible for this hate campaign. As the landlord believes there might be an anti-Semitic element you'll see why I have to investigate."

There's an almost imperceptible pause before Ahmed responds. "I see. And why would this barman think that?"

Ahmed's warmish tone has lowered several degrees over the last few sentences. He obviously hasn't expected a conversation like this with a hack from his own tame rag. Tough. Hook swallows again and when he closes his eyes he sees yellow starbursts on his eyelids. Opening them he stares at the strip-lit ceiling.

"Well, apparently someone representing the mosque called

and asked if he'd considered leaving the area. I believe a cash sum was mentioned."

"And what would this have to do with these 'threats' as you call them?"

"I don't know," says Hook, rashly. "You tell me."

A short silence: bliss. Hook closes his eyes and ear-hum takes over. Then Ahmed's voice breaks through the static. "I *beg* your pardon?"

"Forget it."

The sandwich trolley comes round and Hook waves his arm but the blowsy middle-aged woman in ridiculously high heels who usually makes single-entendre wordplay ignores him.

"Hello?"

"Sorry to bother you, Councillor Ahmed. I'll pursue other lines of investigation."

"You do that Christian. Now I must speak to your boss. Karen Greening, is it?"

"Um –"

Ahmed hangs up. Hook gets the feeling he's done something stupid but isn't sure what. He's tired of gritting teeth, biting tongue, buttoning lip... Why shouldn't he ask questions councillors don't like? What's the point of being a journalist if you only print good news, obsequious love-ins that nobody except the committee ever read? Hook looks at his watch: almost three. His stomach burbles. As he stares at his blank screen a generic email pops up:

From: Head HR
To: all staff
Subject: lift etiquette
Message: Will all council employes please note that due to a meeting of equalities & diversity committee it has agreed that men should not enter lifts in the town hall if only one woman is inside. Some females particularly those of

traditional background can find upsetting or embarrassing to share a lift with a man. Should you be a male and discover a woman lone in a lift please wait for the next one. Thank you for you're co-operation.

By squinting he can see the women outside Da Vinci's, getting smashed in the sun, but he still has that meeting with Karen so Hook surfs the news. The suicide bomber who blew himself up yesterday has yet to be positively identified; police are checking a number of possible sources.

A self appointed Muslim spokesman is warning that any memorial service for Israeli victims of the 1972 Olympic massacre won't be tolerated during Ramadan. Other Muslim spokesmen denounce him for suggesting Muslims are more likely to commit violence when hungry.

Hook clicks on Monica's newspaper's webpage and reads her interview with the new Home Secretary, Clyde Collins, young, black and sharp, a bad lad who's seen the light, joined the big boys. Collins is justifying the decision not to allow atheists to take an active role in the multi-denominational service for peace at the Olympic stadium: what would they pray for, to whom would they make their pledge?

Seeing an item about sea monsters Hook clicks the link. Scientists investigating a gigantic fossil discovered at the bottom of the Atlantic estimate it could be eight hundred feet in length, making it the largest creature that's ever lived. As yet experts are no nearer working out what the creature is; suggestions put forward so far include fish, whale, crab, dinosaur and alien.

Hook's trying to picture an eight hundred foot whale floating over Da Vinci's when a message tells him he's been online for longer than necessary and is now disconnected. Hook stares gloomily at the council's corporate logo, incorporating a cross, star and crescent moon in one unholy mess.

A gaggle of girls across the divide are cooing and clucking at the sight of a workman on a rickety looking harness spraying the outside of the windows. He pushes his groin up against the glass and they cheer; Hook wills the rope to snap, envious of the man's youth and vigour, the way the girls in their secretary skirts want to be filled with his energetic mess. Hook doesn't want to fuck someone from work; he wants to fuck *everyone* from work. His BlackBerry heralds an email:

Thanks for checking out my harassment story. I have some new information. Let's talk soon. I mean what I said – I need you!
   U x

Hook logs off so no-one can sneak a look at his bookmarks (the comment pages, travel bargains, barking blogs) or his treacherous 'history'; time to close down. Turning on his 'out of office assistant', he clicks on 'start'.

Bank station is more than usually harrowing thanks to escalator works, fire alerts and the additional staff brought in to shout at people. Hook squeezes himself into a carriage hoping to read the latest on the ocean fossil and finds himself squashed between a rugger-bugger businessman reading something with a gun on the cover and a Chinese woman in a black dress, whose tome features a pink, perky sketch of a handbag and cocktail. Both seem unhappy.

When the tube stops in a tunnel Hook fears his lungs might detonate in the severe heat; by the time the doors open at Camden Town he knows he won't be going home. He's too scared of his daughter, let alone his wife – how can he explain to Shelley she won't be going to university after all?

As Hook limps along Camden High Street he calls his

brother and gets that same blank voicemail. Jack hasn't bothered to put a message on his own phone, and it isn't the laziness that annoys him, it's the arrogance and security money provides. Hook feels a pain in his chest; hate mail from the mortgage company. Flies fall about his head and he waves his arms.

After taking a deep swallow of a lager in Liberties, Hook watches sweaty shoppers gasp as they fight their way into and out of bargain basements, tat-clothing stores and furniture showrooms. He doesn't wish to consume: he's happiest in a t-shirt and shorts; the sofa on which he often sleeps is adequate. Why does the economy need people to keep buying tat? Is the economy still so fragile? What the hell's *wrong* with everybody?

Hook reflects that his midlife crisis is getting out of hand. His BlackBerry rings: pulling it out of his jacket he makes a face to demonstrate to any voyeur watching that he's unhappy.

"Hello Karen."

"Chris? Where *are* you?"

Even as Karen speaks Hook remembers he's supposed to meet her at four. He looks down at his watch: four-thirteen. Then up at the window:

LIBERTIES

"Sorry Karen, I tried to call but you were engaged and my BlackBerry keeps crashing."

"Well, never mind that now, are you coming to see me or what?"

"That's why I called. Shelley was taken ill from school so I had to rush home."

"Oh. You sound like you're in a pub."

Hook steps outside onto the street. "Sorry, I was at Euston station, bomb scare. It's over now."

"Oh. Look, I need to know what's happening with this

feature. I had to pull a lot of strings to get you unrestricted access. What are you doing with it?"

"Well, I went there –"

"Yes, that's another thing. Councillor Ahmed wanted you to do a proper interview with him and then he said you just sloped off. I need you to see him again. Do you think you could handle another interview?"

Hook swallows, remembering his phone conversation with Ahmed. "Yes, sure Karen, I'll call him."

"This is really important Chris; the service next week will be national news. I need the series, plus a puff-piece on Councillor Ahmed, by Friday."

"No problem," smiles Hook. "Look Karen I have to go..."

His ears are ringing; Karen says something like "walk eggs periods" that he doesn't catch. Hanging up he goes back in the pub, where an over-zealous barman has taken his half-empty pint. Hook orders another and sits by the window. At least she hasn't had any more premonitions about his mortality.

Leaving Liberties Hook limps north through Britannia Junction to the Lock. Car-chains shunt like rusting haemoglobin; vents expel halitosis; insects swarm and crawl up his nose. Pedestrians seem to stagger beneath the weight of the infernal sun and rather than share the load turn on each other like chained dogs. Burnt-out neon tubes are no longer replaced, creating strange hieroglyphs.

Hook smells the dirt in the air, the disease and want: noise-contrasts accelerating so all is silence or uproar. The festering city may indeed belong to the young, but it is not young: London (although immortal) is hobbled, in need of definition, invigoration, new purchase.

After purchasing t-shirts at the Lock, Hook takes a packed tube home. The train sticks in a tunnel and Hook looks round the carriage, aghast. Why do women look so unhappy? Don't they want this cut and thrust, this executive paranoia? Hook isn't even sure what his wife wants, but then they've only been married seventeen years. Even the teenage girls whose eye he caught wear that same furious expression. Maybe it's a front, that antagonism: his daughter seems happy enough.

The lift's out; with bags full of beer Hook trudges upstairs, hoping Monica will be home and sympathetic about his execrable day, but she's still at work and the fish gulp from the murk of their tank like he's their only hope, and a desperate one at that.

Shelley's locked in her silent room, incommunicative, networking: probably has her iPod on, bleating about her parents on Twitter. Strange, this new language, all these new terms; yet apart from the eroding coastal shelves nothing really changes, your parents still fuck you up.

Unable to look at the hoarding but suspicious anyway Hook lies on his back with a beer in one hand, the remote in the other and watches life-sized tennis girls squeal and gasp at Wimbledon. He's sweating despite the grinding aircon, anxious and menopausal, and to take his mind off things he closes his eyes. The delightful feminine yips become a soundtrack for some private fantasy: faceless Susan, or Ulrike, or whoever she is, in a white tennis dress on her hands and knees.

When Shelley opens her door and walks the seven steps into the living room Hook has to roll to face the back of the sofa to hide his erection; his lips kiss fabric.

Bangles jangle as his daughter pulls on her thick woollen cardigan. "I'm going out, dad."

Shelley's accent is like his own: half street, half posh, veering between classes according to need.

"Have fun hon."

Hook's voice is muffled by the sofa and his hard-on has

eloped so he rolls on his back, feeling stale beer sloshing around in his belly. He was right: Shelley has her big pink cardie on, off to the Arctic. She's slight, slim, like her mother, with Monica's big blue eyes and her father's defensive air. Her hair's a tangle of dreadlocks and beneath the cardigan she wears a complicated system of fishnet and cheese-cloth, lace and linen; a life-sized *Bratz* doll.

She looks down on him with an expression of hurtful indifference. What *is* he to her, a whale, a sea monster from the depths of the past, fading before her eyes? She doesn't even respond to the little notes he leaves her anymore – he isn't just disappearing, he's becoming *illegible*...

"Don't you want to know where, Dad?"

"I do, but you know me, I'm not one to pry."

Shelley smiles secretly, checks her appearance in the mirror and pushes hair from her eyes. The closer Hook looks at his daughter, the more he feels there's something not quite right about her face; too much lippy for a sixteen year old kid, and does she need eyeliner at her age?

"Over to Dahlia's for a rehearsal."

"Will you be late?"

"I dunno, maybe."

"Here." Hook reaches up to the table for his wallet and pulls out a twenty. "Get a cab. Order it from your friend's house. I don't want you walking round late at night with all the streetlights out."

Surprised, Shelley bends down and kisses his cheek. He smells good perfume – her mother's, possibly – and the tinnitus in his ears samples alarm bells, klaxons.

Shelley smiles at him like he's ninety. "Thanks, dad."

After she's gone Hook waits five minutes, eyes on the tennis, brain elsewhere, then pulls off his trousers and reaches for the remote. The beauty of Skybox: freezing real life. He tries to find a moment where the young Romanian is bent over waiting for a serve but keeps missing it, so instead he scrolls through the adult section of the menu, settling on some five pound lesbian flick: *Watch Hannah mount Anna!*

Hook watches intently, but on the vast plasma screen the images are so large they don't make any sense: pink hills, glooping mud-baths, deep wet ravines – the intimate geography of a *Koyaanisqatsi* out-take. The brown patch on the ceiling has expanded and looks like a boil about to burst and how can he be expected to pleasure himself with Ken, Deirdre and Van Gogh watching?

Muttering darkly Hook goes to the kitchen for another beer and walks over to the hoarding that blocks off the balcony. Pulling a board away too easily he steps out, gingerly. The balcony seems to wobble: probably just his mind, but he isn't taking any chances. Pressing the board back in place he lies on his bed in his shirt and boxers and tries to catch a breeze.

Still no Monica; is she really seeing someone else? Does he genuinely want that, her lips round some other guy's prick? Would that make it easier for him to play around? Who'd have him? If her uncle's seventy, Ulrike could be anything between fifteen and fifty. How old does he *want* her to be?

The laptop on Hook's bedside table hums so he waves a finger over the touchpad and the fish scatter; typing his ever-changing ID he browses hidden folders and a photograph of a wedding appears, but not the fairytale above the bed, the country church. This is a city registry office – featuring many of the same characters, but most playing different roles.

In this photo Hook's centre-right, Karen latched onto his arm in a short black dress, fishnets and Doc Marten boots; by his side are his mum and dad, looking glum, and on Karen's other side his old friend Michael Mullen and Mullen's little sister: Monica, wifey number two.

Using the mouse Hook zooms in on Karen's young, pre-office, pre-teetotal face, her pale smile and defiant green eyes;

then, using the cursor's little white hand he paws his way across the tell-tale bulge at her belly to Monica, sixteen, terrifyingly precocious in her tight pink dress and matching heels.

That was the first afternoon they ever met, and despite or because of her age the moment Hook looked into her eyes he wanted her. That was when he still got, roughly, what he wanted. That afternoon they escaped somewhere quiet where Monica wrapped her hair around his cock and he ejaculated in her ear.

Hook looks up at the photograph on the wall: Monica as bride. Back to the laptop: Monica as bridesmaid. He knows which image he likes best and it has less to do with age or experience than hindsight.

Sucking on his beer, Hook lies on the bed and watches the warm, insidious breeze shift the blinds, sending stripes across the walls. Far below him children in the park are playing, their cries sounding sad, lonely, and far away. He closes his eyes: blood fills his head, nausea his stomach.

Hook sees a woman whose face he can't identify floating to him in a pure white dress of fine lace. As he lies there unable to move or speak she hovers horizontally six inches above his weary body, held aloft by balloons: her nose so close, her breasts hanging loose so that her nipples brush his chest. It's Monica, as she looked on his wedding day – to Karen.

Hook's dozing – twitching, exposed – when the mobile he's stupidly left by the bed rings. He jolts awake: it's still light, eight, and his brain throbs with dehydration. When he sees it's Monica, his dream date, it all comes back as if she's thrown a diary at his head – they've agreed to have dinner with Jack and Maya. Filled with apprehension, Hook presses *answer*.

"...Hi."

His voice sounds full of guilt; he clears his throat.

"Chris, where *are* you? You know we said eight."

She sounds irritated, but no more than normal.

"On my way. Got caught up in something."

Monica sighs pregnantly. "You sound weak, Chris."

He *is* weak, he knows it – debilitated, fading from view. Hanging up he checks the water in the en-suite basin: working. Hook takes a shower, dresses in a short-sleeved shirt and slacks and feels a tad better. On his way out he takes a lump of cheese from the fridge, the first solids he's taken all day. Luckily Maya's a great cook, and he's famished. If he's quick he can get to Monica before Jack does.

As he leaves the block Hook has to push through the gang of louts gathered around the entrance. None speak but he tenses, then worries about his menopause. What the hell does he care about a few street kids? He's lived in this area his whole life.

Hook walks to the cab office next to the kebab shop, pleased his ankle seems on the mend. The high road seems to wallow in a strange dusky light, a luminous grey, an amalgam of metals and emptiness; something invisible nips his arm. On the side of a pub his father used and he never frequents, a huge poster asks worthy citizens to shop a benefit cheat.

His strange vision of child-like, wraith-like Monica lingers like a premonition. Perhaps he'll arrive at the dinner party to find them sat waiting, hands linked in some parody of a séance, to tell him Monica's dead, his wake-up call from her angry ghost. Some awful part of Hook hopes that's the case but it seems unlikely, with his luck.

The quiet, scrofulous streets the cab passes through seem darker than usual: some areas have had power cuts, others ever-tightening restrictions, and the overall effect seems to be that people over thirty rarely venture out to spend money. Instead they stay home, draining their own resources, order takeaways and drink alone with DVDs and iPods hooked up to the brain.

The cab driver, a sullen guy who looks like Saddam peering through the noose, doesn't speak during the journey. Hook tries to imagine what it must be like, to look and sound like this man then get a call to go pick up blokes from a pub. When they reach Jack and Maya's place Hook over-tips the guy but he doesn't smile, nor does Hook.

Slamming the car door he turns and looks up the four-storey house, the stars above brighter than ever due to the lack of competition from Earth. The next door along opens and an old woman descends carrying a burdened recycle box like a gift for the king, oblivious to the swarms of insects all around her. Hook sighs and presses the doorbell. There's a crackle of static: "Battersea Dog's Home?"

"Jack, it's me."

A childish laugh and a buzz; Hook pushes the door. He's in a well-lit hall, walls lined with modern art and a long staircase to the left which he grimly climbs. His brother's been here a few years; before meeting Maya he lived in Winchmore Hill. Typical Jack: goes straight and moves straight to Soho.

Their dining room is the size of Hook's apartment – another reason he doesn't like coming over. Monica, Jack and Maya are waiting at the oak table with solemn faces and empty bowls. Monica turns away furiously; he looks at Jack, who strokes his hairy chin and shrugs ruefully; then Maya, a stout black woman in her late-forties with bright red cheeks and dark, merry eyes, clad in that tiresome African dress and head-scarf. Maya kisses her teeth sorrowfully, rolls her eyes as only black people can and departs for the kitchen.

The blinds are closed from necessity: one benefit of living with your head in the clouds, you don't care about being watched. Does Jack ever find time to masturbate to the tennis?

The walls of the house are covered in tasteful pictures, ethnic weaves, African art – the walls of a couple without children. Jack tactfully withdraws, muttering something about shelling some nuts. Monica puts down her empty glass; the brittle clink makes him jump. Hook looks at his wife.

"I'm sorry Mon."

He almost laughs: it sounds like he's adopted a Jamaican accent. By way of reply Monica rouges and drinks red wine from a glass about the size of her head. Hook slumps on a high-backed, well-stuffed chair from Camden Passage and munches on a lattice of hardened parmesan as he waits for the shit-storm.

"*Why*, Chris?"

"Why what?"

"Why did you turn down your inheritance without consulting me?"

Hook finds himself looking at the tear of pink moisture that has collected at the bottom of Monica's glass and licks his lips. Why hasn't he been offered a drink?

"There was no point consulting you when I knew what I was going to do. If I'd pretended to ask your opinion first that would have been dishonest."

"So you didn't think it was worth asking me about transforming our whole lives?"

There's a terrific crash from the kitchen; thorough the door Hook sees Jack and Maya play-fight like the kids they'll never have.

"Listen," whispers Hook harshly, "I don't know what Jack told you but he was *loving* it, his little charity bit, helping out his little brother. Do you think I could live with that for the rest of my life? Knowing he'd bailed me out?"

"I don't know what goes on in your head," says Monica, pain in her voice, "I really don't. I guess you knew all along you were out of the will, but you never told me that either."

"Couldn't you guess? I hardly spoke to Mum for years! Why do you think we never even saw her that last Christmas before she died?"

"Er – because you told me she'd gone on a cruise?"

Before Hook can answer Jack and Maya emerge from the kitchen, Jack with a hot plate and Maya proudly holding the centre piece of the meal, chicken yassa, her speciality. Maya comes from Lewisham; she's done him the usual veggie cop-out and he's supposed to be thankful. This is what Hook hates about dinner parties, this more than anything: that he's supposed to be grateful, worse, to *show* his gratitude, despite the fact his hosts invited him over in the first place.

Grabbing a glass by his plate and pouring some Chilean Merlot Hook plonks the bottle in the middle of the table like a flag on Everest. Jack plucks it up, shaking his head. Monica's cheeks are bright red: this is as angry as she's been since finding out Karen was his new boss. Maya clears her throat.

"For what we are about to receive..."

She always does this: says grace, despite knowing Hook and Monica's atheist/agnostic stance. Rude, Hook thinks. He opens his eyes and looks round the table: Jack, to his left, eyes closed, smiling piously; Monica, opposite, staring angrily; and Maya, to his right, face shining with gratitude.

Prayers over, Maya begins to serve. At least, thinks Hook as he watches her expert fingers, something good came from his mother's death. Maya nursed her till the end and, unknown to everyone, was working on Jack – his being gay (happily so, and *energetically* so) was a minor complication for a woman of her fortitude. Sweet Maya, the feisty South Londoner who nursed their mother to death, said Jack, had cured him of his homosexuality.

Soon Jack was telling an astonished Hook that he was now straight, anti-racist and Christian – and attempting to be a father. All of these were news to Hook, who had particular issues with the word 'cured'.

"It's not a fucking *illness*, Jack."

"I found it debilitating."

Even the discovery that Jack was sterile hadn't spoiled the romance; Maya announced that if this was God's will she was fine with it. Frequent foreign holidays, spontaneous activities; even the cutlery emphasises the adultness of their lives. Hook finds himself turning a fork over and over, watching the way it reflects light from the Harvey Nicks candles, liking the weight of the metal in his fingers.

Jaffa Jack beams smugly from within his beard. "Haven't done too bad have I? To say where I started up."

"Oh, give me a break…" mutters Hook, looking at Monica, who's chewing without enthusiasm, staring at a Bedouin print above his head.

Jack raises an eyebrow. "Something bothering you, *bruv*?", emphasising the last word in a way he knows annoys Hook.

Hook tries to respond with a mouthful of sweetcorn. "It's just we *always* have this fucking conversation. You were in the gutter, self-made man, blah blah. What about Mum and Dad, don't they count for anything?"

Jack sips his wine and regards him calmly. "Of course they do. You know they do. They gave us all the love we needed, even when they had nothing. Maybe you just didn't see it because for you it was always there."

"What was?"

"Money, security." Jack smiles at Monica then back at Hook. "You never saw how hard they worked to get out from their situation. You were too young."

"Yeah, it was all so fucking easy for me, the whole deal."

As a self-employed builder Hook's dad worked long hours, and his mum was usually at some Spare Rib conference or anti-nuke campsite, so Hook was brought up mainly by Jack – a cause of resentment even now.

Jack left secondary school the year Hook arrived and was living in a tower block overlooking the school, the George

Orwell; sadly, his big brother was never watching. The bullying got out of hand. Hook was a small, weedy kid and his accent veered all over the place, so the working class kids thought he was too smart and the middle class kids thought he was too scruffy.

It seems to Hook, looking back, while he knows it's probably just his discriminatory memory taking over, that the black kids were the worst. If that were so, he reasons, it's probably because they were more likely to be poor and he was an easy target – as Shelley would become years later.

Maya sighs pregnantly and goes to the kitchen. Monica glares at him so Hook goes to lend a hand. Maya's fat rump wrapped enticingly within turquoise cloth presents itself as she leans to get a dessert dish, so he slaps it hard. Maya turns with a puzzled look. Beneath her crimped-straight fringe her eyes pop out when she sees Hook and for once she's speechless. Her mouth is open wide and he can see her long tongue, smell the garlic and wine on her breath.

Taking Maya's flour-covered hand Hook kisses it and sucks her finger, watching her eyes for any reaction, seeing none except a widening of those dark, shocked eyes; so he turns abruptly and goes to the downstairs toilet under the stairs. Lowering his pants he sits staring moodily at some sort of Saharan tapestry that seems as alien to Hook as if it arrived by meteorite.

His gut feels tight, constipated, and he can barely manage more than a dribble. Dehydrated: no wonder – he's been drinking all day and hasn't had any water to ease the load. His liver pings and needles and he puts his face in his hands. What the hell is he *doing*?

A tap on the door. "Chris?"

Maya's rich soft voice.

"What?"

"Are you... alright?"

"Fine. I won't be long. Sorry Maya."

After a long pause Hook hears Maya's footsteps retreat back to the dinner party; she says something in that sonorous voice and everyone laughs too hard. Hook pulls up his pants and washes his face using some stupid homemade liquid soap, ten quid a spurt. He pumps some more on his hands and even that gives him an erection: he should have opened the door to Maya, soaped up her big brown tits.

Once, in a rare unguarded moment, Jack confided Maya's peccadillo: she likes to be covered from head to toe in food – yoghurt, oil or butter – then ridden like a slippery seal. In Hook's imagination it's always custard: the vivid yellow goo an exquisite contrast on her shining skin.

Hooked tweaks the tap: nothing. Another water cut. Cursing he wipes the soap onto a dainty flannelette and unlocks the door. It isn't good, he knows, this feeling of impotent arousal, this blind groping for sensation. But it's too late now: he's disappearing.

The London bombings presented Hook with an opportunity he'd never realised he was waiting for: to disappear, leave Monica and Shelley behind and follow his dreams. He'd been gone two hours when he realised he'd made a dreadful mistake – he didn't have any.

Hook checked into a cheap hotel off Berwick Street. Sat in his tiny room on that strange day, something on TV made him laugh. A helicopter picked out a train making its way to Essex; as the camera panned back he saw the whole of London sprawling, and it seemed hilarious that anyone had the arrogance to imagine they could take on this vast, ancient city and win.

Lying on a tatty single bed, defeated by the challenge of

finding a dream, Hook tried to conjure up a new identity. After a few hours he realised he couldn't even think of a name, let alone a whole new act.

It became apparent the police could name every one of the victims of 7/7, and they hadn't found one cell or wisp of cloth from his shattered body. So he drank himself into a stupor, threw away his coat and went home, blaming what he'd seen on that terrible morning. It worked: Monica held him tight. She wasn't to know, and CCTV hadn't revealed, that he'd stood on the platform and let the doomed train go because it was full.

Over the next few weeks Hook went home each lunchtime to ensure he got to the credit card bill naming the Berwick Street hotel before his wife. That was the last time he tried to disappear. Maybe disappearing wasn't something you could at will: you had to wait for it to happen.

"You know what I hate?" snaps Hook, "*assumptions*. At dinner parties you're expected to hate the Jews and the Yanks. Down the pub and the greasy spoon you're expected to hate the Pakis and the queers. So arrogant, don't you think, *people*?"

The cocaine has come out early. He's been flagging: his fingers feel frostbitten, his liver like a dead badger sewn inside him, so many possibilities going through his frazzled brain that the conversations around him have lost all meaning, as a chair loses meaning upon inspection. Mortgages, schools, Palestine; who cares, really, deep down?

Obviously everyone else does; Hook can tell by the way they look at him as he yells and roars. He listens to his own angry voice, astonished it's coming from his throat when he feels so placid inside, so docile and loving.

Now he remembers why he's so angry: the cocaine's

politically correct, made by unexploited farmers, shipped to Europe on boats powered by soya. Somehow that led the conversation round to global warming and all the associated evils, which apparently include noise-pollution. Jack and Maya, it seems, chair a noise abatement society locally. In Soho. They move to Soho and they complain about the fucking *noise*.

"Yes, you're so fucking different aren't you?" snarls Monica, who apparently has yet to forgive him. "Never one to judge a book by its cover, never one to judge someone by their skin, their education, their parents-"

"Bullshit!" hollers Hook. "Name me one example!"

"One?" Monica laughs nastily and shakes her head. "Just *one*?"

"Shall we have some music?" smiles Maya. Before anyone can answer she puts on Amy Winehouse. That angers Hook too: how can the woman who wrote and sang *Rehab* end up in rehab? To take his mind off the fact he'll never get a chance to tell her where she's gone wrong Hook toys with his vegetable bake, but it's rubbery and the coke has suppressed his appetite, and all he really wants to do is jump around.

He looks up to find everyone staring at him and he grins. "Anyway, fuck politics – let's party! Come on, let's do something wild for once! Whaddya say folks?"

"Like what?" his brother asks him, a small smile on his hairy lips. So cruel, Jack, sometimes. *Back to Black* still plays in the background but it's drowned out by the white noise in Hook's head. He jumps up, unzips his pants and slaps his semi on his plate: the coke has made it shrink and there's barely room for a couple of kernels of sweetcorn to stick to the underside.

"Let's have an orgy!"

Jack's expression changes to one of disgust; Monica looks ready to pop, an angry balloon; Maya puts a hand over her mouth in mock horror, though her eyes are smiling. Hook pulls his cock in and slumps, reaching for his wine like a drowning man.

Maya chuckles soulfully. "He's in one randy mood tonight!"

Taking aghast eyes away from Hook Jack turns on her quizzically. "What do you mean?"

Hook decides to help Maya out. She's a good egg, really. He smiles round the table, at Maya, who shakes her head slightly, eyes wide now with warning, then at Monica, who looks like a candidate for spontaneous human combustion, and finally at his smug big brother with his big smug head.

"Oh, I was giving Maya a *hand* in the kitchen, bruv, you know how it is..."

Dreamily Hook watches his brother glide round the table on well-oiled castors; within a blink he's looming over him. Hook smiles cheesily. Jack's fist thuds into his nose like a wrecking ball – lights out.

Wednesday 23rd June

A UFO descends from the lightening sky with lights spinning in unfamiliar colours, horns blaring with a robotic bovine quality: vast, circular, the flying saucers' hull stupendous yet suspended in space. Hook feels a surge of gratitude that the race is saved, God will finally vanish up his own fundament, and somebody or something has finally noted his struggle and come to help. Astonishing; almost as astonishing as there not *being* any UFOs, no other life, throughout the universe.

As he surfaces into the harshness of morning Hook sees that what he took for a UFO is actually the post office tower bistro slowly revolving, lights still lit in the hard grey dawn. The blaring horns are from a line of protest trucks that are blocking up the West End. His happiness was an illusion.

Hook spits blood on the grass and sits up in a small patch of greenery in Soho Square. He must have scaled the iron railings – his trousers are ripped, his stinging knuckles covered in blood. Wasps harass him, his nose feels lop-sided and his ears ring like two sets of wedding bells.

Then he remembers the fight with Jack, except all Hook can recall is Jack's fist crashing into his face, after which it all went black. Did he hit him back? His knuckles throb, but he doubts it; he isn't *that* stupid. Even drunk Hook knows sober Jack would eat him alive.

Hook's head clangs, like bin lids, like saucepan and spoon; he runs his fingers through his matted hair to ensure he hasn't been scalped overnight. His throat's clogged with bitter cobwebs and he shakes with nausea and self-loathing. His bones have osteoporosis, his liver's doing Catherine-wheels and a slug's crawled into his armpit to die. Half the buttons on his shirt are gone, as is his jacket; miraculously his BlackBerry, shoved down his pants, seems intact.

By the railings opposite the FA HQ Hook urinates against a bush, watched by a life-sized cut-out of Frank Lampard. Feeling a lump on his bell-end he has a momentary existential panic until a kernel of sweetcorn drops to the scorched earth. Hook espies a young lady with the blasé, resentful expression of an *au-pair* walk towards him pushing someone else's pram. Catching her eye he turns, pissing on his shoes, and he starts to walk away, jets of urine spurting. The *au-pair* screams; tucking himself in Hook begins running, shards of pain pulsing through his ankle, warm piss dribbling down his leg.

Hook staggers inside the small, Catholic church at the east side of the square. Not wishing to be too dramatic he goes to the back row, falls to his knees and prays; it doesn't work. Hook has always had the feeling someone's watching him, and not in a good way; yet here, where he needs that omniscient eye, he senses its absence. Church is the one place, reflects Hook, where one feels self-conscious because one isn't being watched.

Too delicate to contemplate the tube Hook rides a black cab into the sun, swigging warm Lucozade as the cabbie recites tracts memorised from the *Turner Diaries*. The trucks have caused near-gridlock: in their protest at rising fuel costs they have succeed both in wasting tons of the stuff and alienating the entire car-driving public. Hook cares little about petrol prices but this seems like the start of something big, something to add to a list of things that might hurt him.

"Now your Polak," explains the cabbie's haircut eagerly, "he's alright, works hard, likes a pint, nothing weird..."

Festering with alienation Hook buries himself in his paper. Wimbledon's holding its annual festival to the gods of disappointment; another kid's been stabbed in South London; experts examining the enormous fossil found beneath the Atlantic are now considering the possibility *it* – whatever *it* was – had been very young. If that's the case, when fully grown it could have been up to a mile long. The newspaper shows a silhouette of a mile-long whale hanging over Central London to provide an idea of scale.

Fractured moments of the previous evening keep bubbling: Monica's face, Jack's fist and Maya's arse, her expression when she turned to see him standing behind her with that undignified lump in his trousers. Did she feel honoured? Had she told Jack the full story? What if Jack thumped him for some other reason? What will Jack do if she *does* tell him? Hook realises he'll have to make it up to everyone somehow. But first he needs to get to work, to get some rest.

The shaven-headed security guard smiles and raises those vast eyebrows when Hook enters the lobby; it's not the first time he's scuttled in wet and sorry. In the old days, before flirting with sobriety, he regularly arrived in such a state, and worse. Lowering his gaze Hook makes for the lift, praying no-one gets in, Karen especially – though if she *is* in the lift he'll have to get out, by recent decree.

To Hook's delight the vast office floor is empty, apart from the bedraggled army of limping cleaners. What have those eyes witnessed: burning villages, stillborn children, desert explosions? But then maybe even some suits are human. Who knows what horrors they've seen: fights, betrayals and dwindling deaths?

Early morning sunlight sharp-angles over empty desks, over photographs of loved ones and furry creatures impaled on pencils, on confidential files left carelessly open and lockers where people are supposed to keep personal effects but don't. Hook likes the office like this, but the tinted windows are edging closer: soon there'll be no morning light, just that dismal all-day-glow.

Holding his sore nose, Hook scurries to his locker for the holdall containing the spare set of clothes he keeps for emergencies, then walks briskly towards the far doors and the men's toilet with its mercurial shower. Pushing through the door, almost safe, a hand falls on his shoulder.

"Chris?"

He turns to see Karen wearing her most efficient suit, nose rouged. Hook holds his holdall behind his back like a kid waiting for the cane. Behind Karen, almost completely hidden from view by his ex-wife's bosom, stands a young, impossibly pretty Asian girl in a plain white dress and flat white shoes. She can't be much more than five foot tall, with long black hair and a tiny nose. Her eyes are almond-brown, her untainted eye-whites shine with frightening intellectual qualities in the sun.

"Hello Chris, you're in early. This is Farzana – you remember the work-experience student I mentioned on the phone yesterday? She'll join you on the photoshoot this morning."

"Photoshoot?"

"Your interview with the rapper about the knife campaign?"

Hook nods resentfully. "Oh – yes."

Hook leans round Karen and nods morosely at the girl, whose smile seems genuine, if casual. Probably scared; he doesn't blame her. He's scared too, of everything, but mostly of Karen. Karen's nose is wrinkling: time to escape.

"Erm –" he's forgotten the girl's name already – "if you go and put the kettle on, I'll be back in a minute. Dodgy –" Hook is about to say 'curry', but that might be offensive. Actually, asking her to put the kettle on is probably offensive too. Hook smiles, too expansively; Farzana's eyes widen.

Holding his holdall to his chest like a magic shield Hook backs through the doors, smiling cretinously at the two women, who regard him solemnly. In the toilet he drops the holdall, puts his head on a cold sink edge and sighs. Then he remembers the pub in its little island of rubble, his date with Sufi Susan, Urdu Ulrike. The day's looking up: time to shower. Stripping naked Hook turns on the tap: nothing.

Dressing again, Hook sees the potted plants on the windowsill are drooping from a lack of water and light. Taking one of the plastic ablution jugs for believers from its shelf Hook enters a cubicle, washes his hands and face and realises his knuckles are still throbbing. Washing away the blood he sees on his left hand small diamond-shaped dots on each knuckle, borstal-speak for 'kill the cops' and on his right hand, to emphasise the point, four letters: 'ACAB'.

The public housing estate comprises a network of five-storey blocks linked by walkways with two tall white blocks at the centre. Hook's never felt comfortable in the vicinity when it isn't raining and it hasn't rained for over a month. But Prof-SC, the teen rapper he's supposed to interview, has insisted Hook come to his "ends", presumably so Hook can see how 'street' he is.

Fortuitously the temp, Farzana, has a car. Hook had assumed she was too young for a bike without stabilisers, let alone a Fiat Panda. They took it in turns to descend in the lift to the car park beneath the town hall, but according to the Koran car-sharing was fine.

Holding his purpling nose while trying to keep his fists out of view Hook shows Farzana the safest place on the estate to park. The girl seems to find him hilarious, laughing at everything he says as if he's some eccentric relative. It saddens Hook that she sees him more as a shambolic uncle than a potential date.

When Prof-SC opens the door to find a suited mediocrity and a tiny Asian clutching a camera he scowls, but when Hook holds up his council ID the tall, muscular young man sees his knuckles and raises his own fist, laughing, and they exchange a ghetto greeting that hurts like hell.

Hook sits beside Farzana on a dirty sofa in a small, cluttered room, curtains closed and oxygen in short supply, while Prof-SC, surrounded by vinyl records and mixing equipment, paces up and down explaining why the "yoot" should bow to his superior wisdom on pressing issues like knife crime and drugs.

The usual form is for Hook to smile politely as he pretends to take notes, then go back to the office and write something uplifting and non-controversial, but the hangover's still hammering his sensibilities and all he can think about is Monica's fury, slapping Maya's arse and getting punched: no more than he deserved, all things considered.

"What I'm saying," drones Prof-SC, "is drop the knife. Drop the gun. I been there, done me time. It not a pretty place, no way."

"You were in prison?" Hook asks conversationally, dabbing fresh blood from his nose-hole. "What for?"

Prof-SC shrugs, a faint smirk played playing on his lips. He wears a sleeveless vest that shows off a vivid large tattoo on one arm but Hook can't read the gothic writing; he doubts that it says anything nice. Prof-SC speaks with a beat poet's incantation, minus the poetry.

"Look," says Prof-SC, "I ain't ashamed. I was a naughty boy, caught up in crime all my life. Blazing, shotting, marking, gettin' in beef, repping me endz strapped, getting gripped by the feds, slipping through other ends, ripping and jacking for me Ps – but you gotta remember that was all we knew. We grow up on the street. *That* was our school."

Whenever Hook encounters a black boy who speaks ghetto he find them essentially unpleasant; whenever he meets young black men with London accents they seem fine. Maybe it's another racist sub-plot going on within his confused psyche, like his penchant for black women with straight hair.

He tries to write, but every time he looks down he sees his knuckles. In the end Hook closes his eyes and hopes for the best. His head throbs – the windows are closed, he's put on a winter jacket that he doesn't feel like removing in case he has to run away and he's being both grilled and microwaved.

Opening his eyes he re-tracks. "The *street* was your *school*?"

Prof-SC stops mid-flow, sighs loudly and rolls his eyes. His limbs seem to spark with malevolent energy. "*Yes* man. That's what I'm saying. There was no school, so the street was our *crib*."

'Crib': infantilised youth. Hook rubs his knuckles and in the corner of his eye sees Farzana notice them and edge discreetly away.

"Really?" says Hook, struggling to keep the impatience from his voice. "There was actually *no school*? I didn't know that. I thought there were several schools round here –"

Prof-SC appears frustrated that he hasn't managed to impress upon Hook his unique perspective. Perhaps as a direct consequence he becomes noticeably more animated.

"It's a figure of speech man, you get me? What I'm saying is, when you grow up in this neighbourhood it's easy to get involved in stuff. Everyone's beefin', burstin' and blowin'. If you don't steal – you don't eat."

"Oh for fucks' sake, this is preposterous!" Hook suddenly exclaims. "I'm sorry Mr… *DC*, whatever, but you're talking utter crap. You seriously mean to tell me that the only way you could eat was by stealing from little old ladies? There were no jobs, no *dole*? I've never heard such... self-serving *bullshit* in my life!"

Prof-SC seems displeased. Standing a few inches from Hook's knees he towers over him; the earnest rapper's muscles coil and writhe. The lump in his pants Hook earlier took for a sign of attraction appears to be a machete and he swallows nervously.

Prof-SC's voice rises. "Easy for you mister, innit! Where you grow up, Surrey?"

"Holloway, actually."

'Holloway', Hook has learned from bitter experience, sounds better than 'Islington' under such circumstances. Though Prof-SC seems unimpressed. He appears about to do something awful when he remembers the girl, sitting quietly with her camera pointed at his knees, a slight smile playing on her lips.

"This interview over!" roars Prof-SC. "Out my house, white boy! Out of here little Indian!"

"East Ham, actually," snaps Farzana.

"What I care little girl? You all the fucking same to me."

Hook stands, keen to be away. With his rudimentary knowledge of local gang culture he's worked out the tattoo; it signifies the fact that Prof-SC has at some point 'merked' some poor sod. Hook has no desire to be next. Besides, he has a date; time to beat a hasty but dignified retreat. He smiles sideways at his young colleague. "Come along, Farzana."

"Why did you wind him up like that?" Farzana hisses excitedly as Hook follows her down the desolate stairwell. "He looked like he was gonna tear you apart innit!"

Hook sighs, dispirited by the tone of the morning, the puddles of glass, the smell of poverty. Why isn't he country gardens correspondent for *Tatler*?

"I don't know, really. I mean, I didn't set out to be, *confrontational*. I just get so... *sick* of hearing all this... guff."

Farzana looks back at him, one hand on the rail, the other on her camera, a mischievous smile on her face. "What's 'guff'?"

"Nonsense. Horseshit. Sorry for swearing."

"I *am* over eighteen."

"Are you? Sorry."

"You like to apologise, don't you?"

Hook thinks about that one as they reach the ground floor and push through graffiti-daubed doors to the car park. It's not so much that he *likes* it, just he's always having to *do* it. Either for things he's said or done, or not said or not done, or for being what, who, where and why he is: Hook.

"Never complain, never explain" – that was his editor's motto on Fleet Street. That's his trouble, he realises: he's always complaining and frequently explaining.

Farzana's opening the car door when a loud and furious yelling prompts them to look upwards. Prof-SC leans over the balcony, gesticulating and shouting angrily. Hook debates giving him the finger but decides against it. He smiles politely and waves; the rapper waves back, indecorously.

Once safely out of the estate – back to the high street, where there are statutory laws, not just *consequences* – Hook directs Farzana to Gibbet Street. His liver nudges his ribs and he grunts; she shoots a sideways glance so he looks out onto the busy highway.

Farzana pulls up at the bus stop opposite the Anne Boleyn and looks round, bewildered. She's probably never noticed this old building, driven past a thousand times on her way to the coffee shop and the Islamic bookshop, never seen this public house with its living, breathing history.

Hook is about to get out when he remembers his manners.

"Look, do you fancy a drink?"

"Pardon?"

Seeing the look of puzzlement on Farzana's face Hook has to backtrack his words to make sure he hasn't requested some sordid sexual favour.

"A drink. This is a nice little pub."

"*Me*, in a pub? I don't think so, do you?"

"No." He regards her sadly. "You're right. Look, I'll see you back at the office. If anyone asks I'm chasing a story. In fact – don't go back yet, go shopping. Go wherever you go when you have free time. I'll see you about three."

Farzana looks at him with appalling fear in her eyes. She's a slave, reflects Hook: a slave to economics, but then who isn't? Farzana shifts into first, then looks at him. "Won't Karen wonder where I am?"

"If she rings, you're with me. Okay?"

Farzana shrugs unreadably and Hook wonders what he'd done now. The new codes, the new details: he can't read anything anymore. The laws of physics have been rewritten, the constitution revised without his knowledge, let alone consent.

As Hook pushes at the swastika-daubed wood and enters the pub he spots the crusty old barman on his knees picking up shards of glass from the carpet beneath a newly boarded-up window. Hearing the door open the barman jumps, looking scared when he turns, but he visibly relaxes when he sees it's Hook. Standing slowly and rubbing his knee with one hand, a long shard of glass in the other, he goes behind the bar and glares challengingly from his sanctum.

"Did you get anywhere with that phone message?"

"Working on it."

"Pint?"

"No rush, do you need a hand with that?"

The barman looks down at the glass then throws it into a plastic bin: the shard breaks with a sharp crack. "Nah mate, all finished."

He reaches up for a pint pot. Hook looks down at the purple smudge of a carpet, fragments glittering in the sun.

"Guinness please."

"Extra Cold?"

"No, not really."

As he pours, the barman nods at Hook's jacket. "Can I have me phone back? Susan said she had a strange conversation with a posh geezer. Reckoned it must be you."

Taking the pint, reluctantly Hook hands over the mobile, takes off his jacket and hangs it on the peg, then sucks on his Guinness. The barman hangs round like an old dog, so Hook feels compelled to feign interest. He nods at the broken window. "More trouble?"

"It's every night mate. You wouldn't believe it round here, mob rule."

"Have you thought about installing CCTV?"

"What do *you* think? Gets lifted before I can even read the bleeding instructions."

"Can't Ulrike help?"

The barman frowns.

"Oh, you mean Susan? Dunno why she uses that stupid name. That's two weeks at bloody college for you. She'll always be Susan to me."

Hook shrugs, his pint evaporating in the heat. The pub's emptiness puzzles him: on a hot day like this where could be better than a brown old pub, even one with smashed windows on a busy roundabout in the arsehole of London?

From the look of the peeling pink wallpaper the place hasn't been done up since the Blitz, but Hook likes that, and the sparkle of glass, the old Guinness posters on the walls, even the old telly above his head with the sound down, on which a golf ball scoots across a smooth green like a robotic mouse.

The barman's looking into space chewing something so Hook clears his throat. "Quiet again today."

Those pensive eyes bore into him.

"It's always quiet. Everyone's gone."

"Gone where?"

"Essex, overseas, you name it. No-one wants to live round here no more. Not worth the hassle."

"Then why are *you* still here? Why postpone the inevitable? Get out, sell up, retire; there must be easier ways to live than this."

The barman wipes his nose then smears green snot down his shirt. "The arse dropped out of the market in case you hadn't noticed. We're just outside the Olympic zone so I'll get fuck all except aggro when that kicks off. I own this place, been in the family generations, but you can't make money without a chain now. Taxes, inflation, licenses, and everyone who likes a pint's usually skint."

Against his better judgment, Hook prods him. "You own the whole building?"

"Yus. Three floors above this one. Bit ropey in places but it's all mine."

"Don't you have any family?"

"Just Susan these days. Her mum went down the coast years back when she married some tuppenny gangster. Since Rach died, Susan's come back here as much as she can. She's a great help. Gets all sorts of shit when she goes down the high street."

"Does she? Why?"

"Well, let's just say she likes to show off her legs. They don't like it, some of 'em. Don't even like a girl on a bike. They raped one of their own the other day, said she was 'pleasing' herself. On a fucking Raleigh. I wouldn't mind if it was a Chopper."

Hook waves his stained glass. "Another pint please. What happened to Susan's mum – Rach?"

The old man shrugs and looked away. "Suicide."

"I'm sorry."

"Don't be. She was a right old – hello, Susan love!"

The anger and fatalism in the old man's battered face is replaced by something close to affection. Hook turns and jumps; he hasn't heard anyone enter and yet here stands an apparition.

Susan – or perhaps Ulrike – is in her late-teens or early-twenties, with ghostly white skin, dimpled cheeks, black hair tied back in what the tabs call a Croydon-, Kirkby- or some other shithole- facelift. She wears a white shirt with rolled-up sleeves and black jeans, chews gum and stares at him intently.

She has delicate grey eyes but there are worry lines around her mouth and her eyes look puffy, like she's been crying. "You were saying Unc?"

The girl speaks with a soft, warm London accent, laden with pride and resourcefulness.

"I was just telling our journalist friend," says the barman, "what a divine lady your mother was."

The girl snorts and gives Hook a cheeky smile that makes his head swim, then looks at her uncle again. "Fuck me, you been on the hard stuff Sid?"

Sid: that saves him the trouble of asking. The old man smiles sadly. "You know me, my dear."

This apparition looks at Hook again and he feels chills pass through his body as her eyes bore into him, twinkling like uncut diamonds with a seductive quality he finds encouraging.

"Christian, ain't it?"

"Call me Chris... Susan."

Hook extends a trembling hand. The girl takes it. Her hand

is warm and strong, her forearms sprinkled with childish freckles. There's an impudent look in her eye that disarms him, makes him stupid.

"Call me Ulrike. Ignore Uncle Sid. He gets confused."

"Less cheek you!" laughs Sid. "You'll always be Susan to – oi, now come on love, no need for that!"

Ulrike pulls a cigarette from her handbag and is about to light up. She looks round challengingly, the flame of the lighter glittering in her eyes. "Who's gonna tell, Unc?"

"I'll lose me license love!"

"You're losing it anyway, get over it." Ulrike goes to the door and shoots the bolt, Hook's eyes on her tight behind in her jeans. Turning, she catches his eye and as she walks to him on mercury-lubed pins he feels she might walk right through him, but is she a ghost, or is he invisible?

Ulrike stops just in time and looks him up and down, smoke trails gushing from her nostrils into his face. Hook wants to suck it all in, this fire from her belly. No-one smokes now – even Monica packed it in, against his wishes.

"So you're the journalist. The posh one. Least I *thought* you was posh. What happened to your nose?"

"Oh, nothing." Hook touches it tentatively. "Family trouble."

Ulrike laughs. "Fuck me! We related?"

It isn't a question so Hook says nothing. Ulrike smiles wickedly. She hasn't even mentioned the newly-boarded window. "You gonna do a story on our little problem then?"

"I might," says Hook, "if you can convince me there *is* a story. Do you have proof of anything?"

Ulrike is about to speak when something on the TV hovering over Hook's head makes her mouth drop, her tongue loll like a buffoon. She squints, smoke in her eyes; Hook jerks his head upwards to see what she's looking at.

"What?"

According to *Sky News*, a truck has been parked beneath the railway bridge beside Holloway Road station. On examination it's been found to contain several tons of explosives – someone tried to detonate the device using a mobile phone as the 11.10 Kings Cross to Leeds intercity was due to cross the bridge.

If the bombers had succeeded the death toll would have been in the hundreds, both on the train and in the vicinity of Holloway Road, where Hook drinks when he doesn't wish to be seen by people in his social circle and Shelley hangs out to be seen by hers.

Hook shakes his head slowly. "Nutters. One day they'll find an operative with brains and we'll be in real trouble."

Ulrike snorts with a seen-it-all scowl. "Fucking animals. They're taking over."

Hook's heart sinks. "Who are?"

"Muslims."

He attempts to help her out of the hole she's digging. "Muslims, Jews, Christians. I'm sick of the lot of them."

"*I* doubt it was Jews who planted the truck," says Ulrike, "or some mad vicar, disgruntled at his diminishing parish."

Hook snorts impatiently. "Didn't you hear about the anarchists in France trying to derail trains, the ALF and their missions of mercy? Muslims didn't even invent suicide bombs – that was the Tamils. Everyone thinks their cause is uniquely worth killing for. Mossad, some crazy evangelist sect, the scientology brigade – who knows?"

"I do." Ulrike looks over at her uncle, collecting last night's glasses – twelve hours too late, by Hook's watch. "I tell you what. If these pricks ever do get it together and the bombs start going off there'll be a civil war in this country."

"I don't know," says Hook with caution, "Most people aren't stupid. They know you can't blame everyone for one bunch of nutters."

Ulrike stubs out her fag on the bar. "Don't be so sure. There was a lot of anger after 7/7. Mosques attacked, Muslims attacking everyone else. Next time it'll all kick off. You can feel the tension, the anger."

"You almost sound as if you relish the prospect," says Hook nervously.

Ulrike laughs, lifting herself out of the hole. "Don't be silly. I ain't got time for none of it. I'm just sick of being told what to think, do and wear by some medieval nutjob with voices in his head."

"I'll second that. Cheers." Hook raises his pint before realising Ulrike doesn't have a drink. "Will you join me? You did want to see me after all."

Ulrike hesitates, looks at her expensive little watch, her uncle and the bolted door, then goes behind the bar and pushes vodka into a wine glass. Fag in mouth she reaches over and taps his pint, eyes widening as she sees his fresh tattoos; then removes the cig and gulps her measure without flinching.

Hook is childishly impressed: this feels like the crush he had on that long jumper at boarding school, except he feels guiltier. The only thing that bothers him about the long jumper is the cliché.

"Christ," says Hook approvingly. "You must like that stuff."

Ulrike wipes her lips with relish, takes a pull of smoke. "Russian blood. We came in the eighteen hundreds to make shoes."

"Who's 'we'?"

"My mum's family. Been round here a hundred and fifty years, now we're being pushed out."

"Is that what... you wanted to talk about?"

Ulrike looks at her uncle, returning with a teetering tower of mucky glasses; he pulls a put-upon face and disappears through the bead curtain. Ulrike leans over, confidentially:

Hook smells good perfume – *Paco Rabanne*, possibly. Her breasts beneath her shirt are small, uplifting. He concentrates on her luminous eyes, interrogating yet provocative.

"You heard of Iqbal Ahmed?"

"Course I have. I spoke to him yesterday."

"Know much about him?"

"Not much. Councillor, soon to be council leader; pretty straight-up bloke."

Stubbing out her fag Ulrike looks round the empty pub furtively then leans in closer, her lips vodka-glazed cherries. She's barely twenty, for Christ's sake. Maya, Karen, jailbait Farzana – the summer heat is driving him crazy.

Ulrike speaks slowly, calmly, her London accent smoothed out. "He runs a vice ring."

"What do you mean a 'vice ring'?"

"I mean he runs a few knocking shops."

The way Ulrike says 'knocking shops' is meant to convey disgust, but arouses him. Hook moves in closer to the grimy bar so she can't see his lap. Castration: there's an option. Freedom and serenity to read, to investigate life's eternal mysteries, to begin to know and to understand the female sex. Okay, maybe not castration. Maybe counselling.

Ulrike sighs impatiently, her cheeks pink and her lips down-turn. "He runs *brothels*. All over East London."

Hook tries to reconcile this allegation with his vivid mental image of Ahmed in his hard helmet and councillor's suit, and shakes his head. "Ahmed? No way."

Ulrike slaps her hand on the counter: the sound makes Hook jump as if she's slapped his cheek.

"It's the truth I'm telling you! On the surface he's a respectable businessman – runs a few curry houses, a car place – but I *know* him."

Hook notices the pink of her cheeks deepening, darkening, as if she's blushing: impossible. He glances down but his erection's concealed by the bar. He has a feeling there's more to this story than meets the eye, but that means time, effort, and possibly trouble. If he *does* manage to sell something to the nationals it might mark the beginning of his rehabilitation... but so far it doesn't look promising, even if Ulrike does.

"Can you prove this?"

"No. But you can."

Hook frowns and drains his pint. "Me?"

"Didn't you used to be on a tabloid?"

"That was years ago," says Hook evasively.

"You must still have contacts."

Hook thinks about Mullen, sitting in his dark tower in Wapping. "Not really."

"Well, that's a shame. It's quite a story. The thing is, these aren't just normal knocking shops."

Hook jiggles around on his stool as if checking for spare change. Ulrike appears on the verge of laughter: her nose is so small and sweet he has an urge to bite it off.

"No?"

"No. They get young girls involved."

"How young?"

"Fourteen, fifteen. You got kids?"

"No. Yes."

Ulrike gives him a strange look then pulls a perfect pint. Hook reaches out but she pulls the glass to her chest. The top button of her shirt has come undone; he spies black lace. Her eyes tease, the dimples of her cheeks dance. "You don't believe me, do you?"

"I'm not saying that – but I mean, you obviously have it in for this Ahmed character; I mean you said he's trying to force you out."

"He is. But that don't mean what I'm saying ain't true."

"Do you have any evidence at all? A name, a place?"

Ulrike leans yet closer, the pint forgotten; her lips hypnotise, her eyes challenge him to withdraw. "Are you gonna help us then?"

"I suppose I could look into it... I'm not promising anything, mind."

Relenting, Ulrike smiles dazzlingly and passes over the pint. Hook can think of nothing to say and looks up at the screen.

The news is full of the latest incident: red banners, white capitals. Hook thinks it should be the other way round – white banners of surrender in a capital running red. He knows what Ulrike means: he's sick of being pushed around, told what to say, or more often, what *not* to say. Then he remembers his appointment with Ahmed and smiles. He has a feeling the interview won't be what the new council leader is expecting.

"What?" asks Ulrike, smiling as she lights up again. Hook feels he'd do anything to keep that smile.

"You'll see. Would you like another drink, Ulrike?"

She thinks about it, nods; Hook takes out his wallet. Then she looks at her watch and snaps her fingers. "Actually – sorry, no time."

"That's fine," smiles Hook, shrivelling, "I have work to do anyway."

He stands to leave; Ulrike extends her little hand. "Nice to meet you, Chris."

"And you, Ulrike."

His hand folds easily round hers; Ulrike adjusts her fingers so they wrap around his. Hook feels an almost intangible pressure, and she leans in and whispers: "Next time we meet I'll reveal *every*thing. Okay?"

He nods dumbly and backs away, Ulrike's amused eyes following him until the door closes. Hook sees the swastika and sighs. Turning, he begins to walk up the street when he feels a hand on his shoulder.

Turning fearfully he looks into the daunting face of a middle-aged man in a rumpled grey suit, suspicious-looking stains on his tie. His hair's grey and receding, taller than Hook and well-built but with the scholarly air of a professor, as in a way he is – a professor of crime.

"DI Schneider. How are you?"

"Very well Chris, very well indeed." Schneider's whiny accent has always put Hook's teeth on edge. "What brings you round these parts Chris, back on the grog are we?"

"Well – yes – no." Hook decides to ignore the question. "How are you, how's Mrs Schneider?"

The instant Hook says it he remembers and flushes deep purple. Schneider's expression never wavers; his eyes drill into Hook's brain.

"Still dead, thanks for asking. How's your missus Chris, alive and kicking?"

Hook nods miserably and waves at the flies buzzing his crusty nose. "I'm really sorry. It's been a long day."

"No harm, no harm. I see you were in the Anne Boleyn. I'm heading that way myself. Had a complaint about a racist attack. Hear anything like that Chris?"

"No," says Hook, "can't say I have. Well, I must be off. 'Bye then."

"'Bye Chris. Stay in touch."

Hook backs away, Schneider's humourless eyes on him. Behind the cop's head Hook notices a group of youths clustering by the bus stop; one seems to gesture so he turns and walks quickly away. He's never felt particularly at ease around Schneider, even when they were friends; now they're enemies, probably best to steer well clear.

Public transport is suspended following the incident so Hook walks to work. Upon reaching the town hall he sees Bushy

Eyebrows has been replaced by some squat South American, dark, bustling: a little Contra. When the lift opens on nine he looks round the vast office for Farzana but she's nowhere. Hook hopes she isn't still shopping: she might get into trouble.

At his desk, Hook logs on and types in *vivrichards79*. A message pops up hectoring him: six days till the password expires. This presents some difficulty as he's running out of heroes. He writes a 1,000-word hatchet job on Prof-SC and emails it to subs before he can think in any great detail about the consequences, then clicks on the BBC news page.

Police are following a significant line of enquiry over the attempted attack in Holloway Road and are linking it to Monday's suicide bombing. The M1 is closed due to fuel protests. The sea monster doesn't make the top page.

Hook opens his eyes: Owl-woman stands behind him. He begins to write a cheery piece for the youth column extolling the virtues of the city farm. The piece fills him with sadness. Are there any young people out there who still wish to stroke lambs? It seems so hopelessly anachronistic. Hamster juggling, gerbil rounders...

An important part of Hook wants to go back to the Anne Boleyn but Ulrike won't be there and deep down he knows he'd best work things out with Monica. Hook turns on his 'out of office assistant' and shuts down.

The tube seems uninviting with these suicide bombers everywhere, so outside the town hall Hook hails a lost black taxi and asks for Holloway. About a month later the cab's stuck in traffic when it rattles to a halt. The driver – fifties, grey, portly – turns, looking embarrassed.

"Sorry mate, out of fuel."

"*What*?"

"I thought I had enough to get to the garage up Hornsey

Lane but the traffic's so bad at the moment."

Behind them cars are beeping: a short London minute.

"Don't you carry a jerry can?"

The man seems affronted, his steel eyes dart. "Course I do, but I used it innit. I usually go to the one up Holloway Road but that's all cordoned off 'cos of the truck bomb and there's a garage down Haggerston that always has some but the queues were massive so I thought I'd risk it. You'll have to get out here mate, sorry."

"Jesus." Hook pulls on the handle but the red light's still on.

"That'll be twelve pound, please."

"You *are* fucking joking?"

"Hey, I got you this far didn't I? Better than nothing."

"If you don't get me home I don't pay. That's the law."

"Not any more, the mayor's changed the rules. Didn't you see her speech?"

There's nothing Hook can do: the cabbie's a big bloke, and obviously isn't too happy at being stuck in the jam in a dry cab. Fortunately Highbury station is across the road. From there he has to go back into town to get north, and the tube towards Victoria is almost empty; but then he boards the Northern Line and it's jammed with nervy commuters.

The lift at his stop's broken so he trudges upstairs. When Hook emerges into the haze of perennial dusk that serves for London night his stomach growls and he goes to the kebab shop opposite the station. As he queues Hook witnesses an extraordinary thing. The two chavvy Greek girls in baggy tracksuits who hang round the tube and giggle when he passes are knocking on the glass making faces and blowing kisses at the tall, spotty Turkish lad who fries the chips.

One of the girls lifts her jumper and presses her large, bra-encased tits against the glass; the young man smirks as he passes over Hook's parcel of meat. Outside the two girls cackle. Here's Hook with his good suit, his obvious *money*, and they haven't even registered his existence, so engrossed are they in the heroic actions of King Kebab. Ten, fifteen years ago he was the recipient of wolf whistles from women as he walked down the street; now they look right through him.

Shaking his head, holding the warm bag away from his body to prevent grease stains, Hook takes advantage of a three for a tenner deal from the offie and walks up the quiet street to the apartment block waving his arm. At the frontier of his vision he sees the many dark legs of a great spider scuttle malevolently in the semi-darkness: as he draws closer they turn into the gang of yobs that are always hanging around, and he waits for some injurious comment but they part sullenly and he enters the building. Where's security? Why can't someone cast a stone on their collective heads? Hook goes to the lift to find it out of order. Cursing the management and the committee Hook begins the arduous walk upstairs.

When Hook enters the kitchen, panting and sweating cobs, Monica and Shelley are settling down to eat something fresh from the microwave. Shelley, in a smock and big pants, smiles at him; pityingly, Hook thinks. As he leans over to kiss Monica, still in her work skirt, he inspects her face for signs of fury but she looks calm, self-contained: *fucked*.

Hook hangs up his jacket and sits at the table laid for two, one glass beside an open bottle.

Monica looks at him impassively, chewing on her nuked food. "I didn't think you'd be home. Shall I warm something up?"

"That's fine; I got something on the way."

Hook holds up the bag, transparent with animal goo and feels the temperature drop. Why does she hate it when he looks after himself? You'd think she'd be grateful for his *independence*. He's about to reach for the wine when Monica wrinkles her nose then looks at the sordid little package in astonishment.

"What the hell's *that*?"

Hook shrugs. "Kebab?"

"But you're –"

"Vegetarian. Yes, thanks. I remember."

Monica looks at Shelley, who regards her father in alarm. "But Dad, you haven't touched meat since..."

It's twelve years since Hook touched meat. Every time he's tempted to devour flesh a balance sheet flashes before his eyes, a calculation estimating the optimum return on lambs, and piglets, and chickens: quantity of food consumed, life insurance, weight, history, possibility of infection (blue tongue, foot and mouth, Bovine Spongiform Encephalopathy...), heating, re-breeding... Though suddenly none of it matters as much as the fact he needs some *meat*.

Finding a corkscrew Hook slits the cap from a bottle with the metal tip.

"Good day?" Monica asks. Hook looks up briefly then down, watching the corkscrew delve into the cork, pull out flinty pieces, make room for its own volume. Hook remembers his tattoos but thankfully her eyes are on his face. Although he doesn't have a black eye his nose is severely bruised; Monica doesn't seem to have noticed that either.

"It was, actually," says Hook, surprised at her interest. He's about to tell Monica he's met a girl he fancies when he remembers he's talking to his wife. Clearing his throat he addresses Shelley, also oblivious to him, munching lettuce and texting, the bangles on her wrist jangling. "How are the exams going?"

Shelley looks at her father, then her mother, then back at her mobile. "They... finished ages ago, Dad."

Nodding solemnly Hook sips his wine. "Oh, right. I thought – you were studying at your friend's house. Dahlia, wasn't it?"

"That was normal stuff, Dad."

"OK, so how's the 'normal' stuff going?"

He pronounces the word 'normal' testily, with some distaste. "Fine... I've had enough, Mum." Shelley pushes away her plate, most of the food still on it.

Emptying the polythene bag onto a plate he regards the heap of meat and soggy salad with disgust, leaves it on the breakfast bar untouched, refills his glass, grabs the bottle and walks the four steps to the living room and its cardboard wall, glad they only have one child to deal with.

Somewhere along the line Hook and Monica changed their mind about the whole breeding lark. At some point she stopped looking at dates, started taking pills, stopped making plans, taking temperatures; went lukewarm on the subject. Not that he blames her – why would she want another child with him, with *his* genetic codes?

Now their only child stomps around her room as Monica crashes about in the kitchen. The world's running low on energy, Hook reflects: not only coal, oil, gas, solar; eventually, he's read, the energy of the universe will peter out, all the solar winds cease, and he'll no longer hear his wife and daughter negotiating, moving stuff around. And with nothing left to move around there'll be nothing to converse about. The big silence: he can hardly wait.

"'Bye Mum, Dad!'"

Shelley bangs the front door and he's alone with his wife. It seems odd, too personal: whatever will they find to converse about when their girl leaves for good? *If* she ever leaves, of course: now they can't afford to send her to uni and the papers are full of chilling stories, 40 and 50 year olds still living at home, tabloid-framed photos where the doddery parents have that sad trapped look in their eyes... one thing for young Hook: he got out sharpish.

The bottle beside him is almost empty. Hook drifts to the

bedroom. When he pushes open the door Monica's attaching tan stockings to a new white suspender belt; he smiles, closing the door behind him from habit, but she lowers her eyes, dismissive rather than submissive.

"Don't get too excited. I'm off out with the girls."

"'Girls'? *What* girls? You don't *know* any girls."

"A couple of girls from the paper. You don't know them."

"So what's with the porno get-up?"

"It's only porno get-up to you, Chris. Believe it or not, women don't always dress sexily so that a man will find them sexy."

Hook frowns, in spoof concentration. "What then, women?"

"Them – your*self*, dammit!"

Monica's struggling with a fastening; Hook kneels to help, poking the stud through the thin mesh and sliding it down the groove. He straightens, feeling powerful, fully dressed when all she wears is her underwear, and holds her to him so she can feel what she's doing. But Monica turns away and carefully lifts a black satin dress from the ironing board. Stepping into the dress and pulling it up over her gymnast's body Monica turns for him to zip her in; like a chastity ritual, it seems to Hook.

He stands back and whistles, cock throbbing. "New dress. Nice. Expensive?"

"Not really. Or it wouldn't have been."

Hook tries to deconstruct the sentence but not too hard. Monica's applying lippy in the dressing table mirror.

Seeing his big puzzled face she sucks in her lips, puckers, helping him out. "It didn't seem expensive at the time. Maybe it does now, though. With our... *situation*."

Lying with a mortal sigh, Hook watches his wife get ready to go out with the same amount of effort she used to make for bed.

"Are you off to see that politician again?"

"What, Clyde Collins? Why do you ask?"

"You seem to find him interesting."

"He *is* interesting."

"Because he's black."

Monica purses her lips, applying more lippy. "Oh, spare me, Chris, what's gotten into you lately?"

"What's gotten into *you*? Or should I say – who?"

Monica turns, leans in close, lips shining, eyes vaguely contemptuous. "Black people threaten you, don't they?"

"Nope. Well, alright – some do. Young men worry me and a lot happen to be black. One threatened me today: a rapper. Prof-CD or something."

Monica checks herself again then glances at her husband lying there, still in his shoes, messing up the bed. "Were you worried he was *bigger* than you?"

"He *was* bigger than me."

"Oh, you compared dicks? How nice."

"I don't mean that. He was a big guy, a flat-track bully."

Monica widens her eyes, brushes mascara on her long lashes. "Oh come on, Chris, he's just reacting to his environment. He's acting big because he's powerless. It's people like *you* who have all the power."

"It didn't feel that way when he stood over me, holding his fucking sword."

Hook's not sure why he added that detail, that little fib: to emphasise his point? It doesn't work; Monica turns away and puts the finishing touches to her eyes. Why can't men have these fail-safes, these refuges from life's tides?

"Then you leave and come back to your nice comfortable apartment, and he's stuck in some god-awful estate with nothing. Yeah, really empowered Chris, really in control. Come on buddy, *think*, you're so better than this!"

Hook waggles his feet at the ankles so they meet, part,

meet, like Newton's Cradles, until the balls of his big toes hurt. He answers sulkily, looking to escape. "Prof-whatever *runs* that estate. *He's* not powerless: the little white lady who lives next door, *she's* powerless."

"Except she has the full weight of the system behind her."

Hook snorts: the sound's unpleasant, even to him. "Are you *kidding*? What the fuck are you talking about? Do you know how many old people freeze to death in this country?"

"Yeah, I wrote a feature on it, remember? Stop changing the point. Why are you threatened by black men Chris?"

Monica's eyes fix on him from the mirror as she brushes powder on her reddening cheeks. The effect is ravishing. Hook feels sick with rage: for some reason the mortgage materialises in his head like a pop-up.

"OK Monica, bear with me on this. If a racist is someone who treats people differently because of their colour, *everyone* is racist. In fact, even the word 'racist' is racist because it recognises differences between races. You think that Collins guy doesn't notice if the person he's talking to is black or white?"

"I don't know. Maybe I'll ask him if I bump into him."

Now she's doing something with her hair. Her bright blue eyes have a red rim (from lack of sleep, from all that fucking she's doing with someone else); she looks hotter than he's seen her in years. Hook paces the five steps to the living room and picks it up his glass, Van Gogh's puzzled eyes following him as he slouches on the sofa and switches on the news.

Politicians from across the narrow spectrum are lining up to condemn the bombing campaign, first some minister, then Clyde Collins. As soon as she hears his sonorous tones Monica sits beside Hook on the sofa, rapt. When Collins starts talking about the religious service Hook presses 'back' on the remote and some shopping channel comes on, saucepans perched on models' heads like fetish wear. Monica elbows him in the ribs and he grunts.

She tuts. "What did you do *that* for?"

"He gives me the creeps."

"What's the matter, you find a confident black man offensive?"

"Monica, I find *anyone* in a suit preaching about poverty and praising the lord offensive."

She has been waiting to resume the argument; now she pounces. "Bullshit Chris, you're so fucking repressed. You just can't tolerate a black guy who's smarter and prettier than you are."

"Why bring looks into it? Come to think of it – why bring *black* into it? *I* didn't mention his being black – *you* did. Your article does, too: the great black hope, Britain's Obama."

"Because people – because *you* – see him as black. Admit it: that's the fucking first thing you see. A black face."

Monica's New England accent becomes more pronounced when she's angry, and when she climaxes. The rest of the time she sounds Mid-Atlantic, that deep place where monsters lurk.

"Maybe."

"If he was white that wouldn't be the first thing you noticed."

"Maybe."

"So you're a racist."

"Maybe. I mean – I don't think I am, but maybe I am. I don't know."

Monica frowns stupidly. She's ready, but ready for what? Hook wants to kiss her, rub his cock on her cheek, but he looks up at the Van Gogh self-portrait instead. Van Gogh looks back with melancholy airs from beneath his back-sweep.

"You don't know what you *are*?" asks Monica, a long time later it seems.

"No, I don't know what a *racist* is – or me, for that matter."

"A racist is someone who treats people differently because of the colour of their skin."

"But what does that mean – 'treats people differently'?"

"It's pretty simple, Chris. For a guy who thinks he's so smart, you're an asshole sometimes."

"Jim Jones was *progressive* Monica, Jim Jones was *anti-segregation...*"

"Don't talk to *me* about goddamn Jim Jones!"

Hook says nothing. That whole Jonestown thing is a sore point with Monica; he's never asked why. He knows he's needling her but can't help himself, it's like picking scabs. With his tender elbow he nudges her gently. Her warm ribs, soft white stomach inside that dress: so close, so far away.

"Anyway, what happened to *you* the other night?"

"Which night?"

Hook has to count back. "Sunday."

The silence is too long: on some infinitesimal level her reply follows a definite pause. Something dies inside.

"I came home."

"Bull!"

"I did. It was late and I didn't want to disturb you, so I slept in Shelley's room."

The closed door: doubt.

"I didn't hear you."

"You'd sleep through a supernova. I looked in on you. You were in bed with your hand in your pants."

"And whose pants was your hand down?"

Hook's accent is also becoming more pronounced, back to punky old London. She hates that as he loves her wealth, her richness. Hook concedes something and switches back to the news.

"It's *were*," says Monica pedantically. "*Were* your hands down. I didn't have my hand down anyone's pants."

"Okay, I'll re-phrase that, who had their hand down yours, Clyde Collins?"

Bored by the circularity of their argument – not even that, a clash of balloon swords – they keep their eyes on the vast plasma screen, where bearded men on board a ship in the high seas babble excitedly. Hook thinks they look like fishermen but according to the caption they're scientists. More global warming doomsayers; at least they have a boat.

Hook turns on Ceefax to check the cricket scores but up pops a page about long haul bargains. Hook frowns at the three-letter airport abbreviations like they're secret codes. Monica whispers in his ear, her breath as warm as the wind from the city beyond the undulating card. "Why would Clyde Collins have his hand in my panties?"

Hook smiles and sips wine before responding.

"If you were bad he'd have to check. Right up to the second knuckle. Two fingers, maybe three, jammed right up there."

Monica's breathing deepens. Hook turns down the sound, finishes his glass and puts it down on the coffee table. In the corner of his eye he sees Monica lift her dress, put her hand down her panties. She reaches over and presses her fingers against his nose. He inhales, thinks he smells semen but isn't sure; do all men smell like musty armpit?

"See?" whispers Monica. "I've been a good girl."

Her accent lingers on 'girl'. Hook licks her sticky fingers. He closes his eyes and she moves her hand down to his crotch, fondling him through his trousers. She leans over and whispers in his ear: he closes his eyes. "You wouldn't catch me with some other guy's cock in my mouth."

"No?"

He can feel his own hot breath bouncing back at him.

"Oh, no. What sort of girl do you think I am? Think I'd just get down and suck Clyde Collins? Think I'd just go down and swallow his come in the middle of an interview?"

"Wouldn't you?"

"Of course not." Monica's whispering gently in Hook's ear

as she pulls his cock free. "What am I, some sort of slut? How would that look, some black guy's fat cock in my mouth, or fucking my hot little cunt?"

Monica lifts her hand and spits in the palm. Taking her other hand Hook sucks her hard thumb.

"How would it look?"

"You tell *me*, mister racist."

Lifting her dress so he can see her stocking tops Monica begins jerking his cock, her hand slippery with spit.

"Scared you might not measure up? Scared it's not just a myth? Maybe I should hold your pecker against his, see who's boss. I read somewhere that if you have one guy in your ass and the other in your cunt they can feel each other's cocks through the wall. I reckon that's what makes them come: take the woman away they'd still be comparing peckers. I can hardly imagine such a thing. I – Jesus!"

With a sharp groan Hook ejaculates onto her dress and nylons. Monica skips to the bathroom. He grabs a tissue and wipes himself clean. She's left the bathroom door open but he makes for the bedroom, flicks on the main light, pulls out his belt and throws it towards the bed: it writhes and coils in the air like a flying snake. Stripping naked he pulls on fresh boxers and a t-shirt and lies on the bed looking up at the ceiling, feeling reptilian in the harsh light. Monica comes in, stripping off the ruined dress, looking for another outfit.

"So, Mister Griffin, where were we?"

"Stop, Monica. I know what this is about."

"You don't know what *anything's* about."

Hooks sucks up wine. "Bullshit."

"It's true!" blazes Monica, slipping into another dress he's never seen. "You sound like some... BNP activist, you have no concept of money, or time, or – *anything* anymore. What's happening to you? Why are you so bitter? It's like living with a fucking stranger."

"It's still me in here. I'm just trying to work out some... stuff."

"Well when you work it out, send me a text. I'm gone."

And she is. Hook meant to warn her about the gang loitering downstairs but maybe she knows that, with her contacts. Flicking through zillions of satellite channels he finds nothing of interest and settles on the news.

The scientists on their ships speak through their beards onto rain-soaked lenses. They aren't talking about global warming, but a subject about which the common consensus is they know nothing; not even whether or not the thing they've found down there has been dead or alive for a million years.

He turns off the TV and goes back into the living room, velvet shadow punctuated by tiny red lights and standby hums. Hook goes to the wall, pulls away a piece of card and looks over the city, feeling like a child lost at night in a Siberian forest.

Thursday 24th June

Hook stares at the fish; the fish stares back. He opens and closes his mouth; so does the fish. Where's its little friend? Down behind the little plastic castle taking it easy, away from the artificial lights illuminating the tank twenty-four-seven like some terrible god.

Do fish sleep and dream? Is the castle made of plastic? Hook has no idea. He has no idea how most things are made, or of what material: it's only recently he learned colanders are made of nylon. The news depressed him – how many gaps are there in his knowledge? Will he ever fill them and does it matter?

Hook's brain feels welded to his skull with tofu, eyelids rasp against eyeballs like glass-paper, his stomach an acid-bath swamp. But at least he slept. Monica came home after he'd attained unconsciousness; he woke around three, a blanket pinning him down.

As Hook sits groaning into his tea Shelley emerges from her room in a too-short pink gown. His daughter's demeanour suggests she isn't about to enlighten him why and how he's upset her this time. They eat breakfast in a silence so frosty that in the end Hook stands, puts on Radio 4, and, too weak to re-tune, listens.

The morning's main item of news concerns plans to introduce aspects of Sharia Law in Muslim-dominated areas. Monica has gone off to write a feature on the proposed prohibition this very morning.

Coming from a family where the left wing position was non-negotiable, Hook's beginning to find the new order somewhat confusing. He's always believed that to be left wing you need to support equality, freedom and tolerance towards other peoples.

Multi-culturalism for the left, it now seems to Hook, means tolerating intolerance; promoting mono-culturalism; closing one's eyes, ears and mouths to the unspeakable opinions of one's new comrades, the cultists, the medievalists, the paranoid and deluded.

It hasn't always been this way; he hasn't always felt like this. On the day of the anti-Iraq war march through London, Hook, believing the march to be right and the invasion wrong, marched alongside his mother, in her late-fifties, still looking good in her anti-cop t-shirt.

Jack refused to go. Though he didn't think bombing Iraq was a good business proposition, as a banker he'd lost friends on September 11, and became, Portillo-like, something of a cheerleader for the SAS. Hook thought he was wrong and told him so.

On the march Hook and his mother came across some young Muslims holding a banner: 'Jihad is the answer'. He didn't like the men holding it, they were aggressive towards other protesters and wore masks over their faces; one sported a fake suicide belt. When he told Jack about it later he sniggered and said this was just the start – things would get worse before they got better.

Even after 7/7, the sadsacks driving 4WDs into airport terminals, the goon with the smoking shoe, the attempted bombings of nightclubs where there were all 'those slags dancing around', Hook still thought Jack was in the wrong. And yet now, with his brother's Damascene conversion complete, he feels himself being pulled in the opposite direction.

In his shades and long coat Hook feels like a thirties' private eye and wishes he had a hat to keep away insects. As he waits to cross at the zebra he watches with mounting anxiety as lorries snarl and buses sail by inches from his face.

Hook shivers. Everything in this sick multiverse could kill him: every brick, blade of grass, the air he breathes. It's all a question of *application*. Death is inches away at any moment and it frightens him, this motion and noise. He isn't evolved enough for this world; his brain can't adjust, hasn't managed to reboot to a new century already ten per cent obsolete.

The curry house, '*Ahmed Balti*', sits mid-row on an arterial route between the scrimping City and expansive Essex. With its tinted windows it looks cool, inviting, a classier joint than other local balti-palaces. Maybe it's that the shops either side selling strange fruits and phone cards, Polish sausage and polyester saris look so dark and down-at-heel.

A car appears to slow so Hook steps out onto the crossing, but as he does so its occupants – young black men with Harlesden haircuts, Stonebridge stares – scream crazy abuse from lowered windows. Feeling delicate, unable to confront, Hook waves his hand apologetically and scampers over the black and white lines. The noise of the car screeching away makes his heart lurch.

Hook is about to enter the restaurant when a horn sounds by the kerb. He jumps out of his skin, thinking the young men have done a U-turn. Turning fearfully, he spots Farzana in her Panda, smiling warmly as she leans over and lowers the window. She wears a smart suit, cream jacket over a pink t-shirt and a tight skirt that ends mid-thigh; her bare legs are warm and brown.

"Hi Farzana, what are you doing here?"

"Karen thought it might be good for me to come along. Take some pics." She waves her camera. "And pick up a few more interviewing techniques from the schmooze-meister."

Hook feels relieved she's there and worries that's his own repressed racism coming through; if he walks through that door with an Asian girl by his side, they can hardly accuse him of intolerance... can they? Jesus, what's he thinking? What does 'Asian' actually mean, anyway? He'll have to consult *Wikipedia*.

"Come on then, hope you brought spare batteries. That old thing drains them like..."

Unable to think of a suitable analogy Hook pushes open the door, its glass tinted where he can see his own sad face, Farzana beside him as fresh and eager as he was as a trainee reporter on Fleet Street all those years ago.

The restaurant is tastefully decorated with elephants and fake marble, potted plants and watercolours; not an image of the Taj in sight. Unlike his brother, who's been off curries since working in a dole office with Dennis Nielsen, Hook could eat veggie thali every night. When he smells the aromas coming from the kitchen his stomach moans.

A tall young man emerges in a waiter's outfit, dark trousers and jacket over a white shirt. He looks cool: the aircon's on high and Hook shivers with pleasure in his short-sleeved shirt. The waiter regards him without much interest, then Farzana with antipathy; gamely, she glares back.

The waiter drags his eyes back to Hook and speaks snappily, without any discernible trace of bonhomie. "We don't open till five, boss."

"I know." Hook hates being called *boss*. Reluctantly he takes off his shades and extends a hand. "Chris Hook, *Eastern Express* – the council rag? I'm here to interview Mister – erm..." He dithers; the young man glowers and shouts in Bengali over his shoulder and through the door, his eyes still on Farzana.

Hook shivers again, enjoying the unfamiliar sensation.

"Mister Ahmed will be right out. Take a seat."

Hook leads Farzana to a table by the window, eyes unable to adjust to the gloom; his thigh bangs the corner of a table and cutlery falls to the floor. Dropping to his knees to retrieve it the savage numbness of a dead leg sets in and he bites his lip.

Looking up Hook sees Farzana smiling down at him. If anything today she seems even more beautiful: her hair lustrous, her light brown legs smell clean and her small firm breasts fill his vision. He feels an overwhelming urge to prostrate himself before her, to lick her little brown toes as she strokes his hair. Instead he stands gingerly and folds himself into the booth.

The tinted windows aren't working: he can still see out. As they sit staring at the unappetising vistas Farzana plays with the camera. For want of conversation Hook reaches in his jacket pocket and pulls out a print of Ahmed's potted and sanitised biography from the council website. The waiter brings a plate of poppadom and a thali dish containing chutney in a variety of luminous colours. Hook's about to protest then bites his lip again, drawing blood.

"Mister Ahmed has been detained on another matter," says the waiter. "Can I get you something while you wait? A drink, some snacks?"

Hook looks at Farzana with raised eyebrows. This is almost like a date. Except there's less than no chance of his ever having a proper date with this girl, this much he knows; at heart, Hook is a realist.

"Why not have lunch?" says Hook, looking at a menu. Farzana looks surprised.

"I didn't think we –"

"What?"

"Well, I didn't think we were supposed to accept any gifts as part of our work..."

"Who said anything about gifts?" smiles Hook. He looks at the waiter, who's still glaring nastily at Farzana. "We'll have roti, vegetarian samosa, and I'll have a mutter paneer. How about you Farzana?"

Farzana looks briefly at the scowling waiter then drops her eyes subserviently, which annoys Hook. What's she afraid of, being seen with a white man? Even Jack concedes he and Maya get their fair share of stick from black and white people alike; black women are the worst, apparently. Hook rephrases his question to himself: what's the waiter afraid of?

"Nothing," says Farzana.

"Nothing?"

"No."

She shakes her head, eyes down.

Hook sighs. "All right, cancel the paneer, but I'll have a pint of lager."

The waiter disappears. Jabbing his index finger into the pile of poppadom so they splinter like paper plates Hook looks at Farzana accusingly. "What's up? Not hungry?"

"No."

"Suit yourself. Though you could at least have some water. It's baking out there."

Farzana turns those dazzling eye-whites on him and he squints and looks down.

"It doesn't feel hot to me."

"Of course," says Hook, "you're –"

He's about to say "used to it", remembers she's from Newham. Instead he munches poppadom and cranes his head round. He's in luck: the waiter sets down the glass as hard as it's possible to do without spilling any and disappears again. Hook grabs the cold lager, takes a deep draught and gasps, so happy suddenly that he almost chuckles.

"You drink a lot," says Farzana.

Hook shrugs and dabs his brow with a house napkin. "Does it offend you, Farzana?"

"Why would it offend me?"

"Your religion."

Farzana folds her hands on the table and shrugs. "It doesn't offend me. It just saddens me, maybe sickens me a little. The smell..."

Using a shard of poppadom to scoop up lime chutney Hook crams it in his mouth. The pickle's hot: he winces and gulps down more cold beer before answering.

"What is it with Muslims and beer, anyway? I reckon if you lot just lightened up a bit we'd all get along. That's the trouble: you never meet Muslims down the pub so you don't get to know them."

Farzana looks out of the window, where two gangs of men shout abuse at each other across the busy street. "Thanks for that plea for understanding."

"I just don't get it. I mean, it's *haram*, right, but you sell it in your shops, you sell it in places like this..."

"I don't do either of those things. I'm a student, doing an MA in media studies."

"And do your family approve?"

Farzana's eyes widen, almonds marooned in enamel lagoons. "What?"

"Don't they mind you studying, mixing with the *kafir*?"

Farzana looks down, pinking. "Now you are insulting me."

"No, I'm not Farzana – I'm just asking. There's so little I know about your faith, about all faiths. I don't mean to be rude. If you don't want to answer tell me to... mind my own business."

Looking up again, causing Hook's erection to try and bust free like a flower through concrete, Farzana smiles wryly. "You were going to say 'fuck off', weren't you?"

"I was," admits Hook. The word sounds terrible and yet erotic from her lips. His cock throbs – for a horrible moment he thinks he's beyond the point of no return and he clenches his buttocks, sits very still, wood throbbing beneath wood like

113

a tell-tale heart.

"But you thought you'd better not say that to a young Muslim girl."

"Actually, I wouldn't say it to *any* young girl. You're hardly older than my daughter and I wouldn't swear in front of her," lies Hook.

Farzana sighs. "Okay. My story. My family are not so strict. Dad is a chemist. I have two older brothers, one is at Cambridge. Dad goes to Friday prayer but also to Ladbroke's on a Saturday. Happy?"

"Inordinately."

Farzana looks at her nails, painted dark crimson like she's raked his cheeks. "You like to use long words to show you've been to college."

"I didn't go to college."

"Oh."

Farzana looks a little undone, so Hook helps her out. He's always helping women out. Why? When have women ever helped *him*?

"Not really... I mean, not consciously. I just like big words. Trouble is the sub on the paper doesn't, so I have to use them where I can."

Hook breaks up the last poppadom and dunks it in scarlet goo, munches on the brittle crisp.

Farzana points the camera at his face. "Smile."

Hook tries, but it's difficult: apart from the fact he has round-the-clock shadow and sodden armpits, he has stomach cramp and his hard-on is crushed beneath the table. He's trying to think of something witty, inoffensive and yet mildly flirtatious to say when Ahmed appears at the kitchen door flanked by two younger men.

Today Ahmed wears a dark suit and an exuberantly gaudy tie; obviously considers himself a bit of a character. He looks older than he did in his building site gear, late-forties, fifty maybe, his hair short, dark and possibly dyed. He has an impressive moustache but a clean-shaven chin, unlike the two young men in his wake who wear dhotis and long, straggly beards. Ahmed weaves over without bumping into even one table, extending a manicured hand and smiling.

"We meet again, Christian! Thanks for coming. Are you looked after?"

"Very well, Mister Ahmed, thank you."

Ahmed looks down at Farzana coolly and she moves over to sit next to Hook. He feels her bare leg against his own and swallows. Ahmed sits opposite; the two young men stand one behind each shoulder, hands clasped out front like a boy band. Ahmed smiles again.

"Good, good. And who is this?"

"Oh – my assistant for the day, Farzana."

"Good to meet you, miss –?"

"Rahman."

"Ah, a good Bengali name. Peace be upon you."

Farzana looks surprised. "Are you Bengali then?"

"I am from Pakistan but have many brothers in Bengal. We are all sons of Islam."

"And daughters," says Farzana with a beatific smile.

"Yes..." For a moment Ahmed's eyes fix on Hook's tattoos and widen slightly. "So, Christian, what do you wish to know? Do you want another beer to help you through? Ha ha!"

Ahmed finds this amusing, but his two associates glare with unfriendly eyes. Hook looks down at his empty pint.

"That's fine, Mister Ahmed, just a few questions about your new duties as council leader – congratulations, by the way."

"Thank you, Christian. I was honoured to be chosen."

"By the way – Chris is fine."

Ahmed shrugs. As they talk, his eyes keep sliding down to Hook's knuckles. Hook works his way through the formulaic questions and pretends to be interested in the answers. It's a phoney conversation, a speed-date: both have their lines, neither are talking or listening; necessity has briefly brought them together.

The rotis are spicy and tasty. Hook decides if he had to choose he'd be a Jew for the humour, Muslim for the food, Catholic for the booze and a Buddhist for the quiet. Not that anyone's asked him to convert to their cause lately – even the Witnesses refuse to come in when he's home alone.

Hook urgently craves another drink but decides against it: Farzana can always drop him at the pub. He can then tell Ulrike how he put the pressure on Ahmed – except so far he's applied as much pressure as a breakfast TV presenter.

What Hook needs most in his life is to see Ulrike smile, and that means giving her something, no matter how uncomfortable things become short term. He clears his burning throat.

"Almost done here, Mister Ahmed, this is all fabulous by the way. I just want to ask you about that other thing we talked about yesterday."

Ahmed pulls an actor's puzzled face; his assistants swap angry glances. "Which is?"

"That campaign of harassment against the proprietor of a local pub. Do you remember we talked about it on the phone?"

Rahman's composure briefly dissipates; then something clicks. "Oh, that was you? Of course. I have asked around and can find nothing to suggest any 'hate campaign', as you call it."

Hook frowns, smiling faintly. "How do you know? I haven't told you the name of the pub yet."

Ahmed rolls his eyes. "Are you going to tell me the name of the pub?"

"I might."

"You are too coy, Christian. Look, I think we both know which pub we are talking about, but let us not mention any names. Having said this, several local people have expressed deep concerns about this particular establishment."

To Hook's own disbelief he's writing stuff down in proper shorthand.

"'Concerns'?"

Placing his elbows on the table and pressing his two sets of fingers together, a ribbed tent, a burnt-out church, Ahmed shrugs nonchalantly. "Late night drinking, punch-ups outside, the usual stuff that happens around..." Ahmed looks down at Hook's empty glass, "alcohol."

"You're saying the place has a bad reputation?"

"If it's the place I'm thinking of, yes, several respected local people have made that complaint." Ahmed drums his hands on the table. "Now that I'm leader of the borough I will of course investigate. If I find anyone is harassing the owner, then I will do my utmost to put a stop to it. If on the other hand it turns out the establishment in question is breaching its license obligations, then I have to consider whether renewing its licence is justified."

Hook looks him in the eye.

"You'd close it down."

Ahmed shrugs again – his shoulder muscles must be well-developed, thinks Hook – and looks away.

"It is not for me to close anything down. All I can do is listen to my constituents and make their feelings known to the relevant committees. It is all very tedious stuff, as you know, Chris. You have worked in local government for many years now."

"A few, yes." Hook grimaces inwardly at the defensive tone in his voice.

"Then you know. Sometimes you think there is something big, but it is all talk, all – *nuance*. No scoops, just small beer. If you'll pardon the pun."

They walk outside into the dazzling sunshine so Farzana

can get her pics of Ahmed outside his restaurant. Though he has a chain across East and North London, this is the place he always uses for PR. Maybe he has a soft spot, this being the place he started out as a young immigrant with nothing; or maybe he just knows it goes down well with the punters, whatever their politics. Everyone loves a curry, except Jack.

Picture shoot over, Farzana gets in the car and opens the passenger door. Hook looks round and Ahmed leans over to shake his hand.

"One more thing," says Hook casually. "I've had complaints about a chain of under-age brothels in the area. Young kids, thirteen, fourteen years old. Would you know anything about that, Mister Ahmed?"

Ahmed's face shimmers a little, Hook's hand remains grasped in his.

"Would I 'know anything about that'?"

"Yes. I mean, as leader and as a prominent member of the community."

"It sounds like bullshit to me," says Ahmed evenly. "Maybe the Albanians, Turks, Nigerians, I can't speak for them, but I never heard anything about it in *my* community."

"Oh. It's just – you were named as owning some of them."

Ahmed still holds his hand, not hard but immovable.

He leans forward. "The person who is feeding you this stuff," he says, still smiling, "is making mistakes."

"Yes, that's just what I thought," smiles Hook. He gets in and closes the door.

Ahmed leans in the window, still smiling but with hard pinpricks at each eyes' centre.

"Drive carefully Christian."

Farzana drives in silence back towards the office, Hook beside her deep in thought. He doesn't like the direction his conversation with Ahmed took and feels uncomfortable that Farzana witnessed it, a witness to his ineptitude. He glances sideways at her legs, her skirt riding high up her thighs. Hook reminds himself of her age but it makes no difference. To distract himself he turns on his BlackBerry.

He sees a new message from Ulrike:

Need to see u scared

Hook frowns.

"Pull over here."

"*Here*?"

They're on a dual carriageway between two bleak nodes with no turning or turn-offs for miles, and a huge lorry fills the rear-view mirror. But Hook knows where he is and decides it would be quicker walking. Anyway, he feels Farzana has probably seen enough and he doesn't really want her to meet Ulrike.

"Here."

Farzana slows and stops, and the truck sounds his horn as Hook gets out. He turns to wave but Farzana has gone.

Hook slings his jacket over his shoulder and begins to walk. The sky's a light, watery blue, the sun directly overhead. Even in a short-sleeved shirt Hook is soon sweating profoundly, attracting flies and things that bite, so he goes in a shop for a can of beer to calm his nerves.

When Hook reaches the Anne Boleyn he sees another window has been smashed, and on the door someone's written 'Hamas'.

Hook shivers and pushes at the door, but it's locked.

He looks at his watch: one-thirty. Maybe they've closed for the 'clerical', as old-timers call it. Cupping his hands round his eyes like blinkers Hook peers inside, but all is murk, gloom and dirt.

On his BlackBerry he calls Ulrike; she answers first ring. "Hello?"

She sounds like she's whispering, hiding from some awful truth.

"Ulrike, it's Chris. What's happened? Is everything alright?"

"Where are you?"

"Outside."

Hook hears a window above him being pulled open and looks up: Ulrike peers out with bleary eyes as if she's been crying. She wears an old yellow dressing gown that falls open as she leans over the sill. It's hard to read her expression, or collage of expressions: some weird combo of sadness, anger and hope.

Hook hangs up. "What happened?" he calls up in a ludicrous stage whisper. "Was there a fight?"

"You could say that." Ulrike pulls an extraordinary face: a brave, cheerful smile filtered through layer upon layer of resignation. Then she notices her diverging gown and pulls herself together. "I'm coming down."

Over the street Hook notices a huddle of hoodies – what's the collective term, a hoodle, a hassle? – loitering by the bus stop, peeking over like stroppy meerkats. He begins to feel uneasy and is relieved when he hears heavy bolts shoot back. The door opens.

Ulrike stands before him in her tight-knotted gown – an impression of Mickey Mouse over one breast accentuating her childlike quality – horrendous slippers on her feet and a fag in hand. Despite or because of these things Hook feels a strange tenderness he hasn't known in a long time.

Her eyes flicking from side to side Ulrike gestures with her head and Hook pushes past her, smelling that same expensive perfume on her bare neck. The door closes behind him and she slams over the bolts. When she bends to shoot the bottom bolt her gown opens and he sees the top part of her warm thigh; Ulrike looks up and catches him. Hook blushes.

When he looks around the tap room Hook is stunned by the mess. Every table's been overturned, stools broken, the TV torn down, the bar taps bent and ripped out. More graffiti: swastikas, anti-Jewish slogans and other signs he can't place. All the bar optics have been smashed, as if a line of tiny explosions have ripped their way along the shelf.

Ulrike catches his disappointed look and lights another fag. "They hate booze, don't they?"

"Who do?"

"Muslims."

"What makes you think this was the work of Muslims?"

"Oh, give me a break."

Ulrike exhales stale smoke into his face: Hook chokes. Finding an upturned stool he rights it and sits with his back to the bar.

"What happened?"

"I was coming back from the wholesalers this morning. The door was open – it was only ten. I come in and see all this. There was no sign of Uncle Sid."

Ulrike's voice betrays her fear, and her anger at that betrayal. Hook looks round, expecting to see Sid in his old shirt at any moment.

"So where is he?"

"Hospital. I got a call from the ward nurse. He chased them with his baseball bat – right into an ambush. They kicked the crap out of him. He's seventy, nearly."

Ulrike's voice cracks; Hook swallows, cursing the lewd thoughts going through his mind. "Jesus."

"He'll pull through. Tough as old boots is Uncle Sid."

Hook looks around again. The place has been gutted – the destruction is methodical and savage. Did they use that same measured approach to beating up her uncle?

"How bad is he?"

"Broken arm, couple cracked ribs, internal bruising –

obviously another warning. If they'd wanted to kill him they had the chance."

The coat peg's still there so Hook hangs up his jacket and stretches, exposing the damp patches beneath his arms. Ulrike lights another cigarette and looks at him challengingly.

He clears his throat. "How do you know it wasn't burglars?"

"Burglars don't bother with all this crap." Ulrike looks round at the explosion of glass. "They'd lift every spirit for starters."

"What about the till?"

"Well alright, that's gone. But they'd have known it was empty in the morning. No, I know who's to blame."

"Who, Ahmed?"

"Who else?"

Hook sighs, wonders if any of the booze-pipes still work. He wipes sweat off his forehead with his sweaty hand.

"Look, I just met Ahmed. We had a bit of a chat."

Ulrike shrugs and blows smoke, but she's too far away to bother him; plumes rise to the purple ceiling.

"That's nice."

"I put your – erm – questions to him, and he denied everything."

Ulrike's face is overcome by a new emotion: fury. Hook is almost pleased, to finally get through those extraordinary firewalls.

"You did *what*?"

"I asked him about this harassment campaign, and the brothels, and – erm..."

"You fucking *prick*!" blazes Ulrike. "Are you insane? You just signed me uncle's death warrant!"

"Oh come on," says Hook, taken aback by her fury, "he's hardly likely to do anything now, is he? Anyway, I didn't mention this place by name. I'm not *that* stupid."

"Tell me something," hisses Ulrike, coming so close Hook

can almost see himself in her eyes. "You were a journalist, weren't you?"

"I still am."

"No – I don't mean a council yes man who prints good news. I mean a proper journalist on the nationals."

To Hook this feels like the old question, have you ceased beating your wife? He says nothing.

Ulrike stubs out her fag on the bar top. "Why did you stop? Not good enough? One big mistake? What?"

Hook sighs and wipes his forehead with an *Ahmed Balti* napkin.

"Long story."

"I can't believe I wasted my time with you. I should have gone to the tabs; they'd have sorted this out."

"I doubt it. In my experience, there's no bad situation that a tabloid journo can't make immeasurably worse."

"Drop the long words, what I want to know is how are you going to put this right?"

Hook thinks about that one but, the more he thinks about it, the less convinced he is that he can put anything right.

"I don't know, Ulrike. I'm sorry. Maybe I should go down the hospital..."

Ulrike looks startled and bites her lip. "The hospital? Why?"

"I dunno, talk to Sid?"

"He's in a coma."

"He's bound to come round sooner or later. I should get down there."

Ulrike puts her hand on his arm and as she does so her Mickey Mouse gown almost falls open and he sees bare flesh, the shadow between her small firm breasts.

"Look," says Ulrike, conciliatory at last, "we've got some booze upstairs. Do you want to come up and have a drink with me? We need to sort this out."

Upstairs Ulrike relents enough to open a window. Hook looks out over the rooftops to the Olympic stadium shimmering like a spacecraft in the silvery heat. Then he looks down to the street but the hoodies have gone, and traffic stretches as far as he can see without leaning too far. He feels nervous and vulnerable, not knowing this odd little woman or what she really wants.

When Hook turns to find Ulrike has removed her gown and stands almost naked before him, her breasts not so small after all and wearing only white satin panties through which he can see her neatly trimmed bush, he swallows dust and closes his eyes. This is what he wants, but now it's here he feels nauseous. More: scared. Ulrike has a triumphant yet pained expression on her face and that resigned air annoys him as much as the silence appalls him.

When Hook doesn't move forward to sweep her into his arms a new climate enters the room and Ulrike snatches up her gown, covers her body and lights a cigarette.

Hook wipes his brow, leaning back so that his behind is resting on the windowsill. This is an old man's room: betting papers, the smell of fried meat, a dusty smell. What's a girl like Ulrike doing here anyway? Who cares about their uncle?

"Ulrike, I –"

"Forget it."

"I want to but you're vulnerable. I couldn't."

"Oh spare me. Do I look vulnerable?"

Hook looks into her eyes, red with warm tears, her scowling lip with its cigarette, her shaking hands, and smiles weakly.

"You do, actually. Anyway, I'm married."

"So am I."

"Oh! I didn't realise..."

Hook looks at her hand. "You don't wear a ring."

Ulrike holds up her left hand and looks at it wonderingly, like an infant who's just discovered they can move their fingers.

"We're separating."

"I'm sorry."

A car horn sounds; Ulrike brushes past and looks out of the window. There's sadness in her eyes as well as vulnerability and Hook is astonished but pleased that he turned her down – maybe there's hope for him yet.

"Don't be," says Ulrike bitterly. "*I'm* not. Fucking sham, the whole thing. Big country wedding and he was already playing around with some slapper. Me mum was so sad about it. She'd spent thousands on flowers. You should see the photos – lilies everywhere. Then he turns out to be a psycho."

"What did he do?"

"He raped me," says Ulrike flatly, "every night."

Remembering his thoughts about Monica, wondering what counts as marital rape and hating the anarchy of his thoughts, Hook drops his eyes. "Jesus. I'm so sorry."

"Fuck him. I'll get him one day."

Ulrike looks like she needs to be alone with her anger. Hook pushes his behind away from the windowsill.

"I should go."

Stepping aside, Ulrike waves him towards the door. "Go on then."

"I'm sorry, Ulrike. I really like you but I can't do this now."

"Oh, *that's* your problem big man. Prefer mucky emails. A cyber-saddo."

Grabbing his jacket he walks towards her. Ulrike relents. "Look, I'm sorry okay?"

"Don't be," says Hook, smiling slightly.

Ulrike comes closer, puts her hand on his arm: her fingers burn. "Can I ask you a favour?"

"Name it."

"Leave my uncle alone. Let him rest."

Hook thinks about it, nods. "Okay, Ulrike, I won't go near him."

"On your mother's life?"

"On my mother's life."

Hook thinks about Ulrike all the way to the hospital. The situation was too complicated even before she revealed her body. Her breasts remain in his vision, burnt into his retinas like twin suns. Why did he reject her: guilt? That didn't stop him slapping Maya's arse. Something more – that puzzling fear, maybe, or instinct?

The cabbie's tuned to a radio call-in about terrorism, knives and monsters of the deep; not many of the callers appear to have much to contribute in terms of analytical data. It's still hot and the cab has its windows up, the aircon on full, using more energy, heating up the planet.

Hook's mobile rings. Looking down at the display he curses silently and presses *answer*.

"Hello Karen."

"Chris, can you get to the office right away? We need to talk."

"Sounds serious."

"It is. Where are you, anyway?"

"Off to the hospital."

"Oh God, what's happened?"

"Nothing. Don't worry, Just an interview with someone."

"May I ask whom?"

"A victim of a racist beating. Allegedly."

"Oh dear! There *has* been an increase in BNP activity lately; it probably ties in with that. Bastards. Well, come back first then go there. See you soon."

Hook is about to protest that with the state of the roads he'll be half an hour at least, but the line goes dead. Oh well, Sid isn't going anywhere. He smiles to himself, reflecting on Karen's response to news of a racist attack. If he'd told his first editor in Fleet Street the same thing his response would have been "fantastic!"

On entering reception the barrier's out of action. The Contra summons him over to the desk and closely scrutinises his pass, looking from the photo to Hook and back again as if he has Alzheimer's. Probably did the same thing with the nuns back home before they were defiled, buried alive. Finally, he jerks his head and Hook makes for the lift, pressing nine out of habit and emerging onto his own floor where many of his colleagues are working late, treading water.

Hook walks up the back stairs to Karen's office. When he enters she's frowning into her PC and he fully expects her to wear a professional stern look to compliment her prim blouse, but she smiles brightly and wiggles her fingers.

"Ah, Chris, do sit down."

Hook sits and waits to be told of Ahmed's displeasure, but she seems in a good mood as she slaps proofs of the latest *Eastern Express* on the desk. He looks down to see the young rapper glowering back at him – a good shot by Farzana before they ran away. He swallows.

"Your interview with Prof – er – BC," prompts Karen, smiling again.

"SC."

Karen squints down at the proof. "SC: yes. I wish you'd run this article by me, Chris – makes him look pretty stupid."

"He *is* pretty stupid."

"That may well be. The thing is, we sort of need him onboard for this anti-knives thingy. He's rather put out by the tone of your piece."

Emboldened by her placidity, Hook snorts. "Tough. The bloke's sub-moronic. If the youth need him to speak for them they're all fucked."

Karen sighs: she has a love-hate relationship with swearing. Quite religious, deep down, always was. She must take after her mother because Hook doesn't recall her father being particularly spiritual. Hook being a lifelong atheist they only had two things in common as kids: booze and sex. As he looks at her now, that maddening crucifix dangling between her breasts, he remembers how Karen was never, *ever* satisfied in bed. The image comes to mind of a helicopter dropping water bombs on a forest fire.

Karen's still talking; Hook comes to with a start.

"...Chris, I know what you're saying, but this does put me in a bit of an – um – awkward position. Brian's furious – the chief executive, remember? I think he knows his probation officer or something – but on the other hand we've already had mail in support of your article and it's only been on the web so far."

Hook sits back with his fingers behind his head. So far as he can recall he's never in his life adopted that posture before; it feels good. He almost puts his feet on the desk and again wishes he owned a hat, to tip over his eyes.

"So I guess you have to decide what's more important," smiles Hook, "the chief executive or the tax-paying denizens of the borough."

Karen sits back in her chair; her blouse is almost translucent and part-unbuttoned so he can see the white lace of her bra, that lucky dangling fella in the dark valley.

She smiles intelligently and raises her eyebrows. "Hmm... I think we both know the answer to that one, don't we? Chris, can I ask you something?"

"What?" Hook feels surprisingly light, giddy almost: all the daytime drinking has made everything floaty. Already Ulrike's proffering of her body seems a distant dream. Did she really undress for him, did he really turn her down? Karen clears her throat: Jesus jigs.

Hook looks out of the window at Canary Wharf, sitting on the Isle of Dogs with a discontented yet unrepentant air. Hook once read a theory that the lines of the pyramid atop the tower, if extended, follow ancient leylines.

"Are you – alright, Chris? I mean, you just seem... *different* somehow."

"Different?" Hook scratches his hairy chin in what he hopes is an appealing manner, "In what way?"

"Well – I dunno... *driven*."

"You mean I'm usually..." Hook tries to think of the antonym of 'driven' – "sedentary?"

Karen laughs and plays with her hair. Her skin's healthy and her hair shines beneath the light, but she works too hard, worries too much to be truly beautiful. And whose fault is that?

"I wouldn't say that, exactly, it's just – there's something of the old Chris about you at the moment. I mean that in a good way. Midlife crisis?"

Hook isn't offended, though he guesses throwing the same question back might not go down well.

"Maybe, I just – I dunno. I think I'm onto a proper story for once, and that makes me happy."

"The racist thing?"

"Yes."

Karen leans forward excitedly; her breasts squash on her desk and now Hook doesn't avert his gaze. "So who's the victim? What's the story?"

"A pub landlord – reckons he's getting harassed by young Asian guys. He's in hospital now. Reckons he knows who's behind it."

Hook looks up: Karen's frowning, as if the smiley face has been overthrown by some ghostly twin.

"Would this be Sid Cohen?"

"You know him?"

"I know *of* him. I know he's been beaten up."

Hook's surprised. "Who told you?"

Karen sits back and carefully rubs her eyes so as not to mess her contacts.

"A member of the public rang to say he witnessed the whole incident, wanted to know if there'd be money for his story. I told him to fuck off."

Fuck off: the flat, Derbyshire tones are still present.

"Great! A witness should nail this."

"Not necessarily." Karen smiles in that infuriatingly diplomatic way that says '*everything is difficult*'. "According to this witness, Mr Cohen racially abused a young man who then assaulted him. It all sounds very tricky, very... *complicated*, Chris. Too complex for our readership, I would suggest. I wouldn't get involved if I were you."

Hook thinks of Ulrike's breasts, her consenting face.

"I won't, Karen. Nothing in it anyway."

"Good. Anyway one of the nationals is onto this now so we've no chance."

"Oh?" asks Hook politely, doom impending. "Which paper?"

Karen pulls a face and tells him. Hook curses.

"Mullen."

High Dene was what the educational establishment referred to euphemistically as a 'progressive school'. In other words, a bunch of fucked-up kids from across the social spectrum crammed into a freezing wreck in the middle of nowhere with a forlorn collection of teachers and counsellors who were idealists, addicts, perverts and often all three.

Legend had it that a few years before Hook arrived a courting couple froze to death in their car on the road to town. Being a sallow, anaemic kid Hook always suffered from colds, flu, viral infections and the like, and he wasn't taking any chances: the first Saturday he went into the local town and bought himself a scarf using some of the guilt-money his parents had sent him. And so he acquired a nickname: 'Scarf Lad'. It seemed no-one in Derbyshire ever wore a scarf, or indeed a coat, even during winter months. Fucking demented, the lot of them.

By the time he arrived in the autumn term Mullen had been at the school for almost three years. A year older than Hook, nevertheless they shared a small dorm with four other boys. Hook hated this arrogant young Yank: tall, cool and confident; his dad, some big-shot in London, usually turned up at weekends in his Jaguar XJS and took Mullen somewhere warm.

Though Mullen soon managed to ferret the weaknesses, the insecurities, out of the younger boy in the next bed he wasn't quite a bully – he just liked to influence Hook into making mistakes. When Mullen smuggled booze into the dorm it was Hook who got drunk and fell asleep in his own vomit. When Mullen brought in porn mags it was Hook who was found by the ancient matron with his trousers round his ankles.

One dark evening Mullen found Hook alone kicking a ball around the hockey pitch. It was only October but even in his plastic ski jacket he was freezing.

The first Hook knew about Mullen's presence was when he was tackled from behind, and the gangly youth dribbled off into the darkness with Hook in cold pursuit. Finally Mullen turned and booted the ball straight at him, missed, but Hook kept on running.

Mullen put up his mittened hands, laughing. "Whoa... easy cowboy! I surrender!"

His voice was muffled by the cloud they were in. Unsure what to do Hook stopped, gasping for breath, hands on knees. Mullen slapped him on the back.

"I'm sorry kid. Want to do something fun?"

Hook shrugged warily; too many conversations had started

like this and ended in detention. Pulling his scarf tighter he shivered. Daylight was melting away over the hills and the sheep beginning to crowd together. The breeze was picking up and the trees ululating, and from the school Hook heard choirboys sing, the purity of their voices strange and distant. He looked at Mullen, tall and good-looking even then.

"Will I get in trouble again?"

"Not if you're careful. There's a 'gig' on in the village. I've got a spare ticket and a few bob... wanna tag along?"

Disappointed and suspicious, Hook's eyes narrowed. "Why are you asking me?"

"Well, we do share a room and everything, and I hear you like this synthesiser stuff... it's up to you Scarf Lad, I'm off."

Mullen started to walk down the lane past the empty tennis courts towards the school gates. Hook looked round: no-one was in sight. A strange thought struck him: he could kill Mullen right there and nobody would ever know it was him.

He ran after the retreating figure. Mullen slapped his back and put an arm round his shoulders as they walked.

By the time Hook reaches the hospital the early evening sky is blushing pink around the tall blocks and the day's heat beginning to slide down the drains and gutters into the sewers and subways. A gentle breeze seeps through the cab window and he checks the petrol gauge is in the black.

Karen's right: he feels different, re-invigorated, without knowing why. Even the look on Ulrike's face as she realised Hook wasn't about to sweep her into his arms fails to dim his sense of optimism: if she really likes him she'll wait. But if he fucks Ulrike he'll have to leave Monica – is he ready for that?

When Hook reaches the door of the ward he waits in vain to locate a nurse, but the desk's in darkness and the place spookily quiet. Finally he catches the eye of a small Filipino woman carrying a pile of towels; she walks over frowning.

"Can I help you?"

"I'm looking for Sid Cohen."

Resentfully the nurse taps on a keyboard as Hook looks around. He shivers. The nurse, younger than his first impression, looks up. She appears exhausted, and he has a vision of boys left back home, the monthly cheque, the loneliness of her existence.

"Are you family?"

"Yes."

"I'm afraid Mr Cohen has been transferred to intensive care."

Hook tries to read the screen over the desk but she shields it with her arm.

"What? Why?"

"Go back through the main door, take a left, straight down and ICU is second on your right."

"Thanks."

Hook finds the ward and peeks through the doors. Sid's in a bed nearest the door, curtained off from other patients but not the corridor, tubes in his nose and a mask over his mouth. Ulrike sits facing the door holding his hand. Sid seems to be talking quietly; Ulrike leans forward, her ear to the mask, frowning.

Hook pushes the door but it's locked, so he taps on the glass. Ulrike looks up and he sees the redness in her grey eyes: red as the gloaming sky through the windows at the far end of the death-imbued room. Reluctantly she comes and presses the release. She's wearing a bright floral summer dress, hair immaculate.

"What do *you* want?" she whispers angrily.

"He's conscious Ulrike, so it's imperative that I speak to him."

"He's too weak."

"He looks okay to me."

Ulrike sighs and appears to be trying to make a decision. Relenting, she steps aside and Hook's about to enter but she points at a small bottle of clear fluid attached to the wall.

"Clean your hands first."

Taking off his wedding ring Hook squirts oily substance onto his hands and rubs it in. According to an article he's just written (based on hearsay, anecdote and prejudice) alkies steal the bottles because they contain pure-ish alcohol. He's tempted to have a swig but instead looks at Ulrike. She has genuine pain in her eyes and he's glad now that he turned her down: she'd never forgive him.

She leans up and whispers in his ear, her breath hot and smoky. "He's had a heart attack." Her voice is frail, fracturing. "The doctors say it was probably a defect no-one knew about brought on by the assault."

As he draws closer Hook shivers. Sid lies motionless at the centre of a terrifying network of machines, monitors and gas tanks, caught in a web of technology. Sitting by the bed Hook leans forward. Beneath the mask the old man's face is a windswept cliff crumbling into the ocean. Hook swallows, remembering the agonies he saw etched into his own father's face.

"Sid," Hook whispers, "can you hear me?"

Cohen rolls his head and nods slowly, painfully. Ulrike sobs.

"Sid, I need you to tell me what happened."

Sid croaks. "I already told your mate."

"My mate?"

"He means the other journalist," says Ulrike, "The real one." Hook gives her a look and she smiles slightly; he's relieved she's donned her mask.

"Look," says Ulrike, "I told you – Uncle's very weak. If you have any questions leave them with me and –"

The door opens. "Miss Cohen?"

They both look round to see a greying man in an old suit. Seeing Hook the detective's shaggy eyebrows vanish beneath his fringe. "Well well, hello Chris, what brings you here?"

"Just following up a story, Inspector, same as you."

"I don't do 'stories', Chris, I deal in reality."

On hearing Hook address Schneider Ulrike's face darkens noticeably. "Police? What do you want?"

Being accustomed to such a reaction Schneider sighs, pulling out his ID. "My name's Schneider, Miss Cohen, do you think I could have a word?"

Ulrike appears torn, but then stands, kisses her uncle's cheek and leaves the room with Schneider, who gives Hook a curious look as he shuts the door. Feeling edgy, Hook leans forward and speaks quietly into Sid's ear.

"Look Sid, I don't know what you said to the other bloke but remember I know the whole background. Just tell me in your own words what happened."

"I told you," says Cohen, breathing painfully. "That gang who hang round the corner kept shouting stuff. Then one of them burst in and started smashing the place up. I chased ' im with me baseball bat right into an ambush. There were four or five of ' em, faces covered and they done me."

"Did they have weapons?"

"Nah, I was waiting for that. I was on the ground and they was kicking me and I was waiting for a knife in me back."

"Did anyone see this? Was there anyone on the street?"

"A few, but you know what people are like, they just turn their eyes... the lorry driver saw it all though."

"Lorry driver?"

"Yus. There was a lorry at the lights, he shouted and they ran off."

Hook looks round him furtively, but all he can see are the feet of men and women at death's door; from this position they look halfway in, head first.

"Does anyone else know about this?"

"Not yet."

"Not even Ulrike – I mean Susan?"

"Not yet. Not had a chance."

"Keep it that way. Now Sid, I want you to think very carefully. Did you say anything to the boy you chased that might have been seen as offensive?"

"Offensive?"

"Yes. I mean – racist."

Cohen rolls his craggy head again towards Hook. "I said fuck all," he says softly. "And I'll tell you why: I know what those kids go through. I used to get seven shades of shit beaten out of me thanks to Mister Mosley and his cronies. I know what it's like to be shat on ' cos of your background, son. Do you?"

Hook lowers his gaze, ashamed. "No."

"No. Well let me tell you: anyone who says I racially abused them yobs is fucking lying. I wanted to bash them ' cos they were yobs, not ' cos they was Asian."

Hook sighs. "Okay Sid. Thanks."

"Look," sighs Sid finally, conceding something deep, "when they got me on the ground I might have shouted 'you bastard' – something like that. I might have said 'bla-' then stopped. I sometimes get me letters mangled these days."

"So it might have sounded like 'you bla- bastard'?"

"Yus. But it was just me words coming out wrong."

Hook stands up and smiles.

"I believe you. I'm so sorry I had to ask you that, but I have to get all sides of the story or it's useless. Take it easy, Sid, you pour the best pint of Guinness in town so don't go chasing the nurses."

Sid raises a cheery finger and Hook forces a smile and exits the room. Ulrike is alone, rushing frantic back down the corridor.

"Ulrike, can I just have a quick word?"

She puts a hand to her mouth in terror. "Is he-?"

"Your uncle's fine."

Ulrike's expression is blank, numb. They walk down the corridor towards an exit, feet echoing. Far away the sound of a woman in labour brings back memories of Byron's horrendous birth, the C-section, the gynaecological complications that still make him shiver.

"Your uncle looks in a bad way, Ulrike. I'm sorry."

"He'll pull through. He's hard as nails."

Hook says nothing, swallows a lump. He thought his own father was hard till he saw him in that hospital bed crying like a baby.

"Look Ulrike, how much did you tell the other journalist?"

"The other journalist? Oh, you mean the one from a proper paper rather than a council rag?"

Hook sighs, too tired for childish point-scoring. "Yes."

"Pretty much what I told you."

"Oh."

"Apart from the bit about Ahmed."

Hook stops and looks at her. "Thank you."

Ulrike moves closer and he smells her clean body, that unnameable perfume. How can she not stink in this heat? When did she have time to freshen up? Hook's drenched and smells like bin juice.

"Don't let me down, Chris. I'm counting on you."

"Are you? Why?"

Ulrike shrugs. "I wish I knew. Uncle Sid's all I've got now."

"What happened to your mum and dad anyway?"

"Me dad was shot by the Brits."

"*What*?"

"He was an IRA man," says Ulrike proudly. "Vincent Kelly."

Hook frowns, puzzled. "But your name's Cohen?"

Ulrike shrugs impatiently. "I changed it after Mum died. Cohen's her family name."

"And what happened to your mum?"

Ulrike shrugs again and looks up at him calmly, her grey eyes gorged with pain.

"Mum died. Suicide."

"I'm so sorry, Ulrike. My dad killed himself too."

Hook is surprised at himself. Ulrike stops at the double door leading to the exit and looks at him intently. He looks down at her and to his astonishment finds he's blushing. To his greater astonishment, so is Ulrike. He leans over and kisses her on the forehead and she closes her eyes, then he hears running footsteps approach them and a woman doctor call out: "Miss Cohen? Come quickly!"

Ulrike looks up at him sadly, knowingly, then turns; he's grateful not to have to look into her soul any longer. Soon she'll feel what he once felt and there's nothing he can do, least of all prepare her for someone else's journey.

The gig turned out to be punk, not synth: a distinction lost on Mullen. Being old enough to pass for eighteen, and flush, he bought all the drinks. Hook sat by the stage, mesmerised by the passion, fury and noise. A few dozen punks and skinheads bounced around, lashing out with studded belts, spitting on each other, grabbing each other's forearms and head-butting one another to a standstill in a tiny, strobe-lit room full of smoke and cider spills.

Hook felt out of place in his floral shirt and jeans, and particularly by his long, wavy, girlish hair. He looked for Mullen, but the older boy had disappeared. Leaning against a loud speaker, Hook noticed a pretty young girl wearing a long mohair jumper, studded belt and Technicolor leggings. Her hair was black, spiked, her face white as death. When she saw

Hook she stuck up two fingers; Hook coyly played with his hair.

Later Hook walked the girl, Karen, through the dark town towards her bus stop, giggling and swapping details. It was a relief to have female company, and when she suggested taking a detour through an alley to the chip shop he agreed. They were kissing and touching when Hook heard a disturbance from the street; he watched as Mullen backed away from a gang of skins.

"Isn't that your mate?" whispered Karen. He shook his head. "But he bought you drinks in the pub!"

"Never seen him before," said Hook, as a punk head-butted Mullen on the nose, which bust wide open. Quietly he led Karen back the other way, somewhere quiet. He was a lover, not a fighter. Mullen could look after himself.

"He looks peaceful, doesn't he?" whispers Ulrike.

"Very."

Hook and Ulrike are at the chapel of rest where Sid's body was wheeled following his fatal attack. Schneider returned, took a statement from Ulrike, handed Hook his card meaningfully, and disappeared. The girl's tears have dried and now she's smiling to herself as she holds her uncle's cold hand. A lump rises in Hook's throat: seeing dead people makes him nauseous.

The sombre, mellow tones of the room, its neutral paintings and beige walls, relax Hook and he tries to forget about the corpse on the trolley and Schneider's casual curiosity, and think about his scoop: 'Murder victim's dying words: get the thugs who did this...'

"What are you thinking?" asks Ulrike, sliding her hand into his.

"You wouldn't want to know."

"He had such a shit life. Doesn't matter now, does it?"

"It matters to you."

Ulrike's dress is so bright and alive in the room that she seems like a splash of colour in a *noir* movie. Her face seems paler under the fake light and she looks younger, lighter: maybe there's already some relief there now she no longer has to worry about her besieged uncle.

That was how Hook felt when his father died: relieved his torture was over, guilty about that relief, relieved to feel that guilt. He puts an arm around Ulrike's tiny waist, feeling it retract and tighten and he enjoys the feeling.

"What will you do now?"

Ulrike sniffs and smiles up at him. "Go and get plastered I suppose... coming?"

"Yes – no – I mean, in the long term. Will you sell up and get out?"

"I guess so, I mean, the market's crap but I'll probably do alright. Pity, though: they've won, ain't they?"

"Who are 'they'?"

"The fundamentalists."

"You get thugs everywhere, Ulrike. Where will you go?"

"Well," says Ulrike dreamily, "Mum left me a bit of land down by the sea. I always thought it'd be nice to build a house there. I only came back to London to help me uncle out. Now he's gone, what's to keep me here?"

"What about your husband? Doesn't he still live down there?"

Ulrike frowns and squeezes the dead hand as if waiting for a squeeze back. "I told you, we separated."

Ulrike sniffs and releases her uncle's fingers, buries her face in Hook's shoulder. They're speaking in low, library tones, and Hook wants to leave before methane plays some ghastly trick and Sid farts, sits up, does a tap-dance.

There's a tap at the door. Both turn, Hook expecting to see Schneider's annoying face, but it opens on a tall man, leggy as a caterpillar (a Rebel's Large Blue, thinks Hook) wearing a suit. He's fortyish with wavy dark hair, a sharp, clean-shaved chin, full lips, a wide mouth and dark brown eyes. He'd be good-looking if it wasn't for that crooked nose.

Hook scowls. "Mullen."

Mullen smiles that same wide smile. "Hello, Scarf Lad! Small world."

"What are *you* doing here?"

"I could say the same to you, Chris; thought you'd given up journalism."

He's kept the whole range of his accent, so much broader than that of his sister. Ulrike looks from one to the other doubtfully.

"You two know each other?"

"We go way back," smiles Mullen. "Way back." Hook says nothing. Mullen drops the smile so fast that Hook doubts it ever existed. "But I'm not here to renew acquaintances with an old friend, Susan. I'm here to ask about your Uncle Sid. Who do you think did this?"

Ulrike begins to cry in earnest then, burying her head in Hook's shoulder. Hook glares: for a split second Mullen sticks his tongue in his cheek and raises his eyebrows, eyes shining victoriously, then his mask falls back in place.

When Hook stumbled back to High Dene late after his first gig, pint and kiss, no-one seemed to have noticed. Tip-toeing into his dorm he undressed as quietly as he could and slipped into bed – then a naked body straddled him, putting a hand over his mouth.

"It's me," hissed Mullen. "What happened to you?"

Hook found himself whispering back so as not to wake the other boys. "What do you mean? I looked round and you'd gone!"

Mullen lit a cigarette and Hook saw his nose was caked

with dried blood.

"Fuck, what happened to you?"

An orange dot spelt letters in the dark.

"I got jumped," shrugged Mullen, "by some fucking oiks. Didn't you see anything?"

"No, I walked Karen home."

As he dragged on the cig Mullen narrowed his eyes suspiciously. "Which way?"

"Oh, I dunno, she lives miles out of town. Why did they head-butt you, is your nose okay?"

"I'll live," Mullen took another drag. "They heard my accent, started taking the piss, calling me JR for fucks' sake." Hook tried not to laugh. "Anyway sport, how did you know they head-butted me?"

"I... just assumed..."

"Hmm. Okay," sighed Mullen, removing himself from atop Hook and sitting on the bed, "I want to know everything."

"There isn't much to tell."

"Come on, don't give me that! Give me your hand." Grabbing Hook's hand he sniffed urgently at his fingers. "You dirty fucker, you fingered her, didn't you?"

Hook pulled his hand away, blood on his fingers.

"No."

"So what's that smell?"

"I dunno. Chips."

"Chips. Hum. You mean fries." When he pulled on his fag, Mullen looked amused. "Okay. Here's the deal, little guy. You want to see this chick again?" Hook nodded. "I'll cover for you. No problem."

"Thanks," said Hook, surprised.

"No problem," repeated Mullen. "There's just one thing. I need you to do something for me also."

"So there we were," brays Mullen, "sitting with the hardest gangster in North London when Sherlock here goes and spills his pint all over the bloke's suit!"

Ulrike laughs too. Hook doesn't: he remembers it being anything but funny. He'd thought he was about to die, and from what he remembers Mullen was pretty scared too.

The tacky, newbuild pub behind the hospital is packed with off-duty medics, nurses out of uniform, and out-of-it outpatients. A bloke with his arm in a sling starts a fight with a bloke with a broken leg – probably on the ethanol.

"What about you?" Ulrike asks Mullen, blowing smoke in his direction. Mullen smokes, too, and it irritates Hook, this fatalist camaraderie. It's his round but he needs to hear what Mullen will say about their history.

Mullen shrugs and puts on his faux-modest look. "Not much to tell really. My dad knew the editor, he took me on as a junior hack, I worked my way up and here I am."

Ulrike looks intrigued. "Which is... where?"

"Chief crime reporter. Don't be too impressed: pure nepotism. Anyone could have done it in my position. Even Sherlock here."

Bored and relieved, Hook goes to buy a round. The fight has died down, ambulances arriving. Ulrike seems in no hurry to get back to the Anne Boleyn; Hook doesn't blame her. Anyway, the place is now a murder scene, whatever Sid said to his attacker. What if he *did* call his assailants black bastards – does that make it any less of a crime?

He knows he should speak to Monica, before her big brother tells her he's out drinking with a woman. He doesn't like the little digs Mullen keeps making out of Ulrike's earshot, about getting undercover, doing some deep research. This insinuation bullshit Mullen is spouting changes nothing. If Mullen has something on him, he has something on Mullen.

Hook has long been fascinated by the scene in movies

where two people point guns at one another and a long discussion ensues about who's right and who's wrong. Why not just shoot? No-one's reactions are that sharp, surely?

A few years ago – even a few days ago – Hook would have closed his eyes and hoped for the best. Not anymore. That raw energy Karen noticed has got into him and he likes it.

"…think about it," Ulrike's saying when Hook sits with the drinks: lager for him, vodka and orange for Ulrike, a mineral water for Mullen. Seeing Hook with a drink doesn't faze him: maybe Monica has mentioned something about his recent behaviour. Is there anything she doesn't confide in him?

Hook tries to remember if Mullen's an alcoholic on top of everything else, but doesn't think that's it: there are car keys on the table with a Daimler logo. Who does Mullen think he is, Morse? They both look with tedious caution at Hook, who pulls crisps from his jacket pocket.

"Pork scratchings?"

Ulrike laughs; Hook gets annoyed and goes to the toilet. When he returns she's sitting alone eating the pork scratchings. She looks up at him and smiles through her smoke, half-cut. Sitting on his stool Hook looks round.

"Where's Mullen?

"Who? Oh – the hack? Said he had to be somewhere. A family thing."

Hook's amazed, and worried by the family reference, but also relieved: all he has to work out now is how to get Ulrike home safely and whether it's out of the question to sleep with someone whose uncle is still warm.

Anyway he's married and if the feelings growing between them are as strong as he hopes, the physical stuff can wait. But then Ulrike leans over, eyes glazed with drink and grief, and kisses him with those soft lips. He closes his eyes, aware they're necking like kids, and also aware that nothing can stop him now, not this time, least of all guilt.

Karen wasn't quite the down-trodden prole she'd made out, or rather Hook had assumed by her spectacular leggings. Though she went to the local comp at the other side of the valley, each evening she returned to a large house she shared with her drunken father, an ex-military type who had a menagerie of animals but, since Karen's mother had run away with her psychologist, no wife.

Every Wednesday morning they'd go to her house while her father was at the bar of the cattle market a few miles away, and Mullen would inform the house master that Hook was helping him on some project or other.

The first time they made love, in her damp bedroom surrounded by cuddly toys and moody pop stars, Karen produced a condom and showed him how to use it; as she rolled the sheath down over his cock he ejaculated, but being fifteen this was a temporary setback. Karen went and found some Clandew, which they drank listening to Goth records, until he was ready for act two.

Hook came to enjoy the contraceptive ceremony: the sound of the ripping packet, the way Karen's warm hands touched him through this flimsy yet vital barrier, the way she carefully pulled his soft cock out of her, the bag drooping with seed. They were always careful – their undoing was Mullen.

One evening Mullen announced he was away to Sheffield to see a girl and Hook would have to cover for him till morning. This was a tricky ask: each night at lights out a prefect came round counting feet, ensuring each bed had one pair. Though Mullen's plan seemed ingenious: Karen's feet would replace his own.

On this particular night, Hook waited for the prefect to leave the dorm, slipped over into Mullen's bed, and only then discovered that in the rush and excitement they'd forgotten to purchase contraceptives. Being drunk (Karen was always drunk, booze turned her on like he never could) she never

145

noticed that he pulled out and came silently onto her stomach.

As Karen slept Hook took the torch he used to read with and forensically examined her vagina. One of his dorm-mates was from Merseyside and called this fresh, wrinkled thing a 'vaj' – which seemed to Hook the worst name imaginable for something so sweet and intriguing.

Kissing her hairy bush Hook wiped Karen dry, not knowing he was too late: a part of him was already sniffing out the ancient scent, tail wriggling to propel its way deep inside.

Friday 25th June

"What you looking at?" whispers Ulrike behind him. "There won't be any yobs around tonight; there's cops everywhere."

"I know. I just like looking."

"You're an odd one and no mistake."

Hook smiles: the line could have come out of a kitchen sink drama from 1962. Pressing his nose against the glass his breath blots out the world.

"Not really – frighteningly normal, in fact. Watching normality dissolve around me like it's gone out of fashion."

Ulrike says nothing. Hook hopes she's watching him stand coolly, his naked body a silhouette against the city. It's hard to know now what woke him, maybe just his guilty conscience. He likes looking down on the street late at night when no-one's around and the cars and trucks are parked in their holes; especially on a hot night like this, windows propped open and sweaty air pouring in.

A cop stands on guard below outside the front door. He looks lonely too, in his white shirt and stab vest, but then his radio crackles and Hook remembers the incident trailer parked around the corner. He asked a few questions when they returned from the pub in a taxi, drunk and trying not to giggle, but he didn't seem interested – too many other fish to fry, riots breaking out all over town.

When they finally got inside they left the chaos downstairs and sat in her uncle's living room drinking some more; then

Ulrike disappeared upstairs and called down to him. He climbed the rickety staircase to find her waiting beneath a thin sheet in her own room, naked and already wet beneath a bright bare bulb. By then it was too late to worry about Monica, or his marriage, or his story.

Hook gets back into bed and Ulrike embraces him from behind, her breasts squashed against his back and her mound to his rear like she's the boss. After a few minutes he hears her deep breathing and closes his eyes, but sleep won't come. 13,605 revolutions: how many has Ulrike started?

Pulling her hands away Hook goes to his jacket and turns on his BlackBerry: three voicemails and two texts, all from Monica. Turning off the phone he gets back into the other side of the bed and tucks himself in tight behind Ulrike. She turns and he sees her pale face in the orange glow from the light outside.

"I can't sleep either," Ulrike whispers. "It's so weird, lying here, in my uncle's house. I had a dream he was watching us."

Hook shivers despite the humid night. Ulrike reaches for the cigarettes on her bedside table and Hook watches the orange firefly dance.

"He wouldn't want to give up this place you know," says Ulrike. "Been in the family generations."

"Your mother's family."

"Yes. I never knew me dad; he was killed when I was a kid. Mum brought me up down the coast. We'd come back to London to see Uncle Sid and he always said this would be mine one day."

"I guess it is, now."

"I suppose so, I haven't checked." The orange dot glows brighter in the darkness. "One part of me thinks I should take over the place, tart it up a bit, the other thinks get out while you can. The area's changing, I can see that. No room for a bunch of Jews round here now. Dunno what the Gardstein Mob would have made of it."

Hook props himself up on one elbow, liking the way his hand can touch her body, younger, tighter, and most essentially not Monica's. Every time you fuck someone new, thinks Hook, a process of de-familiarisation takes place: the same old story from fresh new angles.

"I thought you were an atheist?"

"I am; a Jewish atheist, proud of my heritage. Do you know who my grandfather was?"

"*Who*?"

"Freddy Demuth, that's who."

"Who?"

Ulrike nudges him sharply in the ribs. "I thought you were clever? He was Karl Marx's son."

Hook pushes her hip with his hand then leaves it there. "Come off it! You're telling me you're a descendant of Karl Marx?"

"It's true! I've seen the papers. We used to go and have picnics up Highgate cemetery. I dunno what he'd have made of all this."

"All what?"

"London. The world of Capitalism. I studied him at uni, you know."

"You're a Marxist?"

That makes Hook's head whirl: can you 'believe' in your own great-grandfather, study your family tree in a subject other than genealogy? Ulrike exhales and Hook sniffs the smoke, touches her hot flat stomach filled with his semen. No condoms, but it doesn't matter; he feels lucky, feels her body next to his. Ulrike holds his hand, pushes it down so he can use his fluids to anoint her lightly as she speaks.

"More an anarchist, really. Left and right meet in the middle, don't they?"

"Maybe."

"I hardly know where I am anymore," says Ulrike. "A

mosque on every corner. When did everyone go Allah-crazy?"

"Do you know, I was thinking something similar just the other day."

"Were you?" Ulrike takes two of his tattooed fingers and pushes them inside; her rising chest quickens. "When?"

"I was looking round the Olympic site. This guy showed me the mosque they're building and I was supposed to write how great it all was."

Hook's enjoying the conversation: whenever he speaks to his wife about politics or religion knee-jerk ideologies take over. To be fair to Monica, Hook used to share many of her beliefs; but he's changing. Ulrike has an open mind, a different take on the new realities. Hook's about to tell her this when he hears the strange noise again and jumps out of bed.

"What the hell's that?"

Ulrike stubs out her cigarette. "What?"

"That clicking noise. Where's it coming from?"

Hook gropes his way round the room then realises he's touching Ulrike's shoulder. She kneels, kisses his penis and takes him gently between her lips. Because he's soft the sensation feels more intimate, and gently he strokes her hair as, almost reluctantly, he hardens in her warm mouth.

"Just tell me one thing," whispers Hook, looking down at the top of her head, though he has no need to whisper – the building's adrift on a concrete island in a sea of traffic. She kisses his thighs, sucks his balls, then her lips are round his cock, her soft warm hands cupping and stroking until he's so hard she has to release him before speaking.

"What?"

"What's your real name?"

She giggles upwards. "What would you like it to be?"

"I'm serious. Is it Susan, Ulrike, or what?"

"Does it matter?"

"I guess it does, or you'd tell me."

Ulrike – the name he likes best – whispers up at him in the darkness. "What turns you on most of all? We can do it, anything you like."

"Anything?"

"If it turns you on it'll turn me on. Anything you want."

"Well," admits Hook, "I've always had a bit of a thing for – for –"

"Yes?"

"I can't..."

"Tell me! Anything. Is it kids, animals, piss? I'm unshockable!"

"Of course not! Jesus! It's... just..."

"Yes?"

"Balloons," he groans, "I get turned on by balloons. The feel, the noise, the whole... shebang."

Hook waits for Ulrike to push him away, to scream; but she sucks his balls into her mouth then kisses his cock.

"Sounds like fun. We can get some. We can fuck in a whole balloon world if you like..."

Then she sucks him deep again and nothing else matters: not Monica, or Mullen, or all the slowly-accumulating dangers beyond that windowsill from which a few moments ago he looked down on the world.

A few weeks later Hook found himself staring down the black hole of a gun barrel, pointed by Karen's father.

"So, young lad," the old man said, unnervingly calm in the circumstances, "are you going to make an honest gel of my daughter?"

Hook looked round for an escape route, but they were in a quiet wood in the middle of fields, miles from anywhere – her dad had suggested hunting and he'd been too gullible to suspect a thing.

"Let me make this easier," continued the old man. *"Marry her and I'll buy you a flat in town. Or I'll shoot you here, right after you dig your own grave."*

Hook looked again at the little black hole, down which his whole future was being sucked; at her Burberry-clad father, with his boozer's nose and yellowy eyes, and a mean shot; and at the vast expanse of sky, across which a great black cloud was rubbing out the blue like an Etch-a-sketch. Even at sixteen, Hook knew this wouldn't be the most difficult decision of his life. He nodded slowly, the black dot following him like Van Gogh's dark eyes.

Uncocking the shotgun Karen's father briefly smiled a tight, painful smile and pressed a small hip flask upon Hook, who swigged and coughed. The Brigadier (as everyone called him, though Hook would bet he was several rungs below that rank) slapped his back hard and they walked to the stile.

"I've always thought," said the Brigadier, too lightly for a man who has just threatened to blow your head off, *"cirrhosis is such a manly way to die."*

When the school got wind of what happened he was expelled. So it was that at sixteen Hook found himself back in London with no qualifications, two disappointed parents, and a pregnant girlfriend who he had to marry before she gave birth or have his brains blown out. Although the old man had promised to buy them a flat, he wasn't putting out for the wedding on top; and as Hook's parents had broken their finances on the wheel of his schooling, he needed a job.

It had been all so easy for Mullen: he'd left that same summer, aged 18, with good qualifications and a job lined up at a newspaper thanks to his father's connections. Hook made a call, pleading for a job and making dark insinuations. To his astonishment, Mullen required little convincing, and Hook was taken on as cub reporter and Mullen's skivvy.

Karen's father bought them a tiny flat in Liverpool Road.

Hook was less grateful for that than the fact his head was still attached to his shoulders.

At 6am some pang – guilt, perhaps, or his needled liver – jolts Hook awake and he lies orientating, listening to the noise of this strange part of London floating through the open window as it comes alive: cars, sirens, pneumatic drills.

Ulrike sleeps, mouth open, snoring softly, short dark hair over her eyes. Resting on one elbow Hook studies her forearms, the soft white flesh sprinkled with tiny brown freckles; like observing a galaxy through another galaxy. He moves in closer to inspect her pure, peaceful face in the day's first blush. Even in sleep she's beautiful.

Sliding out of bed, Hook dresses quietly in shirt and trousers. A sock's missing so he slips shoes over flesh. As he does so he realises his wedding ring is missing. After a few panicky moments he remembers taking it off at the hospital; it's in his jacket pocket. Swallowing his fear he slips it back on.

Still Ulrike doesn't wake – he'll be back before she realises he's gone. Sneaking quietly downstairs as if her uncle's waiting with a shooter Hook closes the back door and walks to the paper shop around the corner. His ankle doesn't hurt for the first time in days and his tinnitus has faded to grey.

There's a weightlessness about the morning as if London's floating on a sea of light: maybe it's his limbs limbering up, adjusting to this new regime. For some days now Hook has abandoned watching what he eats and drinks and feels much better for it. Similarly he's tried to stop worrying what he thinks, says or does, and already new worlds of possibility have opened up.

As he walks through a parched playground Hook realises he's been censoring himself for so long it's become unconscious; and, as his tinnitus is only noticeable now it's gone, so his self-censorship has only become apparent now he's stopped editing his thoughts and taken a fresh look at the world.

Across the park a row of shops cling grimly to a condemned estate; a newsagent is open. Mullen's tabloid isn't one he usually takes but today Hook buys a copy with Monica's usual broadsheet and a can of SuperBrew to clear his head, and sits on a shaded bench in the tatty park to read.

There's one thing about Mullen's involvement that's vaguely reassuring: with his history and that of his paper he's unlikely to take the side of a gang of Asian thugs beating up an old man, whatever Uncle Sid's supposed to have said in the heat of the moment. But, as Ulrike pointed out, these are strange times.

There's nothing about the attack. Monica's left-of-centre broadsheet is calling for the introduction of Sharia law in Muslim-dominated areas; the reliably supine Church of England agrees, and the Jews have some sympathy with this cause because of the eruvs they're busily lassoing round selected areas of the city.

The more strident the various sects become, the louder their clamour for understanding and special treatment, the more Hook disagrees with all of them. He's inclining to a view that a 'clash of civilisations' should not be a war between beliefs but *upon* belief.

Only a few years ago Hook and Monica marched against the filming of Brick Lane; he resented Rushdie and Van Gogh and *Jyllands-Posten* for causing such a fuss; when young Muslims bricked Jews commemorating the holocaust by the Jamme Masjid Mosque he had refused to reveal their identities to DI Schneider, causing a rift that continues to this day.

Watching *Fitma* the other night he begun to think Wilders

had a point: there *was* something wrong, these medievalists, these freaks, these women-hating goons need sorting out – they needed a *taste*. And yet a more benign sector of his brain said: free speech and ban, same sentence? Fallujah, Najaf? Who's braver: Saudi freaks with their pallet knives or American shock and awe? It didn't help Wilders' case that the film was so poor, its interpretations of the Koran so selective, Wilders such a prick.

Hook's finished the piece before realising it's written by Monica, heavily edited no doubt but bearing her pretty feminist face on the masthead. Heart pounding, Hook takes out his phone and turns it on. Like prize announcements, the texts are in reverse order. The newest, sent at 5.38 this morning, says:

if u can read this do'nt ever come back.

She sent one last night around midnight (around the time he first slid inside Ulrike, whispering that he loved her, Ulrike whispering "fill me, make me, rape me, rape me...").

I do'nt care where you are just let me know your safe.

Hook sighs and looks up into the blue, plane-striped sky: Monica never really mastered apostrophes. At around nine last night she sent one which said:

Chris I rang home and Shel said youd not come home are you ok

There are three voicemails, the last sent this morning, just after Monica annulled their marriage. Hook thinks about listening but he's too scared and presses *delete*. Instead he scrolls through his short roll of contacts and calls Jack. Not surprisingly, considering the hour and Jack's leisurely position, his call diverts to voicemail. Hook sighs, clears his throat.

"Jack? It's Chris. Look. I'm sorry about the other night. I've changed my mind. I need that money."

'No Shit Sherlock': that was Mullen's nickname for Hook in his early days as a hack. So named for stating (according to Mullen) the bleeding obvious – in print and in person. Hook's chief fault was a tendency to over-elaborate, when one three-letter word would do.

Writing for the tabloids was harder than people thought, Mullen explained: using eight word paragraphs of one syllable or fewer, you had to explain complex subjects like the Middle East and Northern Ireland; not that Hook was ever trusted with anything more serious than trying to out ancient disk jockeys.

Mullen got all the juicy numbers, and sometimes took Hook along for the ride. Once, they were interviewing a Marchioness survivor, and the "posh young bint", as Mullen called her, began to sob:

"It was just so horrible I... just can't put it into words!"

Mullen smiled pitilessly. "Try."

Mullen's main fault was that he reduced everything to the lowest common denominator: there was no issue so important he couldn't use as an excuse to get a celeb quote, or bribe the staff illustrator to draw a tacky cartoon to make the piece bigger. Hook took to calling Mullen 'El Seedy'. The name stuck round the office but Mullen hated it; Hook soon discovered why.

Hook returns to the Anne Boleyn with croissants and newspapers because this is how he imagined first dates, first mornings: coffee and giggles then back to bed to see if the sober couple match the night-time drunks. This is it, he's ready for this: a new life, running an East End pub and fucking each other senseless every chance they get.

He knocks on the battered old side door, knowing the cops are watching, waiting for Ulrike's head to emerge, her tits popping out of her Mickey Mouse gown as they did yesterday.

Nothing: she must be in the shower. Hook rings the bell and hears nothing, but the old building is so labyrinthine he's not surprised. She'll have the radio blaring and when she emerges she'll skip down stairs, open the door and he'll fall into her arms like a crusader back from the Promised Land bearing an infidel's head.

Hook presses the bell again: nothing. Crossing the busy road he looks up; all the windows are closed so he can't shout, and if he throws a rock the cops in their trailer might think he's harassing her or, worse, Sid's killer.

When he rings Ulrike's mobile it goes straight to voicemail and when he rings the pub there isn't an answer phone, just endless ringing. She must have gone out, maybe to deal with the funeral arrangements. He sits at the bus stop where the gang of yobs clustered night after night, and waits. A poster shows a benefit cheat in the sights of a gun.

After an hour the heat's already unbearable and Ulrike still hasn't appeared so Hook goes to work.

Soon after marrying Karen and meeting Monica, Hook was asked by his editor to help investigate the Drummond family, notorious gangsters who ruled North London with the usual tedious reign of terror. Hook had known of the family his whole life; Jack briefly flirted with associate membership before realising it led nowhere fast and getting into banking and homosexuality in a big way.

Hook despised the Drummonds: they were bullies and cowards preying on the weak and hard-working members of the community, exploiting the poor for their own unimaginative ends. He wanted nothing to do with them, and hated the thought of glamorising their sad brand of fascism.

Mullen, a green Yank from suburbia, had no idea who he was messing with; he appeared to believe Islington was so trendy gangsters used garlic presses as torture implements.

One night the head of the family, Danny Drummond, agreed to meet what he thought were two wannabe dealers in his local. When Hook entered the dodgy wine bar in Essex Road he'd arranged to meet Mullen, the American wore a grey hooded top and white trainers, an attempt to look the part of a small-time drug dealer. To Hook he looked like a class tourist.

Hook, wearing a white shirt with needle-thin stripes and smart trousers, his long hair in a ponytail and with his fresh local face knew he looked the business. More important, despite his year in exile on the moors his accent was North London; Mullen's soft twang would arouse suspicion.

"So," said Hook, swigging his lager nervously, "let's get this straight. You're my cousin who went to America and now you're back."

"Yeah yeah..."

Mullen seemed too excited to discuss mere details and winked over Hook's shoulder. Hook turned and froze: the girl he was winking at was related to the Drummonds.

"Michael, stop winking at crumpet and listen. Danny Drummond is a nutter. He has to think he's meeting two dealers. How are we going to show him we mean business?"

"Easy," shrugged Mullen, producing a small cellophane bag of white tablets from his pocket. Instinctively Hook pushed Mullen's hand under the table.

"What the fuck are those?"

Mullen shrugged and petulantly stuck out his bottom lip. "Just a few tabs of ecstasy."

"Michael, are you crazy? If you get caught with them you're going down. And if you offer them to Drummond that's fucking entrapment!"

"Ah, relax," snorted Mullen, grinning over at the girls. "You worry too much, kid. Come on, one more drink, then let's go see this prick."

Mullen insisted on buying another round, then Hook followed his tall, skinny frame along Essex Road, past the taxidermist with its moth-eaten menagerie called 'Get Stuffed', through rainy back streets to the pub where they were due to meet Drummond.

The pub was a grim bunker built into a council block. As they entered, Hook felt strange: light-headed, dizzy, and euphoric. Drummond was waiting in the snug, surrounded by grizzled cronies. Hook's brain fizzed: he wanted to kiss everyone, to strip naked and jump on the pool table, and had to force himself to concentrate.

Mullen, it seemed, had slipped a tab of ecstasy into Hook's pint back at the wine bar. After a short, inconclusive conversation Hook spilled his drink on Drummond's coat. Somehow they managed to get out alive; as they ran away Mullen was laughing his head off in the sizzling street.

"You fucking nutter!" shouted Hook. "What the hell did you do that for?"

"Ah come on man, take it easy! Gangsters in this country are pussies, I had to liven up the night somehow!"

They were passing a shop called 'Past Caring', which made Hook laugh too; the two men ran up Essex Road, yelling uproariously. Hook had never taken ecstasy before, and a part of him wanted to go home and share his loving feelings with Karen; but she was pregnant, and ill, so instead, insanely, he shared them with Mullen.

When he reaches work, head banging, to be confronted by the bristling Contra, Hook discovers he's mislaid his council pass. The Contra makes a big deal of buzzing Karen, making Hook fill in forms to get a temporary replacement and generally prostrate himself in contrition.

Finally allowed through to the lifts, Hook manages to get to the ninth floor toilets unmolested. He considers a shower, but doesn't want to wash Ulrike's scent away so instead changes into a pair of canvas pants and black t-shirt.

As if bursting onstage Hook opens the doors that lead to the vast expanse of the office floor and walks along the line of squared carpet to his desk, aware that people are peeking and nudging at his casual dress.

Taking the BlackBerry out of his pocket and looking at himself in its vacant screen Hook debates turning it on, but isn't ready for Monica. Instead he surfs for news. The headlines are all about the failed terrorist campaign; even 'thisislondon' doesn't have space to mention anything so trivial as an old man's beating, especially one where there might be 'complexities'.

By ten-thirty Farzana still hasn't appeared; Hook wants to see her, show her how journalism works. It's coming back, the old desire. As he's trying to see through the tinted window an email pops up on his screen, subject: *FUCK YOU*.

Hook starts: maybe this bright clean message of hope originated with Monica. But then he reads it and relaxes.

I read you're aticle you fuckign loser who are you to call me iliterate you prick mind you're back!

Hook presses 'reply':

Hi "Prof",
Many thanks for your message.
By the way, there are two L's in 'illiterate'.
Best,
Chris H.
Ps where did *you acquire your Doctorate? I neglected to ask.*

Pressing 'send', smiling to himself, Hook heads to the toilets, where all he can hear is the ghostly whistle of the lifts. All the plants on the tinted windowsill have died. Hook pulls out his Ulrike-scented cock and pisses all over the plant pots and the sink, hooting as his urine bounces off the windows like inverted rain. It doesn't matter where he's headed, where he ends up – because he knows for certain that it won't end here.

Wonky-nosed Mullen chewed gum thoughtfully, deep black eyes boring deep into Hook's soul. For a moment Hook forgot where he was and looked round to discover they were in the Nags Head on Upper Street. Mullen's light mood had darkened and Hook couldn't recall why.

"So let me get this straight, bud," said Mullen finally, his voice somehow not above but below the hubbub of the busy pub, "you're telling me you want to fuck my little sister."

Hook pulled a face, still buzzing but coming down from the highest peak, and as he came down it all came back and came leaping up his throat; two months he'd been seeing Monica and his feelings were intensifying.

"I didn't say I wanted to fuck her, I said I love her."

The intensity of Mullen's stare diluted a little: Hook remembered Mullen was tripping too, and drunk; and it was noisy in the pub.

Mullen leaned forward, whispered in Hook's ear, his breath hot and terrible: "Well you can't have her Sherlock. She's mine."

"What do you mean she's 'yours'?"

"What I said. I've looked after her since Mom died and no-one's taking her away from me. Not you, not anyone."

Unable to grasp the thread Hook looked behind Mullen at two girls on the next table. One was short and cute with short, dark hair; the other, tall, blonde and busty in bright lemon dungarees, winked lewdly.

Hook, who had learned that his innate sense of style, his almost delicate looks and his long hair attracted women,

*smiled back then looked at Mullen, in whose dark eyes it was
hard to believe ecstasy had ever been expressed.*

"Fucking hell Mike, I only said I liked her."

"Well don't, sport. Don't. Come on, let's get out of here."

*Unwillingly, looking back one last time at the two girls, the
tall, buxom one blowing kisses as the other giggled behind her
hand, Hook followed Mullen through deserted Chapel Market
past Joseph Grimaldi Park to a sleazy side street near King's
Cross. Mullen paused outside a massage parlour.*

*Hook frowned, puzzled, almost in the trough of despair.
"What we doing here?"*

*Mullen pulled his mong face and laughed cynically. "What
do you think, Sherlock?"*

*"Mike, I've never paid for it and I don't intend to start now.
Anyway, there were these two birds in the –"*

*"Come on Scarf Lad, it'll be a gas! There's this tall one
who looks a lot like Monica. You can have her, I don't mind."*

"No way."

*Hook backed away, disgusted at the idea. Mullen shrugged,
turned up his coat collars and went inside. Hook walked home
via the Nags Head, but the two girls had left: time to face the
music with Karen.*

As Hook approaches his desk, increasingly aware of the
nervous glances and lowered voices of his colleagues, he sees
the pixelated pop-up on his screen and his stomach sinks:
maybe Prof-SC hasn't appreciated his free grammar lesson.
Taking a deep breath he clicks 'read it now'. The message is
from Jack.

Subject: your challenge.
Message:
I've got it – a name AND a slogan.
NAPiS – the Non-Abused Paedophile Society.
Slogan: 'there's no excusin' our abusin'!

One night a few weeks back, the will, unread, Maya's arse unslapped, Jack said anyone could do Hook's job; to prove it, he'd come up with a winning slogan for anything his kid brother could imagine, no matter how unpalatable. Hook set the task of trying to promote a society for paedophiles who didn't have the redeeming quality of having been abused themselves.

Hook smiles and shakes his head. This is Jack's gesture of forgiveness; he must have got his message. Hook presses *reply*:

Chris Hook is currently out of the office. Your email has been forwarded to his line manager, Karen Greening.

Pressing 'send' Hook snorts under his breath, feeling an unexpected delirium. Everything's cool: Monica will move on, Ulrike will move in and Jack will give him his money. Hook looks down at his BlackBerry and shivers; eleven minutes to opening time. Until Ulrike turns up his plan is to drink.

The girl with owlish glasses peers over the dividing board, but it's impossible to tell her expression. Smiling, holding up a hand, Hook looks back at the screen to find another message from Jack.

Nice one. Do you want a drink later?

It won't do to appear too eager, even to Jack. While Hook waits he looks out of the one remaining see-thru window. Cars skate across flat-pack blocks, the infidel sun presses the dirty air flat. Trees in the artificial park by the fake canal opposite Da Vinci's wither and writhe and the leaves are browning from sunlight rather than season – the vacant sun refuses to vacate the sky. So many people at heights, in storeys, piled high and crammed in like Tetrus blocks, the empty sky shimmering; dreams pop up and are shot down like target ducks. St George's flags flutter from balconies, red crosshairs and dirty whites: *Come On England.*

Hook shoots back a reply.

Meet you in town, usual place.

Feeling brave, Hook pops his head over the dividing board to confront the owlish secretary. "Hi, did you want me?"

The secretary adopts an incredible expression that cuts him to the quick: she smiles. "Hello Chris, you feeling okay today? Karen was looking for you earlier."

Owl-woman has the most extraordinary accent: English, almost certainly, but Hook can't place the region, a mix of Bristolian, Geordie and rural Midlands.

He shrugs with adolescent bravado. "Good for her. Have you seen the sandwich lady? I need a brie –"

"She's off today. Compassionate leave. Found out her partner was messing around with another woman, some bonds trader from Canary Wharf."

Hook's unphased by the news and shrugs. "Oh dear, that's a shame."

"I wouldn't want to be in Maria's shoes I tell you."

"Is that her name, then – Maria?"

Owl-woman blinks, eyes shining with these happy secrets. "No, silly – Maria's her partner! Maria from Da Vinci's?"

"Maria's a *dyke*?"

This information is too difficult to slot into his worldview so he ignores it. "Anyway – any idea where Farzana is?"

Owl-woman blinks stupidly. "Oh dear, haven't you heard?"

Hook swallows bitter cobwebs. "Heard what?"

"She was attacked on her way home last night."

Hook's aware of his heart thumping slowly, the men blacking out the windows in readiness for the global blitz, some faraway Rick Astley ring-tone.

"'Attacked'?"

"Yes." Owl-woman looks around. "They say she was raped."

Hook feels sick. "Oh. Jesus. What happened?"

"Well," says owl-woman, her frizzy perm revolving independently as she checks to make sure she has eavesdroppers, "apparently she was riding her bike and some boys started shouting that riding bikes is *haram*. Leads to lewd thoughts, apparently. I might have to invest in one meself!"

Owl-woman's eyes look at him accusingly and Hook wonders if maybe he did it; but quickly shakes the idea. His stomach bubbles and he tries to shrug off the image of Farzana – feisty, clever Farzana – being attacked by scumbags. A vengeful mood comes upon him and he wonders who might know something. On an impulse he takes a card from his pocket and makes a call.

"DI Schneider speaking."

"Hi Bill, it's me, Chris Hook."

"Chris! Nice to hear from you. I suppose you're calling about the Cohen murder."

"I wasn't, actually. I was calling about a girl who was raped recently."

"I don't know anything about a rape, Chris. I'm on the murder squad now, as you know. Speaking of which, would you happen to know the whereabouts of Miss Susan Cohen? Only I called there this morning and she'd disappeared."

"No, sorry. No idea."

"I see. It's just a gentleman answering to your description apparently escorted her home last night, and didn't leave the premises till this morning."

Hook says nothing. Down the line he hears Schneider sigh.

"Oh well Chris, do stay in touch. We should catch up soon."

A few days after the Drummond debacle he was called in to see the managing editor, an angry Welshman named Meredith. Meredith's office was a glass box at the centre of the office and through the windows Hook could see men in shirts casting sly glances and talking with smirks on their faces.

He knew right away it wasn't good: Meredith's boozy face was purple – even his usually grey moustache seemed discoloured by rage – and he didn't invite Hook to sit. Instead he waved a sheaf of loose papers and slapped them down on his already scruffy desk – on which an intact nameplate someone had salvaged from the wreck of the Marchioness had pride of place.

"Here he is: No Shit Sherlock!"

Meredith was so angry spittle flew from his mouth in all directions.

Hook cleared his throat nervously. "Is there a problem, boss?"

"'A problem'? I'll say there's a fucking problem dickhead! This story on the Drummond family – we can't run it! In fact, worse – they're suing the fucking paper for fucking libel! Is that problem enough?"

Hook was gob-smacked. "Libel? But how can they, with our evidence?"

"Evidence, what evidence? You took no notes so it's your word against theirs! Now your mate Seedy says you didn't even turn on your tape recorder –"

"Whoa," said Hook, "what are you on about boss? I didn't have a tape recorder."

Meredith seemed about to explode. Hook had long had a fascination about the phenomena known as spontaneous human combustion and it appeared he might be about to witness the event. Through the window he caught Mullen walk past, looking in then quickly away, his eyes dark, deep, disquieting. Hook understood what Mullen was trying to do. There was just one problem: Karen was about to give birth and Hook needed his job. Hook smiled, first at Mullen outside the box, who went very pale, then at Meredith.

"Do you want to know what really happened or are you

going to be taken in by a Yank?"

Hook kept his job; Mullen was sacked. His fury was the least of Hook's worries. Karen had long shown the signs of sharing her father's alcoholism, and Hook had gone along for the ride: even when she got pregnant they didn't let her expanding belly get in the way of a good time. And so it was that when Byron was born with his myriad conditions, none of them fatal but all permanent, Hook realised that what he had mistaken for love had been a situation.

Hook's unable to get a new ID because Karen's at some equalities convention so, leaving work at lunchtime, he heads to the Anne Boleyn. Walking past on the other side of the road he sees all the upstairs windows are still closed.

In the children's park Hook takes off his jacket and nervously turns on his phone, but there's nothing from Ulrike, just more texts from Monica, gradually more conciliatory: if her levels of indignation were charted on a graph they peaked around midnight and are now in the flatlands.

When the time's right, when Hook knows what to say, he'll call. He needs to speak to Ulrike first. Has she had second thoughts? Is she up there now, peeking out from behind Sid's dreary old nets, waiting for him and all the cops to go away? Then where will he go, home?

Walking back past the pub he sees the police trailer round the corner and thinks about knocking on the door, but something stops him. Entering the mega-mart where he bought croissants Hook purchases a can of pimped-up lager to sip as he walks.

The Anne Boleyn doesn't have much local competition; by rights it should be jammed out. Surely not everyone's gone god crazy? Hook finishes his can in several urgent sucks but there are no bins, so sucking the vacuum he limps through the desolate streets, ankle throbbing.

Leaving Ulrike a few hours ago Hook felt he was floating on air, could run marathons. But now, energy sapped by the sun and the city, as he walks slowly, painfully in search of a boozer, he's convinced that his worsening limp is the forerunner of something awful: leg cancer, a calf haemorrhage, some metatarsal blitzkrieg.

The slower he walks the greater his awareness of the shabbiness of the world around him, the drudgery and dust. Hook limps through a bleak shopping precinct full of youths walking with that hobbled gait, as if their feet are lashed to invisible posts, their kecks cacked, or they have extraordinary haemorrhoids. A businessman hurries past with a built-up shoe and Hook pities him almost as much as he pities himself.

Finally he chances on an agreeable-looking pub and steps inside. The barman, a young, dark chap with ear studs, stares at Hook aggressively and Hook blinks. Then he remembers the empty can in his hand, crushes it and puts it in his jacket pocket, which rips. He laughs hollowly.

"Sorry. You know what it's like round here. No bins anywhere."

"With good reason, eh?"

An Australian: good, he likes Australians. "I dunno... Stella please. I mean, one nutter plants a bomb in a bin, and the whole of London's covered in shite for evermore. I bet more people die of fucking – *dysentery* – than bombs in bins... thanks, how much?"

"Three-thirty mate."

Hook checks his pockets for change then remembers counting out coppers to the doleful Sikh. He checks his wallet: no notes, not even the secret twenty he keeps for emergencies.

"Do you take cards?"

"Ten pound minimum."

Hook looks at the menu: chips with everything and he isn't

hungry. "Make it three pints of Stella and keep the change."

The barman looks unimpressed. "Thanks a lot."

"But don't give them to me all at once – it looks a bit sad, doesn't it?"

"Whatever you say – mate."

The 'mate' routine is beginning to grate but the silence is merciless: he feels as if he's walked into the guy's front room uninvited.

"Hot," says Hook as the beer pours.

The barman shrugs. "Known hotter."

"Of course. Australian aren't you?"

The barman looks up, surprised and possibly insulted. "No mate. Croatian."

"Oh."

Hook's disappointed. The pint stands before him. He read somewhere that the extraordinary thing about gravity is its gentle strength: so easy to pick up a pint despite the imperceptible, inescapable forces at work. Hook's lips make contact, a chaste kiss with the glass rim, and he's about to stick out his tongue when a hairy hand reaches over and plucks his pint away.

"What the hell –?"

"Your card's been rejected, mate. Got any more?"

"But that's impossible, I – erm..." Puzzled, Hook checks his wallet: all his other cards are missing. Surely not Ulrike?

"Look, I'm really sorry, I don't. But I mean, I should have lots of money in that account. I get paid on the, erm, twentieth and today's the..."

"Twenty-fifth mate, all day."

"Is there a cash machine round here? A bank?"

"There was one in the precinct but it shut down."

"Right." He stands to leave, the barman's implacable face irritating. Hook smiles.

"So, how's life? Do you enjoy being a barman? Beats my

line of work."

"What line's that?"

"I work for immigration," says Hook. "How are things, enjoying the UK?"

The barman nods and puts down his eyes. Hook looks longingly at the pint in the man's hand then walks out.

Mullen's attempts to warn Monica about Hook failed. Had warnings-off ever worked, with women? 'Don't go near so-and-so – he's trouble'? If anything the dark pictures Mullen painted made it easier to keep Monica interested.

They were sitting in the Nags Head swapping dreams one afternoon when Jack paged him, so he went to the pub's payphone and called his brother who informed him gruffly that their father had been rushed to hospital.

Hook raced to the Royal Free – the same hospital where he had taken his mother and father to see their first grandchild – to be told by a nurse that his dad had taken an overdose of Paracetamol.

He ran to the ward to find Jack sat with their father, holding his hand. His father was writhing in convulsions, moaning in agony; a nurse was trying to administer N-acetylcysteine but the old man was thrashing like a landed eel. Seeing him, Jack scowled, stood, pushed roughly past him and left Hook alone with his dad. He sat on the little plastic chair and leaned in close.

"Dad?"

His father rolled his head towards him, eyes tight, fists clenched, thrashing about as if trying to escape, the nurse still trying to get a shot into him. Hook looked at her and she shook her head sadly.

He knew that look: he'd seen it from the midwife when Byron was extracted from Karen's belly, again when he took his mum and dad to see their damaged grandson in another ward of this same hospital. His dad had taken Byron's handicaps, his invalidity, badly as he had a handicapped sister.

"Dad, tell me why!"

"You!" his father roared, his voice a terrible cocktail of pain and rage. "You ruined Byron's whole future with your fucking... drugs!"

"What? What do you mean?"

"I know! You gave Karen drugs when she was pregnant!"

"No Dad, that's not true! Who told you that?"

His father's eyeballs rolled right back in his head and he struggled to get out his words.

"Not true, why then?"

"Dad, Byron has defects because of Karen's genes, who told you that bullshit?"

"Some journalist," groaned his father, "Curran, Murran..."

"Mullen," whispered Hook.

His father nodded and held his hand, unable to speak any longer, and together they waited for the end.

The absence of money is disturbing to Hook, but also exhilarating. After all, if he doesn't have any money, he can't give it away, spend it, worry about how and where to put it. Everywhere he looks experts say save your money, earn more, spend more... but then, who *are* these experts?

Under a railway arch Hook trips over a bunch of flowers laid to some fallen *soulja*. Young people are pricks. They live in the most exciting city in the world and they're still sore. London, he concludes, is like youth itself: wasted on the young. Watering the flowers with his own steaming tribute Hook zips up his pants and walks away.

On a tube west Hook picks up a freebie but the sea monster has been relegated to page three by the latest celebrity breakdown. They're now saying the creature might have been twenty miles long; creationists say the discovery's a prop from an old film or a remnant of the Ark.

Hook watches a teen black girl with one hand on a pram handle, the other holding her Oyster between her fingers as she sucks her thumb. A foreigner makes himself known by wearing a jersey over his shoulders. Where are they all going? Is this the best they can come up with? How many of these people need to get to work, what do they all do that matters so much?

"We're not *going* to work, you prick," snarls a suit, "we're going home."

"Oh yes, very good," snorts Hook, unnerved by the young man's telepathy. Exiting the tube at the next station he flies up the steps, injuries forgotten, then realises he's at the wrong entrance and stands beneath Centrepoint and the forlorn fountains. The underpass is a druggie frontline so Hook risks the traffic, jogging across Charing Cross Road into Sutton Row. As he hobbles past a tattoo joint a bearded chap in the doorway waves and he waves back – one mystery solved.

In Soho Square Hook's certain he sees Sid the barman sat in a deckchair but he's resolved not to speak to anyone until he's spoken to Jack. He can talk to Jack: Jack understands. Jack's always been there and will always be there.

Hook enters the old pub where they always meet. Smiling through his beard (why does everyone have beards these days, have the Taliban taken over?) Jack advances and makes to shake his hand. When Hook goes to shake it Jack punches him in the face. *Again...*

Saturday 26th June

"I'm quite alright now," says Hook, "a temporary lapse, a psychotic episode. Too much booze, not enough sleep is all."

Hook's tucked up in bed at home, Monica standing over him with her eyebrows raised holding the cordless phone. This is perfect. Now she'll forgive his disappearance – just like that other time.

Except it isn't perfect; it isn't alright. Jack thumped him and won't give him his money. Hook has fucked some spectral nymphet and has no cash to find her, although he does have a wife and daughter and a flat in London. What more could anyone need?

"He says he'll be alright Karen," says Monica into the phone. "He's just been working too hard recently. Yes, that's what I said... a week off? Well, I don't – I mean I don't know if I – alright Karen, thanks. Yes, you too. Bye."

Monica presses a button and flings the phone on the bed looking harassed. It was Hook's idea that she ring in to say he'll be off a few days. That will buy him time to find Ulrike. According to the laws of kidology ringing in sick on a Saturday makes the story more believable.

Quite apart from having to lie to his first wife, Monica isn't happy at the idea, but then she cared enough to come and collect him from the Soho pub where he was laid flat out (Jack's remorseful call, he even waited till she arrived). So maybe she *does* still care – a tad.

He could get a note from his doctor, but Hook knows once words like depression, stress or fatigue got onto your records, you're fucked. Not to mention those other invisible words they add in indelible ink to the notes they titter over with your bank manager, accountant and grocer – words like psychosis, insanity, *demented*.

"So," says Hook, pulling his sheets up to his chin and enjoying the snug feeling, "do you have any plans for the day?"

"Well I *was* going shopping," says Monica resentfully, "but as you don't feel too well maybe I should stay home and take care of you."

Hook thinks quickly. That won't do: apart from his nose, which has swelled up like a baboon's arse, he feels fine; and seeing his wife's sad features every way he turns is likely to give him a relapse.

"Look," he says kindly, "there's no point you moping around here all day, I'll be fine. Why not go get some shoes or something?"

Monica gives him a look that implies he's more important than shoes, but only just. Hilariously, she seems eaten up with guilt. Here's her uxorious husband, all alone, vulnerable in an explosive city, and she threatened him with divorce. What was she thinking? Remembering what he was doing, what he was accused of, Hook decides to let her down gently. He owes her that much.

"I'm really sorry," he says, holding Monica's hand. She pushes her hair away from her face, cheeks pinking with some as yet unrevealed emotion.

"What for?"

"The other night when I disappeared. It was seeing that poor old sod dead, really got to me. Then when your brother turned up out of nowhere it brought back a lot of memories about Dad and stuff. I just walked and walked, didn't even think to turn on my phone. Mid-life crisis, maybe?"

"Maybe."

Emboldened by his wife's passivity Hook moves things on a notch. "Anyway," he says with a little laugh, just to take the edge off his words, "what did you do with my salary? I went to get a cab home and had nothing. That's why I went to see Jack."

"Ah," says Monica, blowing her fringe in a way Hook used to find cute, "sorry about that. I transferred some to my account. Just for a few hours."

"What on earth for?"

Monica shrugs evasively. "I was after a loan, alright? You know you can only get a loan by proving you don't need it, and the way things are going now I doubt we could do that."

Hook wants to enquire why Monica needs a loan on *her* salary, but she leaves the room. Sighing, he looks out of the window at the baking city.

The more Hook considers his erratic behaviour, the more depressed he becomes. The crazy thing is, when he was insane he felt happy; now he's sane it's like everything has come crashing down. This is life's great secret, he thinks: *everyone* is insane. It's the only way humans can cope with everything.

When he thinks about it objectively, Hook's leaving his wife for someone less wealthy, less well-connected and (to a neutral) probably less attractive. He doesn't care. In fact, if anything, it confirms what he already knows: he's found what he's been looking for.

By mid-morning Hook's sanity is driving him crazy. Monica clumps round with the vacuum cleaner then sprays something and unloads the dishwasher until he's quite exhausted.

Worse, the bedroom TV is showing *Soccer AM*: all those middle-class actors pretending to be street kids make him puke. It gives him the same feeling as when he hears swing music on car ads: a vision of anti-PC middle-class boys smoking cigars. Hook can't watch Sky football without imagining himself on a blind date with Andy Gray, those piercing Caledonian eyes burning right through him over the candle-lit table, that sinister smile contorted with barely-concealed lust.

When Monica casually mentions she has to go in to the paper for an unexpected editorial meeting Hook practically helps her off the balcony. Shelley's out too – probably stabbing up grannies or injecting 'horse' – and when the door slams he's alone in the flat for the first time in days.

His emails to Ulrike keep bouncing back. He tries Myspace, Facebook, Bebo, Twitter and the rest of the adolescent zone, but according to Google neither Ulrike Nechayev, Susan Cohen nor any combo of the two exist – at least, not HIS Ulrike, his Susan. Maybe he dreamt the whole thing. An awful thought: Mullen. What if he's got to her, spirited her away?

The Anne Boleyn definitely exists – it gets a mark of two out of ten on *beernintheevening*, which seems unkind – and Sid is listed as proprietor but that's it. Then Hook remembers the big date in Sid's diary. Leafing through the yellow pages he finds dozens of funeral parlours, but only a couple of these have a Jewish theme and it doesn't take long to narrow them down to one.

The receptionist is zealously unhelpful. As she's already told a policeman this morning (Schneider, Hook guesses), Sid Cohen's funeral has been delayed pending the results of a post-mortem and his next-of-kin has unexpectedly gone away. This next-of-kin might well have left a contact address but under no circumstances will he or anyone else (not even the Prime Minister, she adds, unnecessarily) be allowed to have it. All's as he expected. Hook hangs up.

By lunchtime the heat is unbearable. According to a memo from the residents' committee the aircon is to be turned off each day due to environmental concerns; Hook's reduced to fanning himself with the letter.

Stripping naked he prowls the apartment, his erect cock leading the way as if he's being towed by a ghost. In the bedroom he kneels facing the wall and squints at his wedding photo: there's Hook, left of centre on the church step, like an imposter in his loose-fit suit, Monica beside him, squinting in the sun.

The village in which this clichéd church sat wasn't one Hook had heard of; nor had Monica, yet for her it typified everything English: quaint pubs, duck ponds, ancient fascists in the tea shops; a cliché not even based on truth. For Hook, born and bred in London, they might as well have been on Mars.

The day dawned drizzly, dreary, but as they stepped off the porch after the service the sun emerged like a late guest; a shaft of light caught Monica's white dress in its spotlight and Hook held his breath and her exposed arm, scared lest she was zapped away to some other dimension.

Karen, looking deceptively sweet in pink taffeta and a little hat perched atop her vast brown curls, scowled beside the bride. Why in hell's name had Monica asked his first wife to be bridesmaid? How cruel were women?

Mullen senior's flight was delayed and he didn't make it in time for the service, so Mike was forced to give Monica away – to hand over his little sister.

At the reception Monica and Michael disappeared and Hook found himself drunk and alone with Karen, his first wife; to his guilty relief she hadn't brought Byron. A cunning smile lit up Karen's face and they sneaked away to her hotel room and fucked, her silk dress flipped over her head, his tie draped

*across her back. Karen joked as he slid inside her that Monica
and her brother were probably doing the same thing (rather
than, as he suspected, rushing to the airport to meet their
father).*

*Reluctant to ejaculate inside her in case they made another
Byron and not wishing to spoil her new dress Hook slid his
cock inside Karen's pale blue panties and watched as bubbles
of white semen sieved through to the air.*

*Karen had the decency to pretend to sleep with slaked lust
and Hook pulled up his pants and went back to the reception,
where suddenly he was being confronted by the sturdy
forcefield that was Monica's father.*

*The old man stuck out a gnarled hand. "So you're my son-
in-law," he grinned, in a loud, Boston accent. "Where you
been, checking out fresh ass?"*

*Monica laughed; even her brother managed a smile. Hook
regarded the hand, remembered his own was still coated in
Karen's juices, and shook it, smiling.*

"Absolutely not, sir, there's only one girl for me."

Hook shifts on his knees as pins and needles spread north.
'The honeymoon never ends'? It never really started: they
went to Clacton. With a shudder Hook goes in search of beer.
Ken and Deirdre bob joylessly in their fetid waste but rather
than deal with their situation he takes a beer from the fridge
and turns on the TV in the living room; both words seem over-
stated. Hook hopes watching cricket will take his mind off sex
and all these complications; but it's so boring he turns on the
laptop and looks at looner porn.

It's hard to know where his fetish sprung from: he can recall
no obvious startling or transitory moments as a child in which
inflatables played a part; except the balloon dance on *Tiswas*
– and he never fancied Chris Tarrant.

Being a looner is simply something Hook is cursed with

and the internet makes things easier in that respect. In fact, too easy – he began to believe balloon fetishes were normal. Sadly, upon discovering his secret one afternoon, Monica disagreed.

Shelley was sleeping over somewhere and Monica rolled home drunk from some all-day bonding session at work, Hook playing catch-up as she led him to bed, stripped him naked, stuck her tongue in his ear and whispered: "What turns you on, honey?"

"In bed?"

"Uhuh. Anything, come on, you can tell me..."

"Well... there is something I need to tell you..."

Monica put a finger to his lips. "That's okay, I already know."

"You do?"

His relief was great: Monica knew and hadn't begun divorce proceedings.

"When did you find out?"

"Oh, ages back..."

"And you don't mind?"

"Why should I mind?"

"Well I dunno... a lot of women find balloon sex rather unusual... you weren't talking about balloons, were you?"

She was talking about his childhood crush on the long jumper, which was obviously less threatening. Perversion, thinks Hook, is not only isolating: it makes finding and keeping true love that much harder. After a miserable few days Monica agreed to stick around, as long he kept his balloons deflated in polite company.

When he mentioned balloons to Ulrike she seemed *intrigued*. Sexually she's a dream, but the more he thinks about it, that isn't necessarily a good thing: their bodies floated together and penetrated one another and filled each other up with fluids but it was like she wasn't really *there*. No matter what he told her he wanted to do she agreed, immediately wanted to enact the scene; she was like a blank canvas for his perversions, a fresh slate but a slate for all that.

Hook actually has no idea what really makes Ulrike happy and that saddens him almost as much as Monica's belief that men really are so selfish that only their own pleasures matters. How can a man rape when the best thing about fucking is the fact that the woman is letting you fuck?

Bored, Hook watches a fuzzy mpeg of a woman dressed as a schoolmarm bouncing up and down on a space hopper, edging ever closer to a disastrously-positioned stiletto. Apparently there are two distinct fetishes, popper and non-popper, and Hook can't quite work out which he is. He's always thought of himself as a non-popper but, the more he thinks about it, maybe he could be persuaded to convert. It's all too complicated. He sighs and logs off.

Disorientated, Hook looks at the photo of his first wedding day, hidden away in a boondocks folder. The day when he married Karen and all seemed perfect – until that bastard Mullen arrived with his teenage sister fresh off a plane.

Even as Karen walked up behind him on her shootist father's arm, rustling and wobbling in her OTT wedding dress, her boozy breath down his neck, Hook felt a bombardment of doubts, queries, questions he had never before asked, never even formulated in all this rush. He looked back and caught Monica's eye, her face demure above her trifle dress, and was sure she winked. As soon as he saw her he wanted her; for once in his life it had happened: his dream came true. He wanted that moment back.

Opening the picture in Paint, Hook uses 'select' to drag a little oblong round Monica and blows it up as large as it will go without the pixilation becoming too obvious. Absently, he adds a speech bubble: 'Howdy big boy, wanna ride my balloons?'

In 'print options' Hook selects 'highest resolution' and has just selected 'OK' when he realises the printer beneath Van Gogh's terrified glare is loaded with normal A4. Hook curses; the door slams.

"Dad?"

"Hang on!"

Hook hops over and curled up on the sofa, places his can over his lap and tries to look composed as Shelley enters the kitchen with a tall, spotty boy of Middle Eastern appearance who seems familiar. The printer cranks into action. Shelley looks over the breakfast bar, sees her naked father and is mortified. Hook looks for a cushion but it's still in the wash. He raises his other hand as nonchalantly as he is able. The printer slowly reels out the picture. From where she is Shelley can't see it, hopefully.

"Hi Shelley, just watching the cricket."

Shelley loiters in the relative safety of the kitchen, face flushed, eyes on the remorseless cricket, an elaborate and pointless ceremony conducted for the entertainment of nobody. Hook sees that, now. When she speaks it's hard to tell if she's on the verge of laughter, tears or hysteria: probably all three.

"With no clothes on, Dad?"

"Well it's boiling out there, the aircon's off again, and anyway you didn't tell me you were bringing guests home... who's this then?"

The dark, eager-looking boy advances and extends a hand. Hook looks at the hand then at his beer, moves his can over (the cold metal mercifully shrinking his cock) and shakes it firmly. The boy steps back. Hook counts the seconds before he wipes his hand on his trousers: four.

"My name's Mehmet, sir. Pleased to meet you."

"You too, son."

Suddenly Hook knows who this is: King Kebab. There's an

awful silence. Shelley takes something from the dying fridge. When she slams the door it exhales an asthmatic groan, as if it's full of cryogenic heads given a glimpse of the sun only to have it slammed in their faces.

The hummus heartbreaker clears his throat, nodding at the TV. "So, who's winning?"

"Looks like the Windies have us on the hop," says Hook lightly. The printer ejects the print-out and it flutters to the carpet face up. Seeing the poor-quality image the boy's eyes widen a little more. Hook looks back up at Shelley but she appears transfixed by a high-res slow-mo replay of a man swiping at a corky ball.

"Mehmet, would you like to come and see this movie I told you about?" Shelley asks finally, saving them all. Mehmet nods once more at Hook – more sorrowful than anything – then follows Shelley into her room. She slams the door and Hook hears some *High School Musical* pap blaring.

Grabbing the photograph off the floor, Hook feeds it through the shredder, goes into the bedroom and puts on his gown. Skulking in here would be like admitting to something so he returns to the sofa. England have lost another wicket: the middle stump cart-wheels backwards in ultra slow-mo. The greater the technology, thinks Hook, the slower things move.

He sighs and looks at the ceiling. That brown patch is definitely getting larger. In the seven years since Hook and Monica moved in to Liddle Towers no-one has ever inhabited the flat above. Hook's contemplated knocking through, erecting a spiral staircase: who'd know?

Maybe the patch is the cadaverous puddle of some no-mates pensioner. Maybe he should call the residents' committee. Maybe he should get dressed and leave his daughter and her friend to whatever it is the young do these days: text each other to death, probably. Maybe he should throw King Kebab out the fucking window.

Shelley's door opens, then mercifully the front door. "See you at the thing tonight, Dad!"

The front door slams. Karl Marx has never been his favourite author but Hook has to admit that sometimes he has a point; today, for instance, he feels profoundly alienated from the fruits of his labour.

Monica didn't enjoy pregnancy; the only thing she enjoyed less was getting pregnant. By thirty weeks she was enormous, complaining of headaches, swollen hands; the usual litany.

One afternoon Hook went to meet Karen for their regular hand-over; Byron wouldn't come to him at first, till he started singing "pop goes the weasel".

As they walked around the duck pond Hook told Karen how Monica never stopped moaning and suffered permanent headaches, and Karen said it sounded like pre-eclampsia. Karen had read about the illness as part of a course she would never complete. Monica went to the hospital and they said if it hadn't been diagnosed she or the baby – maybe both – might have died.

Why tell Hook his wife was sick, the woman he had left her for the first time – some inner goodness, some aimless faith? Or maybe because Karen still believed he was capable of doing good, of being not only a good man, a good husband, but a good father? For this, she had saved one, maybe two lives. And of course when it all came out years later he threw it back in Monica's face: "If I hadn't fucked Karen you'd be dead." Monica wasn't grateful.

Hook remembers Monica's anti-depressants in the bathroom cupboard, dating from some mini-crisis (passed over for promotion by a former assistant – again); the label says they mustn't be consumed with alcohol. Hook roots through the drinks cupboard in the kitchen, settling on a liquorice-flavoured liqueur she brought back from Eastern Europe and uses to strip wax off wine bottles.

Wearing an old fluffy dressing gown that feels safe and swigging liqueur from the bottle Hook drifts through the flat. It doesn't take long. Shelley often jokes that the view of the Wharf is its only selling point as its hardly large enough for a canary dwarf, let alone three adults. And an adult is what Shelley has somehow become: one minute she's playing *Tomb Raider*, the next she's off out in heels and nylons, grown-up in all but years.

By the front door Hook stops then turns right: Shelley's room. He opens the door as furtively as a burglar. For some reason he can't look at her bed, the scene of recent crimes. The curtains are drawn, clothes lie round the floor and the fan of her laptop hums quietly. He looks at the screensaver, some new-age animation bollocks, with its slogan: '*The only escape from a nightmare is to wake; the only escape from reality is to dream.*' What the fuck does *that* mean?

He wiggles his finger and the screensaver dissolves into her desktop image: Shelley as an eight-year-old alongside her mother, by a pool in France. He smiles: he took the picture, happy to be back in the bosom of his family after their brief separation. Then Hook stops smiling – he isn't in the photo.

Hook looks at Shelley's posters, tributes to boy bands, broad-stroke eco-clichés from cod-selling charlatans. As he turns on her ancient Spice Girls rug, wincing each time he sucks on the liqueur, Hook decides life can be summarized in a word: frivolous. As he watches he sees the walls of her room catch fire, melt, drain into a liquid pool; drip, slip and blaze away.

Idly, using his dirty index finger, Hook positions the cursor over the *Explorer* icon and taps the pad. Up comes Shelley's home page, some teen-zone meeting place, and a message: *you have mail*. Hook's finger wavers but then he hears the front door open.

Rushing into the hall Hook tries to think of an excuse for Shelley but to his relief it's Monica, carrying several dozen shopping bags bearing decadent names. And to his greater relief she looks happy.

She waves a paper. "They printed my Sharia piece!"

"I thought that was yesterday?"

"Yesterday?"

Monica's bubble, or possibly her balloon, bursts; Hook doesn't want that so he shrugs. "Oh, I read something you'd written about... oh, Islam."

"Yes, that was an op-ed. This is the real thing. This is a feature!"

"Congratulations." Hook pulls the gown together and hopes his semi has disappeared. Monica looks down at the bottle he's holding by the neck.

"Ugh! What are you drinking that stuff for?"

"I feel much better now so I thought I'd celebrate."

Monica looks vaguely disquieted but heroically holds onto her bags. "You do know you aren't to mix those pills with alcohol, don't you?"

"I didn't take any in the end, feeling better already."

The second half of this statement is true. Hook feels light as air and leans forward to kiss Monica's mouth, pink and pretty from a tube. Maybe it's not too late to resolve things? She grimaces, draws back and looks at the bottle.

"But – drinking that crap?"

Her eyes widen and she smirks. Hook looks down, sees he's poking out of his gown. He places the bottle strategically.

"Oh, that... just for old times' sake. Remember when we drank it before, at that BYO Afghan place down Dalston?"

"Yes, I had one mouthful and threw up."

"Ah, yes, but I had a few glasses with my Biryani. Before throwing up."

Monica smiles brightly: she's always like this when they consent to publish one of her articles. Now he supposes she'll make him read it. Hook squints at the paper she's holding out like an Olympic torch and is suddenly disorientated.

"That's not your paper, that's your brother's!"

Monica drops her arm to her side, smile fading, thank Christ. Come to think of it, he prefers his wife when she's in a bad mood. When she's happy she makes inane little jokes; quirky remarks dance off her tongue like party figurines.

"Er – yes, I know that, so?"

"So how come you're freelancing? I thought you were on a contract?"

Monica's about to say something then seems to catch herself and says something else.

"Champagne," she says with a smile, kissing Hook on the lips, patting his arse. "That's what we need! Why don't you go down and get some while I put on something *nice*?"

Grimly Hook goes to find his shoes.

'Islam unveiled: guest columnist Monica Mullen lifts the burqa on barmy Brent.

'The first sensation is one of suffocation. Niqabs come in a wide variety of colours and cloths, but for some reason, the garment I'm given is a kind of thick Hessian and I pray it won't rain.

"Don't worry,' laughs my guide, Sita Khan, morality adviser to the new council, 'you won't get waterlogged! When I first wore the niqab it was pouring down, but I didn't even get wet.'

'To my surprise, the garment is quite comfortable. And as Sita takes me for a walk round Brent Cross shopping centre, a strange feeling of security comes over me' –

"No, not like that – that's it, *there*."

His ears muffled by her thighs Hook hears Monica lift the tabloid she's been reading. He's been licking her clit for what seems like minutes but finds it hard to get enthusiastic. He returned from the offie carrying three bottles of *Moet* to discover Monica lying on the bed in some faux-cheerleader outfit: blue and yellow pleated dress, high socks, even the pom-poms. She won't say when she bought it but the outfit makes him uneasy – as she stripped him naked he felt embarrassed, as if with a stranger.

Although she looks cute Hook finds it hard to hide his disappointment: he thought maybe she'd finally consented to some balloon-themed action. Added to which he still remembers Ulrike, the things they said and did in the dark that night, and guilt threatens to overshadow fickle feelings of desire.

Hook raises his head and looks into his wife's eyes, his face coated in her juices – or, to be more accurate, his own drool. That's men for you, Monica often complains: two minutes under the sheets and they expect full-on orgasm, as if any woman who doesn't drown you is somehow repressed. But then why does she always need to be fulfilled? Occasionally Hook imagines he'd be happy to satisfy her with no thought for himself, so why doesn't she feel the same?

She sighs, dropping the paper onto the bed beside their tangled limbs. "Darling, my arms are tired."

"Think yourself lucky you don't work on the *New York Times*," grumbles Hook, wiping his mouth and reaching up for his glass of whiskey on the bedside table – he's always hated champagne. "Though there's fat chance of that."

Monica closes her legs and jabs him on the top of the head with her finger. "What do you mean? That's a damn good article!"

"Bullshit Monica. If you hadn't written it they'd never have printed it. It's patronising, condescending, and confused."

"What do you mean 'confused'? It's a straightforward account of my day as a Muslim woman. I just told it like it is. What's wrong with that?"

"Let me give you an example." Sitting up with his back to their wedding picture Hook snatches up the crumpled paper and scans down. "Here, for instance." He adopts a whiny American accent. "'I'm beginning to understand what Muslim women mean about the liberation of this much-maligned religion. It's a relief to go into a shop and not be confronted by a row of women's breasts when you want to buy cigarettes. However, I do experience racial prejudice on a number of occasions. One white man in a shell suit tells me to 'f- off back to Mecca'.'"

Hook puts down the paper. Monica's bottom lip sticks out and, hilariously, she pulls up her socks.

"What's wrong with that?"

"First, there was no chance of rain – it hasn't rained for weeks. Second, it's not *racist* to slag someone off for wearing a burqa. I'm sorry – it just *isn't*. The very idea is demented. Third, fags are *haram* – and you haven't smoked in years."

Monica jumps off the bed and glares at him, hands on hips. She seems about to launch into a tirade, but it's hard to take her seriously when she's still attached to the pompoms.

"Chris, you are *so* full of shit. You lie for a living *every day*. That's your job, that's your *life*. So what if I add a few colourful touches to one of my stories? It's not Dostoyevsky but it's my job, and I'm proud of that. And oh, by the way – here."

Reaching into her handbag Monica produces a pack of fags and lights one with a challenging expression. Something about his wife's indignation, the way she blows smoke, makes Hook horny. His eyes move slowly down over her body. Dangling his legs over the edge of the bed, moving his glass to his left hand, his right hand begins to slide up beneath the crumpled blue skirt. To his surprise Hook feels wetness there, somehow definably different from his bile. Still standing, legs apart, Monica closes her eyes, still inhaling nicotine; blue lace clouds fall about Hook's ears.

Hook pulls his wife closer and moves down her body, kissing her through the cheapo outfit, ducks beneath the skirt and tongues her slit. Monica moves her legs apart and wobbles slightly, so he pushes them closed. Her white cotton panties are round her ankles, but Hook pulls them slowly up her legs until they cover her cunt.

"Do you like my new panties?" breathes Monica, her hand running through his hair. For some reason her East Coast accent transforms into Deep-South trailer-trash at times like this. "They're real clean and pretty. Do you like my white panties mister? Would you like me to wrap them round your dick?"

Putting down the glass and pulling Monica down on top of him, her legs astride his head, Hook moves her panties to one side so he can lick her clitoris. He wants to drink and eat all of her: a keepsake for after she's gone.

He hears the wet singe of her fag being extinguished. "Mister, that's mah virgin pussy. I ain't never been fucked there before." Hook turns her round so she faces the window – he imagines all of London watching indifferently. His tongue slips, slides into her cunt. "Oh mister, that's mah secret place – you wanna fuck my puss? Is that what you wanna do mister?"

Pushing her down to her hands and knees Hook spits on his palm. Coating his cock he pushes against the hairs strong over her cunt. "Go ahead mister, ah ain't never been fucked before. Only by my – ouch!" Monica suddenly shoots forward and Hook's cock sniffs the air.

"What the fuck's the matter?" gasps Hook.

"I can feel the whisky! Burning!"

"So?"

Hook makes a move forward so does Monica and they move across the bed in some grotesque parody of a steam train.

"It hurts, Goddammit!"

"*Jesus!*"

Hook stands and goes to the en-suite, locking the door. He looks at himself in the mirror; the man looking back looks haunted, fatigued, like he's done 20,000 turns. Maybe he isn't better after all. Maybe Karen's right: his liver's on fire and his ankle burns with empathy. Worse, he's betraying Ulrike.

Not only had he betrayed Karen with Monica; he betrayed Monica with Karen. When Monica discovered (from her brother, of course) about his wedding-day fuck with his ex-wife she was displeased; more so when she discovered he was now working with her at the council.

If they'd been together when it happened, maybe Hook could have explained; but in fact she was with Shelley in Massachusetts visiting her sick father. Hook had refused to go; he hated flying. Mullen took whoever he was fucking at the time and one night Hook got a teary call to say Monica was taking Shelley to New York and might stay there for good.

September 11 brought them back together: seeing the planes hit, wondering if Monica was anywhere near, almost killed him. As soon as planes resumed crossing the pond he went to America and brought them both home. Monica called it the most romantic thing he'd ever done, conquered his fear of flying for her. Hook wasn't so sure romance was involved. Booze had played a big part, that and loneliness. On the flight home, petrified and drunk, he took some of her pills and had a strange dream.

There's a tap at the door and Hook holds his breath so she'll think he's vanished down the plughole. He doesn't need another argument.

"What?"

"Mister, did ah do wrong? Ah brought you a present mister, wanna see it?"

Hook smiles but isn't surprised; Monica usually gives in eventually. He opens the door and she stands with one finger in her mouth. He wonders what her feminist friends on the newspaper would make of her performance: probably wouldn't bat an eyelid, the hypocrites.

"Get on your knees," orders Hook. Monica kneels with difficulty in the tiny bathroom – the main reason they'd taken the flat. "Suck my cock." She opens her lips, and he watches in the bathroom mirror as she blows him. From this angle she could easily be a real teenager. Not that he's into the real thing – too much like hard work, all that acne and attitude.

At the same moment Hook realises his cock might still taste of Ulrike. Monica spits on the bathroom floor.

"What the *fuck*?!"

Hook acts innocent. "*What*?"

"You taste... *odd*."

"'Odd'?"

"I can taste beer on your fucking *dick* Chris. I didn't know you loved booze *that* much. But there's something else..."

Hook pulls back, his uncut cock weaves blindly towards the light. Monica wipes her mouth then shoves him away in disgust to stand and gargle with mouthwash.

"What's wrong?" says Hook, wishing he was dressed, willing his hard-on away.

"You taste funny."

"'Funny'?"

"Yes. I don't know... *different*."

Monica squeezes paste onto a brush and scours her mouth.

Hook sighs and looks up at the ceiling, feeling vulnerable under a bright light that exposes all his blemishes. When she's finished Monica turns to him with a sad look in her eye. He tries to look thoughtful and considerate, but it's hard with that thing between his legs deflating as the air escapes.

"What's happened to us, Chris?"

"We simply haven't evolved, babe."

Monica frowns, baffled. "What? What do you mean, 'evolved'?"

Hook sits on the cold toilet seat and wipes corrosive sweat off his face. "Our brains are the same size as when we went out gathering nuts, wiping our arses on nettles, throwing stones at the sun to knock it down and make fire."

"I mean, what's happened to us?" says Monica. "I sometimes think that if we'd never met, fucked, got married, we'd have been better people."

"You're saying you think it would have been better if we'd never met?"

"I didn't say that –"

"But how else could I hear it? If we'd each been better there would have been more... good in the world. That our sum is less than our parts."

"Chris, you are so damn insensitive."

"That's not true!" Hook tries to lighten the mood. "I have a very keen sense of *schadenfreude*."

Sighing, looking sadder than ever, Monica goes into the bedroom and he hears her strip off the uniform, take it to the machine and load the powder; the quiet rumble begins. Pulling on his gown Hook goes back in the living room, turns up the cricket and reaches for his drink. Through the cardboard wall to his right he sees it's dusk. Monica comes through dressed in her silk gown, holding her champagne, deflated. He catches her eye: she blushes.

"You OK?"

"Fine."

Monica sits on the sofa sipping her drink. She hardly drinks during the day as it makes her tearful. Probably shouldn't drink at all as it doesn't agree with her. But then what would they have in common?

Hook nods at her empty glass. "Another?"

"No thanks. I have a headache."

A funny thing, with Monica: she often gets headaches after sex. Doesn't want to talk about feelings or futures, just wants quiet and, ideally, sleep. Except they haven't had sex, not even close. Suddenly Hook knows they never will again. Monica watches the cricket, smoking her cigarette.

"Why did you give up, anyway?" asks Hook dreamily.

Monica looks down absently at the cigarette in her hand. "Smoking? I just didn't think it suited me."

"It does," says Hook. "It does suit you Monica."

This is it: twenty years is a long time, it's natural that in the end the energy dissipates and there's nothing left: no noise, heat or energy, just two self-absorbed masses of cells.

Lighting another fag and standing Monica goes in the bedroom, shuts the door. Hook pours himself another whiskey. Ken and Deirdre gulp grimly, swimming around in their de-oxygenated sludge. No-one's fed them for days – despite being top of every shopping list nailed to the fridge everyone forgets to buy fish food because the pet shop is two blocks out of the way.

Hook looks in the fridge, finds some slices of ham, pulls off a few lumps and drops them into the tank. Ken and Deirdre tear off sections and gulp bits down, spit them out, gulp them down again. Then he gets bored pulling off bits and throws whole slices in the water; the fish swim over and though them, tearing holes in the meaty walls, Hook watching, mesmerised.

After a few minutes Hook tears himself away from the fish's revolting mouths, their awful desperation. On an impulse he checks the internet and discovers *fish* do need their sleep after all; they've had the lamp on 24/7 for ages, no wonder they look so frazzled. Hook turns it off, feeling benevolent.

Slumping on the sofa he switches on the Saturday night TV but it's like the Sky dish decoder's broken and all he receives is unintelligible gibberish; is he really the only person who doesn't like ballroom dancing or auditions? Why not just book people who can already sing, dance or swallow swords? Who needs the back story?

Sipping another whiskey, Hook's eyes glaze over. Monica emerges from the bedroom, handbag in one hand, phone in the other, wearing the new black dress he almost ruined. Hook feels guilty: not about fucking Ulrike but about not fucking his wife.

Monica grabs her coat from the hook. "I'm off."

"Do you know anyone who's ever been to Wimbledon or Ascot, who's ever been on a yacht or bought shoes for six thousand dollars? I sometimes feel like we're receiving TV signals from some parallel planet. It makes no sense. Has the world gone crazy, or is it me?"

"I said I'm going out."

"Where are you going, Monica?"

"If you can't remember I'm not telling you."

Hook tries to focus on dates and places but the medication's setting in: his brain's slipping and sliding like the fish in their tank. Instead, he nods down at the red heels Monica's wearing, bought today. How much, he ponders, sixty, six hundred?

"In *those* shoes?"

Monica looks down at her heels, shrugs. "Maybe I'll find me a real man."

"Good luck with that one, darling."

Monica slams the door – portentously, it seems. Then he spots the pack of fags on the breakfast bar. As he smokes his way through them he tries to find something of interest in the Sky Box, fails; searches the internet for something about Ulrike, fails; texts Shelley to see when she'll be home; back comes the mortifying reply:

After the performance, Dad.

Now Hook remembers: Monica mentioned something about Shelley having a role in a school production. Hook looks at the calendar on the wheezing fridge and there it is, a great black hoop round the day and the initials: ***HSM***!

The washing machine light's blinking to signify the cycle's over. A fag hanging from the corner of his mouth Hook takes out the damp uniform and throws it into the dryer. He shivers with disgust and feels ill; Monica must have taken it from Shelley's room when he was out.

Hook suspects the reason Monica was so pleased with herself earlier was because she could still get into her daughter's clothes. The realisation that he forgot all about the musical makes him feel sick. Maybe he should take the uniform to Shelley? No, it would never work, it'd be all wet.

His head begins to spin like the tumble dryer: what did Monica say about Librium and booze? Hook lies on the bed and puts on the news, smoking a final cigarette. Something's happened to someone, somewhere, sometime, for some reason, but he can't quite focus: the drugs and booze have knocked him skewif. He sleeps.

He dreams the house is haunted, that there's something in the basement, something else trudging across the loft. But that can't be right – they no longer have either. Maybe that's why flats are never haunted: no cellars, no attics. Hook doesn't miss either, but he misses the garden at the old place.

The garden was short, wide and large enough for foxes and Shelley's friends to play. That was why they had to leave the terraced house: a misunderstanding. Shelley and her friend

(Hook can't even remember the little bitch's name) were inseparable that last year at primary school; they were ten or so, little faux-ladies. At seven the friend was still in nappies; by eight she was wearing thongs. Hook never felt easy around her, a feeling that increased on discovering her thuggish father was loosely linked to the Drummonds.

One cold April afternoon Shelley came home from school to find Hook watching re-runs of the Test match in Australia.

"Hi babe," said Hook, "where have you been?"

"To my friend's," said Shelley. "She has a lovely room, Daddy, it's pink."

"That's nice", said Hook, distracted by the cricket.

"Would you like to see her bedroom dad?"

Hook shrugged, half listening, watching Nasser Hussain swipe at, and miss, another McGrath special.

"Sure, why not..."

So Shelley told her friend, who told her violently unhinged father that Shelley's Daddy wished to see her bedroom. They had to buy the apartment in Liddle Towers when prices were at their peak, Shelley lost her friend, Hook his garden. His mother took it worse than anyone; her cancer was crushing her from the inside, and the thought of losing the patio on which she sat watching Shelley grow up was all too much; she went downhill fast.

Hook did have one thing to celebrate: at the age of thirty he became a property owner. Monica threw a belated party and flat-warming; he arrived home to find the front room covered in balloons. Jack arrived early with a moving-in present: an aquarium and two small fish.

"That's fantastic, Jack, thanks," said Hook, secretly cursing; he'd always been intimidated by the thought of pets.

"Now Chris, I know you don't like pets much," said Jack, laughing, "but I also knew Shelley really wanted something to make up for losing her garden, so I thought I'd get you

something that didn't need much maintenance."

"Yes, great." Hook smiled, watching as Shelley popped all the balloons. What was a goldfish's lifespan anyway? None of the ones he'd won as a kid even made it home from the fair.

"With TLC they could last forty years," Jack said with a malicious smile.

"Great. Thanks, bruv."

The apartment was too small, right away Hook could see that: they only had a few guests and the kitchen stroke living room was packed.

Hook pulled Jack aside. "Jack, where's Mum? She was meant to be here early so Shelley could show her her new room."

"Ah," said Jack, gloomily. "Bit of a problem there."

"Problem?"

Jack stroked his beard thoughtfully. "I'm afraid I made a bit of a boo-boo."

"A 'boo-boo'? What the hell are you on about?"

"Well," shrugged Jack, "I... kind of let it slip – why Dad topped himself."

Hook looked at Jack and waited for the laughter, the wink; none came. The balcony was just a few short feet away. It would have been so easy to pick him up and throw him over; maybe even easier just to hold on, to fall together.

Sunday 27th June

At 3am, hearing noises in the attic, Hook wakes. The drug cocktail makes him nauseous and the cigarette taste sends him over the edge of the toilet bowl. As he barfs he hears Monica return three sheets to the wind and stumble into Shelley's room, leaving him staring down the dark pan.

The light goes out; another power cut, as if at this time in this insomniac city no-one'll notice. All over the house, the great deflating sound of things shutting down.

When Hook emerges from the toilet to a living room full of soft velvet shadows and looks out over the city he becomes afraid: not for London, which will always be here, gleefully soaking up pain and ghosts, but for himself, his life; his diminishing returns.

The contrast between the bipolar hours astonishes him. Not twelve and twelve, noon and midnight – at twelve noon most people still retain hangovers, night-horrors, and at midnight work still impinges on sleep, drink and sex. The real contrast comes later, three versus three.

At 3pm in the office, surrounded by wisecracks and sandwiches, daily gripes and daylight distractions, Hook can almost convince himself the world's under control, that life can be segmented, as pioneers segmented the American plains; digitised and pixelated and reduced to byte-sized chunks.

Yet when he awakes from some internal horror at 3am

Hook senses there's no control, order, plot, history or sense to any of it, only the slither of life's light being crushed from all dimensions by darkness, and darkness conquers and all will be still and cold and (most of all) silent.

Hook looks down at the bottle of anti-depressant pills: time to increase the dosage. That or get out more.

There are night lights beneath the sink and Hook lights a few and places them round the apartment so it looks like a place of worship and his shadow dances on the cardboard wall as Van Gogh watches with baleful eyes.

Alcohol is unthinkable so Hook tries to find something that doesn't require electricity to keep him occupied. Unsuccessful, he skims his iPod but music doesn't seem to matter; nor do the books he's been putting aside and the DVD box sets he's hoarded all become suddenly redundant.

Is Shelley stopping with a friend? Hook doesn't know any girl called Dahlia, has never come across her parents during school events or PTAs. Maybe there is no Dahlia: only Mehmet. Does it hurt more because of the boy's name?

Maybe there's no Ulrike either; he'll go back to the Anne Boleyn to see if it exists and not just some sixteenth century ghost. There's nothing in the papers about Sid's murder so did it happen? Hook isn't sure – even his conversation with the funereal receptionist seems disconnected, dreamlike.

Holding a night light like an ancient cobbler Hook goes and inspects the fish: they bob and gulp water, seemingly no worse for the ham. Taking a pint glass from the dishwasher Hook scoops out the smaller fish – he can never remember which is which.

Carefully holding the glass in his crabbed fingers Hook walks to the toilet, the fish gulping at the change of scenery. Placing the flickering night light on the cistern Hook opens the pan and it still contains his vomit as he'd been scared to flush in case he woke Monica. But he can't do it; he can't flush the fish away in all that puke. So instead he goes to fetch its twin and puts that in another glass and leaves the two glasses touching, the fish seeming puzzled that they slide from each other's kisses like reverse magnets.

He cleans out the tank for the first time in months; it isn't as difficult as he imagined, in fact it feels good to be doing some good for once. When he's finished Hook discovers he might be able to face a beer, and feels he deserves it for his show of mercy. Clicking open a can he goes to the family laptop on the desk. Its battery's hanging in there, he has mail.

Sender: unknown. (How can that be? How can anyone send a message and the computer not know who it is?)

Subject: I know where she is.

Message: let's meet.

MM.

"I thought I might pop by the office today," Hook informs Monica over breakfast. Her eyes peer at him over the top of her paper, which she's inspecting for some response – good or bad – to her Sharia story.

Bad timing: the papers are full of the latest failed bombing, some mad mullah at the Tower of London. The detonator on his belt blew his beard off but the tower seems intact. The incompetence of the bombers is a national joke; one near-the-knuckle comedian called the IRA from onstage to see if they could give the terrorists some tips.

"Are you sure? It's Sunday darling. I told Karen you'd be off for a week."

Monica's eyes are bloodshot and despite his failings the night before she looks guilty. If he licks her cunt now what would he taste? Whom? Neither of them mentions Shelley's show, Hook's no-show.

Hook looks up into Van Gogh's eyes. "I don't mean I'm

going back to *work*. I just need to make sure my feature about the reconciliation service is right. I won't be long."

Monica sighs and tosses the letters page on the table, where a corner falls into her bowl of cereal and milk eats its way through the column inches.

"I might go into town too. We can get the tube together."

Hook's heart sinks: crammed together, noses meeting, not sure whether to kiss or close his eyes, not sure how best to make it clear to other passengers that he and Monica are married without speaking...

He shakes his head. No. Be normal. There's nothing wrong with getting a tube with his wife. In any case he can always get off.

"Are you going to shave today?" Monica asks him casually as she dons her coat. Hook looks in the mirror at the shaggy growth and strokes it with pride.

"No."

His wife's out in the shared hallway and he's having a last look round when he notices Ken and Deirdre floating dead on top of the water. Quietly Hook shuts the door and hurries after Monica, disappearing down the stairwell. At the top step he stops, dizzy, then carefully follows her down.

As they pull into King's Cross a bunch of apprehensive-looking Yanks board the tube. They probably booked their trip months ago and by the time the bombing campaign got underway found it was too late to cancel. Hook smiles at the idea: all sat on the plane as it lands, wondering what they're in for.

Seeing them with their suitcases on wheels Hook decides he'd like to visit London as a tourist: quaffing fine wines, eating sweetmeats with ladies and overlords, clutching at bright parcels from Harrods and Harvey Nicks, catching taxis, attending dire musicals, sleeping sweetly in faceless hotels.

Monica changes at Euston. Hook kisses her hard on the mouth and she seems surprised, waves awkwardly from the platform as his train whizzes into the tunnel.

The morning heat's stifling when Hook emerges at Embankment, but as he walks up the steps and crosses Hungerford Bridge towards the clamped London Eye a slight breeze cools him through his short-sleeved shirt. Halfway across the bridge he passes a dark, Eastern European tramp staring intently into the water and considers talking him out of it, but that will make him late. He can't save *everyone*.

As Hook reaches the south side he looks down and spies Mullen on a bench by the Thames, in front of the crumpled cardboard box that is the National Theatre. Hook limps slowly down the concrete steps, squinting in the sun; Mullen reaches in his jacket pocket and pulls out a pack of cigarettes.

As Hook approaches Mullen turns as if sensing his presence, blows out old smoke and smiles calmly. A rook from the Tower swoops, sits on the arm of the bench, caws at Hook then flies away.

"Scarf Lad. Glad you could make it. Do sit down."

Fag in smoky mouth, eyes narrow with smoke, Mullen pats the bench beside him as if he owns it; maybe he does. Hook remains standing and rather than look at Mullen in his suit and tie (on a Sunday of all days) he stares out on the brackish Thames.

A pleasure boat growls past. A few years ago Hook made the mistake of treating Monica to an anniversary lunch that consisted of being broiled beneath acres of glass as obstreperous waiters filched his wallet; all so they could watch the uninspired riverside passing torturously by, car parks and apartments no-one could afford to buy. Now there are forests of these buildings – the city keeps expanding yet nobody seems to notice, no-one seems able to stop it. No-one has any money and yet the city keeps growing with a mind of its own.

Hook turns and leans against the hard wall, folding his bare arms. "What do you want, Mullen?"

Mullen inhales, forcing smoke out through his nose. "I need you to find Susan Cohen."

"You mean Ulrike? I thought you knew where she is?"

Mullen sighs, puts the fag to his mouth and squints up at the sky as if it disappoints him, puts his big nose out of joint.

"I lied about that. Look, it's... complicated. Let's just say there's a lot riding on this story."

"Like what?"

A MILF-type woman passes between them pushing a pram, a baby in front and a two-year-old on the backboard with her long blonde hair streaming behind her like Boadicea, or Isadora Duncan, eating ice cream. The mum's a size 18-20, maybe more of a BBW. All the new acronyms, all spelling out the same old story: M.I.S.O.G.Y.N.Y. Hook closes his eyes. Mullen continues.

"There's been a lot of tension recently. Susan appears to be the only reliable witness to these alleged attacks at the pub. If we can get her to speak, maybe we could cool it all down before things get out of hand."

"I don't see how," says Hook, puzzled. "If *Ulrike* says young Asians targeted the pub because it was a pub wouldn't that increase the tensions?"

"That's the rumour anyway, but on the other side people are saying Asians are being fitted up. You know how it is."

"So you're actually saying 'the truth must out'?"

"Doesn't it always?"

He leaves that one floating and turns back to the river. Up on the bridge the tramp leans over the fence – armed police patrol. Another cloudless day: eight-something and he's sweating. Even the breeze has died. The weatherman on the radio sounded jubilant – the drought continues, rejoice! Hook, who gets nervous after an hour of sunshine, looks for a black cloud to brighten up his day.

He turns again to Mullen, who's lit another cigarette and watches him impassively. To take his mind off the cigarettes Hook wipes his nose with his hand and dust crumbles out. Apparently that's all dust is: snot. You wipe it on the sofa and it dries and turns to dust and you breathe it up your nose...

"What's in it for me?"

"Twenty grand," says Mullen instantly. Hook knows this is negotiable but doesn't care: he isn't taking money to betray the woman of his dreams.

"I won't do it."

"Thirty."

"It's not the money, damn it! Why the hell should I help you, of all people, get your scoop?"

"For the public good?"

"Oh fuck off, Mullen... anyway, I'm busy."

"What, drinking yourself to death?"

"I do have a job, you know."

"I thought you were taking a week off."

"How the hell –?"

Hook remembers Monica, shuts up.

Mullen speaks softly. "It won't take long. Yours is a small island after all."

Hook shakes his head. "No."

Mullen sighs and stubs out his cigarette on the arm of the bench, apparently placed in memory of *Sarah Noone, 1991-3*.

Flicking the smouldering fag so it shoots past Hook's head into the water Mullen smiles again. "Does Monica know where you were the other night?"

"What night?"

The faux smile drops at last and there he is, the same old Mullen.

"The night you spent with Susan. Oh, sorry – I mean Ulrike-*ka-ka-ka*. I take it you couldn't find her on Facebook, huh?"

Hook looked at him, startled and scared. "How the hell do you know about that?"

Mullen runs his fingers through his hair and examines his nails, as if to minimise the impact of what he's saying.

"Chris, there are trails everywhere you go, every place you visit. Not just DNA, CCTV: I mean *electronic* trails. I happen to know IT-bods are working on software that will reveal the contents of everyone's 'history' folder, everyone's browser, to anyone who has the money. It may even work retrospectively. Essentially there will be no secrets anymore."

Hook looks up to the sky for rain. For the first time in his life he wishes there was some god to pray to, to dance for.

He turns on Mullen. "Fuck you, Mullen, I won't help you. Tell Monica whatever you like. I'm with Ulrike now."

"Oh, get real!" snorts Mullen. "You fucked her once and she disappears. Hardly the romance of the millennium."

Hook shakes his head, remembering the whispers in the dark, the sliding hands; the way their back stories and dreams fitted together.

"You weren't there."

Mullen lights another cigarette and blows white gas. What does smoke do to the ozone layer anyway, Hook ponders? Maybe, if everyone lit up together as one, we could save the world, take a deep breath and believe. Yes we can.

"Did she tell you she was married?" asks Mullen.

"She did, actually."

Mullen's face registers a minute expression of surprise; Hook grins. "You didn't think she would, did you?"

Mullen shrugs that one off. "Did she tell you who her husband is?"

"You mean, 'was'. None of that matters, Mullen. She's left

him; she's with *me* now."

"He's still in the picture, Chris. Look."

Mullen gestures and hesitantly Hook steps towards him. Behind Mullen a tin man stands frozen for the benefit of passersby. He catches Hook's eye and it looks for a moment like the performer's trapped inside a metal prison.

Clamping his fag between his lips Mullen digs in an inside pocket and produces a photograph of Ulrike, next to a young white guy with a ponytail, chains and a tracksuit. Both are laughing. By the look of the wallpaper they're in a grungy pub; on the wall above the bar he reads a banner: *Happy Birthday Vic from all at the Ship Inn.*

"Who's this?"

"Gary Cooper. *Susan*'s husband."

"*Ex*-husband," corrects Hook.

"Bit of a nutter by all accounts. Comes from a vicious family. His dad's Vic Cooper; they reckon he's had a hand in every big bullion job in the South East in the last twenty years, runs this pub and a builder's yard as cover. Susan on the other hand is a bit posh: private school, trust fund, slumming it."

"What are you saying, you think Ulrike's in trouble?"

"If Ulrike knows *Susan*, yes, it's possible."

"Ha ha." Hook peers at the weedy-looking kid next to Ulrike, tall but skinny and pale. "Ulrike told me about this Gary bloke. She says he raped her."

Mullen shrugs. "Doesn't surprise me. He's done time for assault on a minor."

Hook jerks his head upward at Mullen. "Where can I find this guy?"

"Gary and Susan were living over the pub. Might be a place to start?"

Mullen writes down the address of the pub in a small town on the Essex coast. Hook takes the paper and puts it in his wallet.

"Thanks," says Hook, grudgingly.

"Good luck," smiles Mullen. "Oh – and give my regards to Monica when you see her."

Hook walks away without another word and, buying cigarettes from a kiosk, lights one with trembling fingers. The moment he inhales he feels better. He's only been smoking for twelve hours and he's hooked.

When he reaches the middle of the bridge he sees the tramp has vanished.

The police trailer's still parked outside the Anne Boleyn, whose windows are all boarded up. Hook walks round the tiny block, but there's no other way in. Buying a cold can of SuperBrew from the doleful Sikh Hook sits at the bus stop opposite the empty pub. Now it looks like it's never been open, or maybe built as a tourist impression of an old East End pub.

They do walks round this area, showing where the Ripper carved his victims, where the good ol' Krays smashed kneecaps and the Luftwaffe incinerated families. The East End: a living museum commemorating man's inhumanity to man, now an audio tour on iPod.

Around the corner, away from view (if anywhere in London fits that description), Hook throws a small stone up at the window from which he once looked out; he's certain Ulrike's looking down. The stone makes a sharp crack but nothing happens. Far away he hears truck horns blaring, as if that'll provide safe passage through the streets.

"Haven't you heard of the broken window effect, Chris?" asks a familiar voice behind him. Hook jumps and turns. Schneider, in that same old suit, the same humourless face, looking down at his tattooed hand round the can of lager.

"Look," says Hook, "I want what you want, Inspector. To

find Ulrike – Susan. That's all, isn't it?"

Schneider sighs, shifting foot to foot. He seems shambolic but Hook knows him. For a few years they were acquaintances, sharing beers and swapping tips; they even visited his weird old place on Hackney Marshes for dinner, Monica getting on well with Mrs Schneider, his dead wife. Then, just because Hook did what any good hack would do, protected a source, he got the hump.

"Maybe we should have a proper chat," suggests Schneider. "I need to find out a bit more about this problem Sid reported."

"Problem?"

Schneider scratches the back of his neck ruefully. "You know, the anti-Semitism malarkey. Sid contacted me about it a few weeks back, but no-one seemed to know anything. Sounded like a bunch of kids to me, but then he gets murdered and this Susan goes missing. Seems you're the last person to see her, would that be a fair summary Chris?"

"I suppose it would, yes."

"Hmm... as I say, an odd case. But old Sid was a good friend of mine. I'll get to the bottom of this one." Schneider winks cheerily. "See you later Christian. And oh – people in glass houses, know what I mean?"

He doesn't. Schneider lopes off round a corner; Hook limps in the opposite direction, throwing his empty can into a skip. He feels a great rage at his powerlessness. Being sane: *that's* his sore heel. If he was still crazy he wouldn't care what Monica, Mullen or Schneider thought.

Hook walks back toward the shops where forty-eight hours ago he bought a newspaper thinking a whole new life was opening up. He bought croissants thinking this would be the new routine – they'd run the pub, fuck every night and live forever.

Trains to Essex depart from Liverpool Street but the tubes are down so buying another can for the journey he walks west, into the sun. It's so hot now he can't remember it ever being cold, being winter.

By the time he reaches Liverpool Street Hook's drenched in sweat and in a bid to throw the insects off buys a new t-shirt from a shop in the mall before purchasing a ticket. There's a train to Ulrike's hometown in twenty minutes so he pops into the elegant station bar to change, then takes a treble whiskey surrounded by morose Essex boys in suits.

London's out of order, incommunicado, on voicemail: Hook tries to contact his brother, his daughter and each of his ex-wives in vain. At one point cops with machine guns scream at everyone to leave the pub immediately, and in the panic an old woman gets trampled; Hook helps her to her feet and she backs away as if scared.

Hook's feeling giddy and the journey ahead seems daunting so he buys some cans to keep him company. On the train he drowses and thinks he's dreaming when he glimpses a giant headless horse in the distance before realising it's the unfinished Wallinger across the estuary.

When he wakes the train's pulled into the final stop: a tiny seaside town. According to the disinformation board there are no trains back to London till morning. Hook grabs his last can and begins the slow walk into the centre, shivering with the unfamiliar cold and trying to ignore the hangover that keeps threatening to catch him up.

Whenever Hook leaves London he feels lost, and usually that's disagreeable, but today it feels different. He still feels alone and alienated but he also feels light, knowing that if he removes the SIM card from his mobile nobody will be able to find him unless he wants them to, and in the meantime he can pretty much please himself. Once, Hook had had this giddy lost feeling in London.

He'd been married to Karen for two years, Byron was hard

going, Monica temporarily engaged to someone from the paper, and having been sacked thanks to Mullen he'd taken a job in a factory. He was still only eighteen, and missed his father: more, it seemed than either his mother or brother.

The job was mundane but not too hard, and Hook liked the other workers more or less, though the problem (there was always a problem) was that this job was in the outer suburbs, a fifteen minute hike from the tube through endless semis and cul-de-sacs.

One rainy lunchtime Hook set out from the factory with the intention of visiting the chip shop across the road but instead he carried on walking through the endless streets, searching for the countryside.

He'd walked for over half an hour and knew he was already in essence late, and couldn't afford to lose the job, but his legs kept pushing him on, pulling him away, and he had fantasies of becoming a man of the road, sleeping beneath hedges and disappearing forever. Only the relentless rain stopped him – dispirited and cold he finally turned back.

By the time Hook got back to work he was an hour late and drenched through; he had to make up some cock and bull story about being attacked in the street, and everyone apart from the boss laughed. He went home to Karen and Byron and ever since he'd wondered what would have happened had his conscience (or cowardice) not got the better of him and he had carried on walking down that long, dark road.

Hook walks along a dismal high street past boarded up charity shops and B&Bs, downhill toward the shiny air over houses that signifies water. It's dusk and he shivers at the difference in temperature. A middle-aged man urinates against a tourist information doorway and glowers at him as he walks, sucking his can, arms bare and goosebumps spreading, to the sea.

The harbour isn't pretty enough, a horseshoe cluster of tat-themed shops and desperate pubs: the crunch has frightened away the tourists and only a few people pass as Hook stands on a raised promenade, leans on railings and watches dreary waves roll in. How many summers did he spend in resorts like this as a kid?

Hook's adventure at boarding school had always been blamed for their lack of holidays; it was also blamed for a lack of presents, new clothes and friends from either of the social classes they hovered between, neither of which ever wanted to claim them. Hook had felt not so much aloof as aloft: suspended on a gravity-hammock between two competing worlds, neither of which was his own.

It was unfair, really – it wasn't like the school cost his parents anything, so how could they blame that for the two weeks of hell (parents at the clubhouse, crapping in a bucket as rain dented the roof) on a caravan park? Or, come to think of it, when he was sixteen and waiting for his first wage from the newspaper, and went to his dad for a loan, to be told his schooling had cleared him out?

Then, when his father took the hero's way out, there had been whispers of bankruptcy, negative equity, debt; were they blaming Hook's blighted school days for his father's death? His mother never quite managed to reassure him on the subject – or of much else, for that matter.

Hook crushes his empty can, puts it in a bin, and walks down some slimy steps to a pebble beach mussed by the tides. Reaching the surf and wetting his boots he stoops to scoop up a handful of water. He sips the sea, hoping to taste monsters, but all he can taste is salt so he spits out the Channel and limps up the beach, liver twanging like a mistuned banjo.

Back on the high promenade Hook turns on his BlackBerry to tell Monica he's leaving her – has in fact left. The welcome tone sounds trivial here, at this meeting point of the elements. There are no messages: maybe Monica's guessed what's happening? He scrolls: home or mobile? Home. He'll need to edit his numbers soon.

As Hook walks towards the Ship Inn, which looks warm and inviting, he hears the phone ringing in distant London: Heat City. Someone answers. He closes his eyes and to his surprise tears are squeezed out by his heavy lids.

"Hello?"

Mullen's voice. Hook drops the BlackBerry on the pavement, stamps on it hard, so its intestines squirt out the sides, and keeps on walking towards the pub. A part of him feels relieved, that he isn't the one to break the news to Monica; a larger part feels a surprising fury.

On entering, the pub seems busy but that's because of the number of men at the bar; most of the booths and tables are empty. A few gnarled faces look his way as he approaches then turn back to their conversation; Hook thinks he hears the word "miscegenation".

"I'm looking for a girl," says Hook to the first person at the bar, a burly, grey-haired type in his fifties wearing a fisherman's sweater. Hook would lay good money on him working as an estate agent. The man laughs lewdly at his friends, then back at Hook.

"Aren't we all?"

Hook takes out the photograph and the man's face changes. He throws the photograph at Hook, who tries to catch it, misses; it falls on the floor. As Hook picks it up the man moves closer, looks down on him menacingly.

"I'd fuck off if I were you."

"But you're not."

Hook stands. The man eyes him up and down, appraising

him. Hook knows he looks tougher than he is and stares back evenly, heart bumping.

"This Vic Cooper," says Hook. "Who is he?"

The man jerks his head; his friends fall silent but the jukebox suddenly kicks into Kylie Minogue. *Sha-na-na-na-nah – na na- nana- nah...*

"What are you, filth?"

"Nope."

"Then fuck off. I'm warning you. He don't like people sniffing round his business. I'm saying this for your own sake, son."

"Can you tell me if you've seen him lately? Or his son, Gary?"

"Listen," says the man quietly, leaning his face in, "just fuck off out of our town. *Now!*"

He barks out the last word; Hook and most of the pub jump. He's getting nowhere.

"There's nothing I'd like better," he says, "but there are no trains. Can you help? I don't mind paying."

The man stares at him coldly, but the tension drops a few notches.

"Nope. Ring your mum."

Some of the men laugh. Hook sighs, picks up the picture and waves. "Okay. Thanks a lot."

Leaving the bar Hook begins walking away from the pub when he hears running footsteps behind him. Tensing and turning, he finds himself looking into the face of a young man with shiny eyes, long hair and pierced ears. He's wearing a t-shirt, combat trousers and a woollen beanie hat.

"You're the journalist, ain't you?"

"I might be."

"You looking for Ulrike?"

"I might be."

"What do you want?"

"That's between me and her."

The young man seems taken aback and thinks for a moment; Hook sees the cogs turning painfully.

"Tell you what," says the young man in a strong, estuarine accent, "you go and get a drink from that offie, meet me in the car park at the back of the pub and we'll go see Ulrike. She likes vodka."

"Yes," says Hook sadly, "I know."

Its fully dark now and on returning from the off-licence Hook has to squint in the car park before seeing the young man, loitering beside a sturdy-looking jeep. Wary, Hook holds onto the bottle. In the gathering gloom he sees a snide smile floating as if detached; the kid steps forward, nose inches away.

"'Gis a drink, then."

"Will you take me to see Ulrike?"

"Maybe."

"No Ulrike, no vodka."

"I don't want your vodka."

"Then what do you want?" The boy's eyes go down again, to his crotch. "A blow job?"

The kid looks astonished. "Do what?"

"Is that what you want, a ride for a ride?"

The kid pulls a small knife from his jacket. "Give me your wallet you queer."

Hook's relieved; that's what he's been looking at. Then he's hurt, frustrated and outraged. All his life he's lived in London, staggered home through dark streets, partied on dodgy estates, danced at shebeens, drunk with gangsters, and never once has he been mugged. Yet five minutes down the country and some fish-fucker's trying to take his money. Hook laughs.

"Don't fucking laugh queer boy," says the kid quietly, stepping in, prodding the knife into his ribs. "Think I won't use this? I'll tell them inside you fucked my wife. I could kill you now and the cops'd believe me."

"Alright, alright." Hook puts down the bottle and holds up his hands.

The kid looks down then quickly around. "Throw me your wallet."

Hook takes out his wallet. "This?"

The kid again looks round quickly. "Yeah."

Hook throws it; the kid catches it, backs away.

"Don't try anything funny. Come back in that pub I'll tell them what you said. You best fuck off. Don't come back."

"Where is Ulrike, Gary?"

"None of your business. Ulrike don't wanna know."

"OK – which way's the road to London?"

"Erm – head down to the sea, turn left, go about a mile then you'll see a sign."

"Thanks."

The kid backs off further and puts away his knife. The moment he disappears around the corner Hook picks up a half-brick he spotted in the road and runs after him. His mind is clear and composed, though his actions seem unrelated to his thoughts.

The kid appears round the corner again. "Here – you never gave me –"

Decades of frustration channel themselves into Hook's right arm as on the run he hits the boy in the mouth. The boy drops to his knees, blood and teeth spraying in all directions. Hook hits him again, hard on the crown and he's on the floor. Hook's on top holding the brick aloft quaking with a rage he can't control. Something terrible has overtaken him: the more prostrate the boy becomes the more his rage intensifies.

Looking up, the kid sees the tattoos on Hook's knuckles and it seems to dawn on him that he's made a terrible mistake. The kid shakes his head, spits out teeth, making a strange gurgling noise from the blood, tries to push Hook off but his arms are too weak. There's no going back now: no point. Hook lowers his face so it's an inch from the kid's and hisses, like a dark gas from some unholy well within.

"You dirty little fucker."

The kid shakes his head, gasping for breath.

"You fucking little pedo." Hook hits him in the face with the brick again, hearing an awful squelch. "You fucking nonce, you *raper*. I'm going to cut your eyes out you fucking prick, you know that?"

Making a terrified noise the kid shakes his head. Hook roots through his jacket and grabbing his wallet stuffs it down his crotch.

"Where are the keys you fucking cunt? Where's the knife?"

The kid shakes his head; Hook hits him again and hears his nose crack. The kid's hands are covered in blood, his face unidentifiable; he moans terribly and tries to protect his face. Hook looks around and sees the knife glinting, within reach. Grabbing it he holds it to the kid's eye; he shakes his head in a desperate attempt to evade the point.

"Where's Ulrike?"

"Why?"

"What's it to you?"

"I'm her husband..." 'Huthband': the kid lisps through broken teeth.

Hook holds the blade to his cheekbone. "Yeah, the one who raped her."

"Me? No!" The kid's eyes widen then close tight. "Never! I'd never do that to her, I *love* her! It was you what fucking raped her!"

Hook leans in closer, hissing. "It's *love, cunt*!"

"That's not what *she* said!"

"OK, where is she? Let's sort this out!"

"I don't know! I swear! I just wanted to get a few quid out of you..."

Hook has read that in American prisons the inmates use rape as a form of hierarchical device, it having nothing to do with homosexuality. He hadn't bought it at the time, but crouched over this prone man, knowing he can do as he wishes, the thought crosses his mind – he could fuck his arse and there's nothing he could do about it. He's a rapist – how would *he* like it?

Hook decides it's a bad idea. In any case, he hasn't brought a condom. What if you fuck someone then they say they've got AIDS: how does that affect the hierarchies?

Hook sighs. This is getting him nowhere. "You're going to take me to Ulrike right now. Keys."

The kid gestures down to his jeans. Hook pulls out a key ring with a fish on it, which almost makes him laugh. Using one hand to grab the boy's hair and pull it sharply backwards he holds the knife to the kid's exposed throat.

"Where is she?"

"I don't know, I swear to you! She came back then fucked off back to London, said she was going to find you –"

"Then I'm going to cut your throat you fucking pedo. Say goodbye."

The kid shakes his head, crying, and Hook smells urine. He looks down: the boy's trousers are soaked.

He hears a shout: "Oi!"

Hook looks up; the grey-haired bloke and some other men from the pub are running towards him. Standing, Hook backs away from the kid and gets in the jeep, looking frantically for the ignition. There isn't one. The men are just yards away. He presses a button on the key. The jeep starts first time, a satisfying throaty noise – an automatic, thank Christ.

The jeep's lights light up the boy in the road. The grey-haired man almost has a hand on the door handle when Hook lurches forward. The men are just behind him banging on the sides. The kid's legs shake uncontrollably as if he's having a fit. Hook accelerates towards him, but at the last moment brakes hard, steers round the prone body and puts his foot down.

At some points in the car chase across flat country it seems Hook's pursuers are gaining on him: three or four sets of lights fill his mirror. But he's in the fastest, most sturdy vehicle: only a JCB could force him off the road. The jeep has enough gas to get him home. He can hardly remember how to drive and the headlights are still on his tail; crash now and even if he survives the impact he's a dead man. He hopes they haven't called the police but it seems unlikely, fish-boy doesn't seem the type.

There's one lucky side-effect of the fuel shortages: none of the speed cameras work and the police have better things to do with their petrol than waste it on chasing speed merchants. Rooting in the glove compartment Hook discovers a toilet bag and roots through it as he drives. The bag contains a selection box of drugs. No way is fish-boy calling the cops. Finding some white powder Hook dabs with a wet finger.

When Hook hits a long straight section between overhanging trees and pushes the accelerator, he starts to laugh: a blow job would have been easier than this. He's a glorified admin assistant, what the hell's he doing? More by luck than judgment Hook finds a turning for the M11 and flicks his indicator. The sound's a cold thud, like someone bouncing potatoes off the bonnet.

Driving straight means he's able to snort a thick line off his hand; then he hits the accelerator harder and streaks back into London. The sinister lights behind him have merged with the other traffic but he puts his foot down to be sure.

The half-lit towers of Canary Wharf are rearing up in the distance when a police car behind him turns on its lights.

Hook looks down and sees he has the bottle of vodka between his legs. He can't remember opening it. Grabbing the bottle and taking a quick scorching swig Hook drops it behind the passenger seat and fumes fill the car. If the cops stop him he's finished: drunk and in charge of a stolen car full of Classes A-Z, GBH, TWC and god knows what other TWAs... Hook takes his foot off the gas till the cops turn off.

When he parks up behind Liddle Towers Hook notices something odd: the block is swaddled in darkness and looms like an obelisk framed by the stars. As he drove down the North Circular he'd noticed the streetlights were off, most of the shops fronts in gloom and he thought it must be some new council green initiative (funny, he always thought an initiative meant *doing* something, not *not* doing it) but now he guesses there's a blackout.

A couple of the apartments have mini-generators and their windows glow. Hook counts up to his floor but his windows (and the cardboard wall) are in darkness. Leaving the jeep in the car park he thinks for a second then locks it and puts the key in his pocket.

The main lobby doors are jammed open with an old fridge. Hook's too impatient to get upstairs to work up indignation; it isn't like they're selling up any time soon. By level three he's out of breath and has to stop for a breather. On seven he stops again, has a snort and runs on up.

Strange noises echo down the hall like a cat being strangled. Apparently in blackouts the birthrate usually shoots up: there's nothing on TV, what the hell, make a baby, use some more resources. Hook walks quietly to the front door and puts his ear to the letterbox: quiet within. Not sure why he's sneaking around, he inserts his key and twists.

The flat is silent and black. He listens at Shelley's door: nothing. In the kitchen he sees Ken and Deirdre bob up and down by the light of the moon. Monica's always been squeamish; he can't see her taking control of that situation. As Hook approaches his bedroom door it opens and someone holding a torch screams.

Hook holds up his hands. "Monica, it's me!"

"Fuck!" Monica shines the light in Hook's face and he squints, shielding his eyes with his hand. "What the hell are you doing sneaking around? I nearly killed you!"

Shelley opens her door, looking scared and indisputably naked; behind her Hook makes out sheets billowing. The door slams again. Flushed with rage he turns back to Monica, who he now sees has a carving knife in her other hand.

"What's the big deal? I just got home, didn't want to wake you."

"Did you call earlier? Michael answered then the phone went dead. I tried 1471 and it was you – why didn't you *answer* Chris?"

"Flat battery."

Though she's put down the knife Monica still waves the torch around and the strobe-effect gives the apartment a confusing quality.

"Jesus Chris, you look terrible. Where the hell have you been?"

"Down the country. What was Mullen doing here?"

"It's *Michael*, Chris – I'm a Mullen too, remember? He popped over to see *you*, as it happens. But you didn't leave a note."

Hook sits at the kitchen table, hearing voices in Shelley's room. With his head down he points at her door, breathless with pain. "What the hell's going on *there*?"

Monica sits down with a sigh. "Oh come on Chris, don't be so goddamn naïve. I'd sooner she did it here than in some bus shelter."

"On the pocket money we give her? She could get a room at the Ritz. Gordon Ramsey could knock up a fucking...

omelette while they're doing it."

"Forget Shel: she's fine and happy. What happened to you? Jesus Chris, what's with the blood?"

Hook stands and looks in the mirror; helpfully Monica plays the torchlight on his face. Fish-boy's blood is all over his hands and t-shirt. No wonder he feels clammy and cold. Shivering he strips in the living room and stuffs his clothes into the washing machine as Monica shines her torch.

"Chris, what the hell have you been doing?"

"Nothing. Just got in a fight. I'm fine."

"And the other guy?"

"He'll live."

Mentally Hook crosses his fingers, then physically.

"We need to talk, Chris. But first, will you put some damn clothes on?"

"Why? Do I offend you?"

"We have guests."

"We do?" Hook looks around, puzzled, then laughs. "Oh – King Kebab? I doubt he'll be offended, he's seen it all before. Anyway he's got other priorities."

Then it hits him. A cat being strangled: that's what he heard, Shelley and Mehmet. Well, hang out the sheets in celebration.

A cool breeze comes through the hoarding and Hook shivers. "I need a drink."

"Chris, you *know* what we agreed about mixing medicine."

"I'm not taking any more of that crap. Makes me... stodgy."

In the wine cupboard Hook finds an ancient bottle of *Beaujolais*. Levering the temporary cork off with his teeth he swigs from the bottle, gasping with delight as the tough grain sandpapers his throat. Monica's close behind him, stroking his back as if they're still married.

"Chris, you have to see this from my point-of-view. You come home, no explanation of where you've been, covered in blood, then put all your clothes in the washing machine – despite the fact you never mix whites and coloureds –"

"Monica– *don't*. Just shut up a minute and let me –"

"Don't tell *me* to shut up! Who the hell are you these days? What's gotten into you?"

"And who's gotten into you?"

The anger and shock take up so much of Monica's complex facial expression it's hard to make out if guilt's in the mix. "What?"

"Oh come on Monica, I'm not blind here, I –"

Monica slaps his face; it hurts. Hook takes a draught of rancid wine, gasping, and waves. "I'm leaving."

"No! Fuck you Chris, you'll stay and –"

She's pulling at his naked body; Hook tries to wriggle free and thinks about smearing himself in margarine and sliding out the door. Instead he yanks free and stomps to the bedroom. Monica's left a drawer open in her dresser – probably where she keeps the knife – and he bashes his shin.

"Argh! Fuck!"

Dropping the wine bottle, which thuds harmlessly as it spills its contents on the carpet, Hook yanks open his own drawers, pulling on boxers while Monica screams. Shelley comes and joins in, clothed now thank Christ, and grabbing a tracksuit Hook barges past them with his hands over his ears singing "*na-na-nah*."

In the bathroom Hook grabs the pills then pushes through the women into the kitchen. Unable to find the car keys he remembers the trousers in the machine and thanks God there's a power cut. His wallet and house keys are retrieved while his wife and daughter scream. Hook puts on the tracksuit and feels impregnable – sound waves bounce right off.

There's a mobile tucked away at the back of the kitchen drawer: Hook slips the heavy block into his pocket. If he'd hit the kid with that, he reflects as he feels his way carefully down the darkened stairwell, shouts and sobs tumbling down after him, he'd be up on a charge of murder. Maybe he will anyway. Right now, that's the least of his problems.

The instant Hook slams the jeep door he feels safe, self-contained. After taking a couple of snorts of powder he catches his breath, composes himself, and points the bonnet at Canary Wharf. He's been between cars since Monica's mother's unhappy demise, but night-driving brings back memories of Shelley as a horrors-haunted toddler back at the old house. When she woke screaming at night Hook strapped his daughter in the booster seat of the old Mondeo and drove from the slightly bruised Cally down through the 24-hour bustle of the lit-up and prosperous Angel streets to the empty City, playing Mary Coughlan or Grace Jones to help her sleep.

Sometimes when Shelley dropped off Hook was so happy and awake he'd carry on driving through the night, out to Sussex or Essex, arriving home at dawn so Monica could take over. It wasn't fair – she was working and he wasn't – but being a parent was no pushover and nor was Hook, not back then, in his early-twenties, young enough to take on the world and old enough to play it along. Fifteen years on his body, soul and career are fucked; and so, it seems, is his daughter. By King Kebab.

Nerves shredded by the cheap coke, Hook swigs vodka from the bottle and turns on the radio, tuned by fish-boy to what sounds like a pneumatic drill with less melody. Hook looks for a dial, can't find one, remembers he's in the digital age, presses a button and scans the ether, settling on a talk-radio station whispering right-wing lullabies.

Hook's concentrating so hard on driving under the influence that at first the intercutting monologues on the radio pass him by; then he stops at some late-night roadwork snarl-up (Ukrainians in orange vests shining search-beams, digging tunnels home) and realises the callers are talking about the monster.

'*...news once again, scientists involved in the examination of the creature's remains now say they believe it to be The Devil. Yes ladies and gentlemen, that's what senior zoologists, palaeontologists and marine biologists are saying right now. Have your say here on 92.2...*'

On closer listening, it seems the allegation's been made by a scientist no longer involved in the dive; apparently he felt an incredible sense of unease every time his boat floated over the search zone, and several members of the team claimed to have fallen ill. Since then this particular scientist has been struck off. Naturally, the late-night crazies who frequent the station take that as yet another ingredient of yet another conspiracy.

Calls come pouring in: it's God's way of testing humanity's faith; it's Gaia's brain, more powerful than any super-computer and able to influence thought, to warn society of the perils of global warming; it's the endlessly reproducing cells of Henrietta Lacks; there *is* no monster, it's the government's way of diverting attention from the mess they've made of everything.

One balloon-head even claims it's aliens telling the mayor not to hold the Olympics in London, lest she anger the gods. That's the one Hook buys into, mainly because of his council tax bill, but what the hell, he's no expert.

Parking up in the bus lay-by opposite the Anne Boleyn, Hook peers through the windscreen and up the building but there are no lights on and the windows are boarded up. No way would Ulrike keep them closed on a sweaty night like this. As he sits in the quiet street a great drowsiness swamps him. The coke's wearing thin, cheap but free. Hook sleeps, slumped over the wheel, dreaming of monsters.

Monday 28th June

He's woken at five by a terrible blaring noise that seems to fill the universe; sitting upright he stares wildly around and realises he's in a bus lane. Starting the ignition he lurches forward, the bus driver apoplectic in his mirror, shaking his fist and screaming obscenities. Hook pulls into a side road, the bus driver sounding his horn a final time as he sails by with his empty load and his heart's tachograph ticking.

Parking up Hook gets out and stretches, hungover, hungry and cramped, and it seems the only things that makes his continuing existence bearable are the clean clothes he pulled on during the domestic storm up at the Towers; hooded top, tracky bottoms and trainers.

He remembers the altercation and zooming back to London with a load of angry fishermen in hot pursuit. They probably explode if they get too close to town, he supposes, like deep-sea fish when they reach the surface.

The talk show is still droning on about the monster and then some advert comes on for an evangelist church; he's been tuned to some crazy religious station all night, the background burble chattering away like a schizophrenic. Maybe that explains why Hook's dreams prominently featured a young long-haired boy with bleeding palms.

Hook turns off the radio, snorts two lines off his hands, puts the toilet bag in his jacket pocket and reluctantly leaves the safety of the jeep. Feeling light-headed but better than he has on a Monday for months he goes to the dolorous Sikh and buys a SuperBrew to wash down his depression pills, plus a few tablets he's found in the cup-holder of the jeep. Then he limps sorely back around to the pub, followed by his gang of insects. No sign of life: the cop trailer has gone, a corrugated wall erected to keep crackheads out and ghosts in.

Despite the coke Hook feels drained, so he decides to go to work. It's the one place he can be sure of some peace and quiet and a brie and lettuce roll.

First he heads back to the jeep to check for anything that might identify him, but apart from fingerprints and the vodka bottle it's as he found it. Traffic wardens lurk like short-sighted train-spotters; the jeep will be destroyed within nanoseconds. Hook once wrote an article explaining why crushing cars to metal cubes an inch across helps combat global warming; now, he can't recall why.

To his amazement there's a tube station he's never heard of or seen before just around the corner. From a phone booth inside its shady entrance Hook rings his old mucker Mullen.

"Hello?"

"Mullen, it's me. Chris."

"Hello Chris." Mullen's tone is neutral, strained. Hook shivers.

"Mullen, I can't find her. She must have gone into hiding."

"Did you check the hubby?"

"Yes – no."

"Hmm, thanks for clearing that one up."

"This ex," says Hook casually, "are his family in the same league as the Drummonds?"

"Maybe, why?"

"Just wondered what Ulrike had got herself mixed up in."

"Chris, it's *Susan Cohen*. Have you ever wondered why she chose the name Ulrike Nechayev?"

"I dunno, a Marx/Russian thing?"

"In a way, yes. Sergei Nechayev was a Russian anarchist, 19th century, friend of Bakunin. A very dangerous man, old Sergei. Killed a guy in cold blood, died in prison for it."

Hook snorts. "So?"

"'Ulrike' probably comes from Ulrike Meinhof. The German terrorist of the movie. Are you sure you know what you're getting into bed with here?"

"This is bollocks, Mullen. Ulrike studied Marx at uni. She's his great-grand-daughter."

"She is *not* related to Karl Marx, Chris. *Susan* studied Marx for about a week at Canterbury before being thrown off the course for... shall we say irrational behaviour."

Hook says nothing. Instead he looks blankly at the tube entrance where police with dogs are checking all who enter; people with burqas and beards more than most. He sighs.

"Look, Mullen, I don't want to find her anymore. I need to go to work."

"'Work'? I'd have thought you'd have more pressing concerns."

"Like what?"

"Like trying to save your marriage. Monica seemed most upset last night."

"Is that why you went round, to tell her about Ulrike?"

"No, I didn't say anything."

"Why not, Mullen, what you playing at?"

"Why should I want to hurt my sister when you've done such a great job over the years? She'd hardly thank me for telling her about your sordid little affair with a psychopath would she?"

Hook says nothing and has to resist the urgent temptation to bang his forehead against the wall. Some sunshine boy has spat blood-flecked phlegm that stars out in all directions, a supernova of snot.

"Anyway Chris, you go to work, put your feet up. I'll just have to find Susan myself. Must fly."

Mullen hangs up before Hook can answer. The tube's out so he has to get a series of buses through a cityscape on the verge of nervous breakdown.

The Contra's disappeared from the front desk and the new security guard, a sleepy middle-aged African, waves him inside without asking for ID. He's just going to the lift when the sandwich woman exits, trolley empty.

It feels odd, coming back in the office. People smile vaguely as if uncertain who he is. Hook puts his hood down and the tension dissipates, curiosity dims.

Stroking his week-old stubble he walks towards his cubbyhole, ignoring the furtive looks from Owl-woman across the divide. Hook toys with the idea of getting a huge card made up: '*you don't have to be a fucking psychopath to work here, but it helps!!!!!!*' As he reaches his desk he sees a Muslim girl in a Burqa typing on his PC. Her face is covered, even her eyes hidden by mesh.

He shivers and addresses her formally. "Excuse me, may I help you?"

The mask looks up. "Hello Chris."

Hook struggles to recognise the voice, muffled by thick cloth.

"*Farzana*? What the hell –"

"Hope you don't mind, I was just catching up and this was the only free desk. Do you want it back?"

"No, you go ahead."

"God Chris, you look terrible."

Hook thinks this unfair. Rubbing his rudimentary beard he asks, "Farzana – what's with the outfit?"

Farzana lowers her head, says nothing. She doesn't need to – he's read enough bleeding heart articles on the subject, usually by Monica. By being raped Farzana brings shame upon her family; this is the only way she can show herself in the street. Everyone from Karen and Ahmed down will commend her for her bravery in returning to work, having the guts to wear traditional dress despite the hostile reaction of the ignorant public.

Hook bounces up and down on the balls of his feet for a bit but it hurts so he stops and sighs. "Is Karen in?"

"I'll just check for you."

Farzana opens an online diary and leans in to the screen, visibility impeded. Hook decides if he ever gets on a plane and the pilot wears a burqa he'll get off and hang the consequences. Remembering his dream he shivers.

"She's... free this afternoon between two and two-thirty, then she has a meet–"

Hook frowns over her shoulder at the screen. "Hang on, what are you doing opening her diary?"

"That's one of my responsibilities now, managing Karen's appointments."

"You mean you didn't get my job yet?"

"Well, I am taking over editorial duties, but Karen felt –"

"Has your salary gone up since you started acting up?"

"Well no, but –"

"Karen felt she'd like a secretary instead of someone out chasing stories. I'm sorry Farzana, I hope things look up for you soon. Did they get the guys who attacked you yet?"

Farzana goes quiet. Perhaps if Hook could seen her eyes he'd feel more empathy, but right now he feels detached from Farzana's trauma, Karen's power trips and the crappy little paper residents use to line budgie cages.

An ancient ring tone sounds from his desk – his archaic work phone, now his only and reluctant option to replace his BlackBerry.

"Hello?"

"You fucking asshole."

Farzana looks up: her super-hearing must have heard Monica's mellifluous tones like an owl hears a mouse in the corn. Meanwhile the original Owl-woman doesn't flinch. Hook smiles and backs away towards the stairs.

"I'm sorry honey bunny?"

"You slept with some fucking barmaid!"

Hook closes his eyes: it's over. Banging into a locker he opens them. "What the hell are you talking about?"

"I know *everything*, don't even deny it you – animal!"

"Monica, I honestly don't know what you're talking about."

"Oh yeah? I got an email. Some fucking barmaid on a story."

"An email? From *who*?"

"Well, it doesn't actually say but it sure sounds genuine."

"That's bullshit, Monica. I *am* investigating a murder at the moment and I *did* interview a barmaid, but that's all."

"So where did you stay last night?"

"In the –" Hook's about to say 'car' but so far as she knows they don't have one. "Office."

"Chris, gimme a break! You slept in the office? Come on, you fuck!"

Odd, thinks Hook, now her accent's veered off down the last exit to Brooklyn. "It's true! Ask Karen, she was in early and found me asleep under my desk. Thought it was hilarious."

"I fucking will ask her; I'm emailing her right now. Stay on the line."

"Oh come on babe, don't bring Karen into this, of all –"

"Right. It's sent."

Hook's already halfway up the stairwell. "Well, fine," he gasps, his voice echoing. "You're *so* fucking insecure Monica."

"I wonder why. I bet you're fucking Karen too, aren't you?"

"Monica, Karen Greening's a fucking *lesbian*!"

A team of senior managers walking downstairs exchange

startled glances as he pushes through.

He reaches Karen's door; she's frowning at something on her screen. Hook knocks. She glances up looking lost, then smiles wanly and waves him in. She's wearing a severe black cardie and blouse: funeral clothes.

"I have to go now, Monica. Let's talk later."

Hook hangs up, and watches Karen's face. Her eyes go back to the screen but there's no obvious reaction. Maybe Monica sent it to the wrong email. Maybe she was bluffing. Karen looks tired and surprised – Jesus has deserted her and her cleavage gone into mourning, covered in black cloth.

"Chris. You're back."

"Couldn't stay away Karen, you know me – a workaholic."

"Hmm." She looks closely at his hairy chin, his tracksuit. "Well, as long as you're OK, let's catch up over lunch."

"Great."

Hook goes to leave then remembers something. "Um, while I'm here Karen, do you think you could sort me out a new ID? I seem to have mislaid mine."

Karen looks up a little impatiently. "Chris, those passes are extremely important! We're supposed to notify site security if they get lost."

"It's not lost – it's at home. Monica had a spring clean. It'll turn up."

"Okay, I'll issue a temporary pass as soon as the network's up and running. It's been out for hours."

"Oh, can't you receive emails?"

"Sadly not."

Hook smiles and scratches his greasy beard. "See you at twelve."

"I'm glad you're feeling better Chris," smiles Karen over lunch at Da Vinci's, "because we need that feature on Leader

Ahmed by tomorrow. He keeps asking when he can see the copy – seems quite impatient."

"Yes, I got that impression as well."

To his surprise Hook has wolfed his starter (anchovies in something) before starting his pint of lager and feels worse than ever. Chips would go down better but Maria doesn't serve them. This might be a good time to bring up Monica's looming email. Instead he looks around the quiet murmuring bar, the football shirts and photos of Italy, the blinding light from the water outside.

Karen, such a hearty eater as a kid, picks at her salad like she's looking for beetles and Hook hopes she's ordered a main course; when Maria came over with a face like thunder and he ordered Karen wasn't ready, and he was in the loo snorting when she finally decided. He hates eating alone, especially when he's being watched.

Karen's face had been a picture when she returned from long-term leave to find him one peck beneath her in the food chain. Hook hadn't known she worked there until his first day; the money was so good after years of scavenging round the edges of Fleet Street that when he found out he decided to stick it out whatever Karen said.

Fortunately for Hook, nobody likes him; he has a feeling if he was Mister Popular she'd hate him. Apart from moving Hook from a private room to the centre of the office, Karen has more or less left him alone until now.

As Hook toys with lunch Karen keeps peeking at his knuckles but she's too polite to comment and too posh to know what the letters represent. As she sips her water Hook holds his breath. Why does no-one *drink* anymore? On Fleet Street in the old days anyone who didn't stand a round over the Stab got sent to Coventry. Now every hack he knows (not that he knows many) spends every spare minute in the staff gym.

But then, of course, Karen doesn't drink – every day she has to live with what drink did to her boy, *their* boy. Now she's looking at him expectantly and Hook tries to spool back to hear what she said, but it's all tattered ribbon.

"Sorry?"

Karen almost laughs; Hook hasn't seen her *this* happy in years – if ever.

"I said, 'did you get anywhere with that victimisation story?' I heard the nationals were sniffing around; I suppose they got the woman to sign a contract?"

"Not so far as I'm aware. I did speak to the niece, and warned her about the tabloids. But she's disappeared – probably got away from it all."

"Maybe some hack took her to a safe house."

"Maybe..." The beer kicks in: time to make his move. "Look, Karen, can I ask you something?"

Now Karen's nervous and looks down at her plate, the lettuce untouched. "You can *ask*."

"My... marriage is a bit... tricky at the moment. Monica's rather jealous for some reason. If she asks, could you tell her I slept at the office last night?"

Karen pinks, looking peeved, and scans the wine bar then back at Hook, who resists the urge to look away but colours dramatically.

"And did you?"

Hook frowns, lost in words. "Did I what?"

"Did you sleep at the office?"

Now Hook understands: Karen can't lie, but he can. "Of course! I had to get out of the house so I came to do some... stuff."

"Then of course I'll vouch for you Chris. That's fine. As long as you don't expect me to lie for you, I could never do that – least of all to Monica. Obviously."

"Of course."

They finish lunch in silence – or rather Hook plays with his, as Karen hasn't ordered a main course, unless that fold of leaf counts for something. He feels pretty lousy, but Karen insists on paying for his meal. As they leave Maria ignores him completely.

Upstairs Hook finds a desk, logs on and turns off his 'out of office assistant' to find over a hundred emails. As he scythes through them deleting anything from Prof-SC, Equalities, Payroll, and all the other stuff that keeps the world turning, the post boy gives him an envelope with his name on it: his new ID, the photo taken just days ago, the smooth face cleaner, but not exactly happier.

He's contemplating nipping out to the pub when he realises he didn't ask Karen about Byron. This makes him feel bad. Hook snaps his fingers: he knows what he needs.

"Give me Horse," he mutters to himself. "I must have Horse."

Sadly there's no ketamine in the selection box. Having swallowed several tabs of acid Hook decides to leave work early to go to the Anne Boleyn and then on to Soho – anything, rather than face Monica – but just as he's turning on his out of office he has a message from Karen asking him to pop upstairs.

Gloomily Hook knocks on the glass of his boss's door. She looks up but doesn't smile and beckons him in. She has a red face, which means she's cross. Ominously, she doesn't ask Hook to sit, so he stands, arms knotted defensively, a naughty schoolboy.

"Chris, I've just had Councillor Ahmed in here asking all sorts of questions! What the hell *happened* between you the other day?"

Hook swallows, then worries he's swallowed his tongue.

He sticks it out to make sure it's still there. "Nothing much... I just asked him about his new role as council leader, stuff like that?"

"Did you ask him about that harassment case you were looking into?"

Karen's Bolsover accent is poking through: a bad sign. Hook swallows again, sticks out his tongue. "Erm... I might have."

"Councillor Ahmed also said you mentioned an alleged link to some underage brothels."

"It came up."

Karen looks aghast. "But *why* Chris, *why*?"

"It's on his manor. I just thought he might have heard something. I didn't... *accuse* him or anything."

Karen puts her head in her hands and when she speaks her words are muffled by her fingers. "Jesus Chris, you asked our Leader if he runs underage *brothels*?"

Hook hates the upper case 'L' she always puts on 'leader', even in speech – the way she talks about Ahmed you'd think he was emperor of some Pan-Galactic Federation rather than council spokesperson for toilet roll.

Hook rubs his beard, which feels prickly, anachronistic. "I was investigating a legitimate tip-off. I thought that's what we did."

"Oh spare me the crap! You aren't a journalist Chris, you're a PR man!"

"That's bull, Karen. I can't ignore a story just because it's inconvenient. The paper would be seen as a laughing stock."

"It *is* a laughing stock. YOU are a laughing stock. I think you're forgetting, Christian, I could have had you sacked the day I came back from sick leave to find you lording it here. Instead of which I kept quiet for Monica's sake – and to ensure you contributed to Byron's fees. I thought we had an understanding?"

Hook sighs and looks out at Da Vinci's, which seems to be floating downriver. "Then I'm sorry you misunderstood."

Karen glowers; even as the LSD surges through his veins Hook knows he's gone too far. He sticks out his tongue.

"OK Chris. We both know I can't sack you. So you're taking leave. How many days do you have left this year?"

"Nine or ten."

"Take them. Use them to get a new job. Because after I speak to accounts your position will be under permanent review."

Hook shrugs and turns to leave, touching his tongue with his fingers.

"Oh, and Chris?" He stops, not looking back. "The answer's no. I'm not going to lie to Monica. If you're fucking around *you* deal with it. I can't believe you asked me, of all people."

Quietly Hook shuts the door behind him and goes to clear his desk, but a hooded figure is hunched over his keyboard. He takes a guess: "Farzana?"

"Oh. Hi Chris, how are you?"

"I'm good, thanks..."

Farzana seems remote, disinterested. Hook heads to the toilet, snorts a couple more lines and feels much better: the coke seems to get the acid moving more efficiently round the system. He bounds upstairs: as he's been sacked, he may as well give Karen a few home truths. He's about to march into her office when he sees she has company: Ahmed. The two are deep in conversation: it looks serious. Knocking brusquely, Hook walks in. Both turn and look at him, surprised. "Afternoon."

"Chris!" says Karen. "What are you –"

"Still doing here? Just clearing my things. Be out of your way in a jiffy. Hello Mr Ahmed, are you well?"

"I'm fine thank you," says Ahmed in a strained voice.

"So," says Hook, smiling maliciously, "what are you two plotting?"

Karen laughs. "What on earth are you on about now Chris? Mr Ahmed is Leader of the council, *ergo* it's perfectly natural that –"

"That you give him some media advice? Not really, Karen, not really. I mean… you're employed by the tax payers of the borough, not just the ones who voted for his party."

"Oh, spare me the technicalities please," sighs Karen. She flushes, furious, yet also nervous.

Hook smiles again at Ahmed. "Congratulations Mister Ahmed."

"On what?"

"Well, that barman's dead, the pub closed and so your problems are over."

Hook backs out of the room, Karen's hot and Ahmed's cool eyes on him all the way. Bounding back downstairs he reaches his floor and is about to keep going when he changes his mind and goes back to see Farzana.

She looks up, he thinks, hard to tell.

"Forget something?"

"I did, yes." Hook sits in a spare swivel chair and rolls towards her. "Look Farzana, I'm really sorry about what happened to you. You do know it wasn't your fault, don't you?"

"Of course I know!"

"Then what's with the outfit? Seems like penance to me. Did your family say you'd brought shame on them, is that it?"

"You wouldn't understand."

"You're damn right. But I do understand this. If someone attacked my daughter I wouldn't tell her what she should be wearing."

"No? What if she wore a short skirt, what then?"

"That's totally different. I –"

"Please," Farzana shakes her head, "spare me your Western 'guff'."

"Listen," says Hook, rolling closer with his elbows on his knees and folding his fingers together, "you're a journalist. Come with me and I'll show you a story that will make your name. No more arranging Karen's fucking... lunch-dates, no more burying bad news. What do you say Farzana?"

"I am happy here Christian. Karen is a good manager."

"Happy, *really*? Being told what to wear, do, and think every day for the rest of your life? Come on Farzana, you have a brain, I *saw* it."

Farzana says nothing; time to go. He goes to clear his desk but there's nothing in it he needs. The striplights are stretching into interesting shapes and suddenly he finds the burqa intolerably oppressive.

"Take it off," he says quietly.

Farzana looks up. "What?"

"This." Hook reaches out towards Farzana's head-dress and she pulls back; his fingers close on the fabric but they're weak, like the crab in a seaside booth.

"Get off me!" snaps Farzana, jerking away. "Have you gone mad? Don't *touch* me!"

Heads turn at the commotion. Owl-woman stands and Hook finally sees her mouth: thin lips, a dirty smirk.

He looks at the ceiling sorrowfully. "I'm sorry Farzana," he says. "I tried. Remember that – I tried."

Hook backs away, not sure if Farzana's looking as he heads to the stairwell and waits for the lift. When it opens it contains another girl in a head-dress. Hook gets in and she backs away into the corner as if he's someone of whom she should be afraid.

Stomping out of the town hall he walks, taking in new sights: cars skating across rooftops, yellow cranes saluting, dreary trees waving silent protests, garages and car docks and wine merchants, new apartment blocks abandoned, red-grey DLRs weaving tragically, Canary Wharf's time-share cluster propping up the moon, the sun hidden behind a grey ceiling of concrete dust, the dense thick air carrying rain so thin it can't be seen but you feel it cross your skin and wet your hair, you forget what weather's like in this place it's so good to feel this rain, these cool soft clouds like a grey paint brush splashed in water, anachronistic planes pulled along by propellers from Stuttgart and Leuven, piles of scaffolding build themselves up by day and into lofty towers then crumbling down to form new piles like sand beneath oceans –

Hook steps into the road: a cab bears down, Cyclops eye yellow. Hook holds up his palm like Knut.

In the taxi Hook tries Ulrike but the call goes to voicemail; he doesn't leave a message but looks out at the passing city. What he took for rain was spray from a building site, damping down dust. The sun's as hot as ever.

It's getting late but few streetlights are on. When he reaches the Anne Boleyn he sees it's unoccupied. Hook walks around to the shop where he bought croissants – although he's been there at least three times since to buy booze, it remains to him the croissant shop – and sees to his amazement the jeep's still there, un-cubed.

As he drives carefully home it strikes Hook that north and east London aren't so far apart as he's always imagined: in fact, they melt together. As he passes the church at Bow he recalls that poignant, perfect jingle Byron liked as a toddler: *oranges and lemons*. From Liverpool Street he heads up Moorgate. Byron loved it when he read to him, and in an old book of nursery stories he found in a charity shop one comes to mind, or at least fragments of a song:

'*Up and down the City Road, in and out the Eagle…*

That's the way the money goes, pop goes the weasel...'

The Eagle pub he passes is new by London standards, but stands on the site of the one in the song. He likes that sense of history: not the official one he learned at school, all kings and queens and coronations, but the oral history, the myth and legend of the street. Hook drives around Old Street roundabout up City Road to the Angel. After walking out on Karen he lived here briefly, for appearance's sake, alone, before getting the place off Liverpool Road with Monica, much to her brother's disgust.

The Brigadier was as good as his word and died like a man when his liver detonated and melted his insides. He left Karen the flat in town; his country house was re-possessed. Now her financial security was assured Karen made it clear Hook's input was no longer required.

Despite his ongoing affair Hook didn't really want to leave; the one time he had almost left something had pulled him back, something he could only conclude was love. He'd formed an easy bond with Byron, reading him stories, taking him for walks, smiling in restaurants as the boy made delighted sounds while the people on the next table furtively peeked over, lowered their voices.

They had a child-minder for a while, a stout, roseate neighbour in her fifties who'd take Byron to the park. One morning the mobile phone Hook had given her for emergencies went off in her pocket, dialling the house. Hook picked up the landline to hear this jovial woman crooning to his son as she pushed him in his pram: "little cunt little cunt..." After that, Hook agreed to give up his factory job and look after the kid full-time.

One afternoon, with Karen at work, Hook stood on the corner of the living-room carpet, making as if to dive into an imaginary pool, Byron lying there laughing out-loud, when

Hook felt something in his pocket: the crenulated lid of a squeezy juice bottle he'd taken up off the floor so his son wouldn't choke.

Byron squealed with delight as his father prepared to swallow dive, but even as Hook did so – arms raised high like a diver, a trapeze act, holding his breath and about to jump – he realised that he or someone else would be picking choking hazards off the floor for the rest of Byron's life. He knew then, deep down, deeper than this imaginary water into which he was about to plunge, that it would never get any better than this; it would in fact become harder, longer, deeper. He couldn't do it. Hook left a week later.

He made too many mistakes with Byron – his whole life was a mistake. If it had been down to Hook, following the routine scans and then the extra ones where no-one smiled, and then the apocalyptic warnings from concerned doctors, they'd have aborted the child. But it wasn't down to Hook: he had no say. Which was right, even now he knows that was right.

Then when Byron was born with all his ghastly defects and the realisation set in that things would never improve Hook ran away; there's no other way to put it. He can't pretend any longer that Karen pushed him out, that he refused to give up alcohol and she couldn't face seeing him with that stuff in his hand. He left her with a child who cried for his daddy day and night; and he never grew up.

The lift at Liddle Towers is working, to Hook's relief; he's too hot and sweaty for the stairs. When he reaches the flat he puts an ear to the door: silence. For all he knows Monica has already cleared out. Opening the door he sees her best coat still in the hall, her *Louis Vuitton* handbag over it. Hearing murmuring voices Hook's heart pumps but her house keys are off the hook.

Shelley's door's wide open but she isn't in either. The fish tank and its contents have disappeared but the voices drift from the living room. Hook realises he'd sooner face intruders than his own wife and child. Grabbing the nearest thing to hand – an umbrella – Hook tip-toes into the living room and sees something that makes him smile: King Kebab, watching the cricket with a bottle of beer in his hand, naked.

"Yo!" says Hook, and the boy jumps, beer spills down his rug-like chest and puts a hand over his balls.

"Mr Hook!"

Hook puts his brolly on the breakfast bar. "Hey Mehmet, what's the score?"

Mehmet hides behind a cushion, surface area blushing. "I am so sorry Mister Hook. Mrs Hook said you were gone for good!"

"Hey, don't worry about it kid, you're fine. Where's Shelley?"

"She has gone to meet her mother for shopping sir. I was very hot, so –"

"As I said, don't worry about it, though I'd get dressed before my wife gets home if I were you."

"I will! Of course! Sir, you will not tell my family about this, will you?"

"What, sitting around naked watching cricket? That's not *haram* is it?"

"No sir, but drinking beer is."

"Tell you what – give me a swig and your secret's safe with me."

The boy passes over the bottle, Hook takes a swig. Warm. He's probably been nursing it for hours just to enjoy the forbidden feeling. He hands it back. Mehmet covers himself; LBW, someone giving an umpire the finger.

"Where are you from, Mehmet? You don't go to Shelley's school do you?"

"No sir, I am from Turkey. I been here a year now."

"You like it here Mehmet?"

"It is very good sir." The boy's eyes are downcast.

"You don't sound convinced."

"Well... there are always problems. Everywhere. But what can you do?"

Hook smiles. "What can you do?"

Collecting his clothes he leaves Mehmet to his cricket and beer. Before leaving he makes two ragged lines in the bathroom. The sun vanishes. It's a long time since he's seen it set or rise over an actual horizon. He debates leaving Monica a note, decides against it. What the hell would he write? Heart thumping, he calls as he walks down the stairwell.

"Hello, Monica speaking." Her voice sounds dead.

"Monica?"

"What do *you* want?"

"Well, I just came home and you weren't there."

"I had to go out."

"Listen honey, we need to sort this out."

"It's too late, Chris."

"You think?"

There's a slight, terrible pause at the other end. Hook's steps echo. "Do you know what day it is Chris?"

"Monday."

"Monday, 28th June to be precise."

Their anniversary; Hook pulls a face as he emerges into the courtyard at the rear of the block.

"I actually trusted you," says Monica, "so I emailed this guy back and said I didn't believe him. So he sends a video of you fucking your whore. I notice you weren't wearing your wedding ring. Nice touch!"

"Monica, I –"

"*Fuck you!*"

Terribly, Hook hears her voice break and she hangs up. He's about to call again when he's hit from behind with something heavy. He drops to his knees and is kicked to the hard pavement. Two or three men begin to beat him with measured punches and slide-rule kicks until his body's a hornets' nest of pain and just as someone raises a baseball bat he loses consciousness.

Tuesday 29th June

Hook's dreams are lurid, warped and mutilated by fresh agonies, and some deep part of him knows when he surfaces the pain will be terrible and he might be better off drowning, but something pushes him back to the surface. As he reaches consciousness a noise screams deafeningly in his head and bright lights blind his eyes and a terrible thirst makes him gag.

As he slowly emerges Hook finds his left leg excruciatingly painful but otherwise he seems intact. The ward he's on is quiet and there are plants; this is altogether a superior hospital to the one in which his father died. Hook sees the logo of a private company on the wall and mentally curses, then thanks whoever brought him here. Feeling fingers close round his left forearm he slowly turns his head to see Monica, his missus, a nervous smile on her sad, teary face.

"Wakey, wakey."

"What happened?"

"I don't know. Someone found you in the street outside the apartment. They found your mobile and you still had me as 'home'."

This saddens Hook, that she feels this need to make a point, even here.

"Where's Shelley?"

"She popped out for a fag."

The word 'fag' sounds strange in an American accent. Hook has changed her: maybe not only for the worse.

"Where am I?"

"A hospital."

"Private. Who's paying?"

Monica bites her lip, exasperated. "Does it matter?"

It does, but he says nothing. Looking distracted Monica strokes his arm; even that hurts but Hook hardens, then rages at his disconnections. She leans in and kisses his cheek and he smells *Yves St Laurent*. Nodding at his leg he feels a searing pain rip along his spinal cord, disrupting his train of thought.

"How bad is it?"

"You'll be okay. The doctor says you're a fighter."

He doesn't feel like a fighter, except maybe a beaten one. Agonisingly he looks round, but the only other bed in the room is empty.

"May I have some water?"

"I'm not sure... nurse?"

A nurse who's been hovering beyond his vision gives him a straw; it feels like his jaw's broken but it's only bruised. Remembering the sight of the raised baseball bat he concludes whoever battered him was disturbed.

Trying to assess Monica's mood Hook looks at her curiously but she lowers her eyes. Then Shelley returns, waving, smiling and crying at the same time, wearing a smart dress suit he's never seen before. He realizes Monica's dolled up too. Shelley runs to the bed, kisses his cheek and he tries not to cry out.

"Daddy!"

"Hello beautiful, what's all this about you smoking then?"

"I'm a big girl now, Dad."

Monica checks her watch: Hook summons enough energy to get annoyed. "Late for a date?"

Monica looks at Shelley, who flushes pink. "Yes. I'm afraid we are."

"'We'?"

Hook looks at Shelley, whose lip quivers. Remembering the photograph of Monica and Shelley in France he feels left out again. Too late to complain now; in a few mad days he's demolished a family unit that took decades to build.

Shelley looks at her mother and puts a hand to her mouth in horror. "We can't go now, Mum!"

"Oh come on darling," Monica snaps, "we've been through this. Remember what you said the other night when he forgot your concert?"

"I don't care, he's not been well! He still isn't well can't you see?"

"Don't be silly Shelley, your father will be fine."

"But who's going to look after him?"

"Look, we talked about this. Jack will take care of everything."

"Whoa, hang on," croaks Hook, looking impatiently between them. "Where exactly are you two going?"

Monica looks at Shelley then into his eyes, and sighs; but there's definitely a triumphal glint there. "We're going home, Chris. Back to America."

"*America?*" Hook says the word like he's never heard it before.

"Things are different there now. I just think Shelley will have more opportunities. A new era's dawning."

Hook looks from mother to daughter in utter bewilderment. "You're emigrating because of *Obama*?"

"Don't be silly, Chris. We're going because it will be a new life for us. You know our marriage is finished. We both know it."

"We do?"

Shelley's lip trembles and Hook looks up at the ceiling, at a chessboard patchwork of heat-resistant tiles. In his imagination upside down pieces are dancing across the board, but his king lies on its side. Hook looks back at Monica, who already seems further away, her mind in the departure lounge.

"Can I ask you something?"

Monica sighs reluctantly. "Okay."

"Is anyone getting on that plane with you?"

Monica messes with her hair absently and touches her ear. "Do you mean am I having an affair?"

"Yes."

"Chris – it's you who fucked the barmaid, remember?"

Shelley looks tearful and closes her eyes, bites her lip.

"Who sent the email, Monica? Your brother?"

Monica shrugs. "No."

"Then who?"

"He didn't exactly introduce himself, does it matter?"

Hook closes his eyes so he won't have to meet his daughter's. Whoever beat him up will be back to finish the job and Shelley might be in danger. The only thing he can do is let them go: make Shelley think he *wants* her to go, however much he doesn't want that, doesn't want to fail her as he failed Byron.

"Aren't you going to say anything?" says Monica coolly.

"Such as?"

"To make us stay? Don't you even have anything to say to your daughter?"

"I don't want to go, Dad!" sobs Shelley. "I was just cross with you for missing that fucking show, I want to stay here with you!"

She breaks down and puts her head on his chest, shoulders heaving. Monica sighs. Hook's lip trembles. He knows he has about enough self-control for one sentence, so mustering all his energy he gathers in his breath and speaks through a throat suddenly painfully sore.

"I don't want you here Shelley, go with your mother."

He hears Shelley crying and feels tears squeeze their way out through his lashes. Hook tries to think about the pain in his leg, but his heart hurts worse. As he lies there and Shelley sobs, his mind flashes back over the years: her tears starting secondary, and periods, and primary, and solids; her floppy four-year-old body when he carried her at midnight to the toilet (laughing in her sleep, chatting nonsensically as he put her safe back in bed); the time she got sick aged six and they rushed her to the hospital to pump her with drugs; and he wonders how much she'll really remember, and how many of her memories will be tainted by these last few weeks.

Finally, just when he thinks he can stand it no longer, he hears them stand and someone's lips – Shelley's, he can tell by the chaste affection bestowed – touches his cheek. Then they're gone and he sobs great heaving sobs until a nurse comes with something merciful and pricks his arm. Soon the drowning sensation returns and mercifully he's sucked under and dreams of sea monsters.

With Shelley, Hook went to the other extreme: did all in his power to be with her, to give her his love, to make amends for what he'd done wrong first time around. Monica wanted to pay for childcare but Hook refused; his argument was that childcare didn't make sense. You pump your kids into this machine and for what, so you can leave them something when you're gone?

It turned out the reason Monica was holding out on this, determined to get her way, was because she thought he expected her to stay off work but he didn't – he wanted to be home, to read to Shelley, to be with her, in the same way he had tried to do for Byron and failed.

Like Byron, Shelley loved stories. Her favourite had for a time been Where the Wild Things Are, but there was one line that she couldn't grasp at all:

"Oh please don't go! We'll eat you up, we love you so!"

Hook tried to explain to her, but couldn't, that when you understood that line was the moment you reached adulthood.

Hook sits with Jack and Maya at the table in their large, cluttered kitchen, shelves overflowing with herbs and spices, cookbooks and glass jars containing unidentifiable condiments. Formal guests see the ordered dining room with its great oak table; the kitchen is for family only.

Jack's in boxers and a t-shirt, damp patches under both arms like some old Queens boxer. He looks at Maya, worry-eyed, holding a cream silk gown around her shoulders. Through an open window comes the sound of traffic, sirens, drunken shouts and slamming doors. Jack passes Hook a glass of water; Hook pulls a face but drinks it anyhow.

"First things first," says Jack, "I'm sorry I hit you Chris."

"Both times?"

"Well, the second time. Not the first time. You were out of control mate."

Maya seems uncomfortable and leans over and holds his hand in hers. Her hand is large, warm and hard from all the hard, useful work she does. She looks at him worriedly. "What's going on, Chris?"

"I wish I knew."

"Why not start at the beginning."

"Where is the beginning? I'm fucked if I know."

"Why don't you start," says Jack, "with what happened after you left here – you know, that night you went a bit crazy."

As best he can, Hook tries to précis the events that lead back to that night: sleeping rough, Sid's brutal murder, his problems with Monica. Though it forms a loose narrative too many events seem unconnected, the result of chance; he begins to lose the thread.

Jack frowns. "Why *did* you and Mon split up? There's someone else, isn't there?"

"There might be."

"Who? Monica said it's a barmaid."

"I suppose she is. Or was..."

"Chris, are you *sure* about all this?"

Hook looks at him intently. He's been asking himself the same question for so long he has a tailormade answer.

"Sometimes," says Hook, "you make the mistake of thinking someone is 'The One' when they aren't, not really... you just want them to be that special person so much that you blind yourself; you don't really listen to your heart – you lie to them and yourself. It's all a big mistake and everyone can make it. But when someone really *is* the one, you never, ever make that mistake – you always know. Don't you?"

Jack and Maya look at each other and smile. Maybe it's true, then, maybe their love is real, not just a cover story. Nervously Hook combs his greasy hair with his fingers.

"Actually," says Hook, "she's part of the reason I'm here."

Jack raises his eyebrows, and Hook empties his glass.

"I've changed my mind," says Hook.

"About what?"

"Mum's Will."

Jack frowns; not the facial expression Hook's hoping for. "What about it?"

"I mean I'd like my half, if you haven't spent it all on hookers and drugs."

"Chris mate, what the hell you on about? I gave you half already. Remember?"

Hook frowns, head buzzing. "*What*? When?"

"When I got your email the other day I zapped it into your account."

Hook feels the bottom drop out of his world. "What account?"

"The one you share with Monica."

"The *bitch*!"

Hook jumps to his feet but Jack puts a strong hand on his arm. Shaking it off Hook turns on him accusingly.

"When did Monica tell you she was going to America?"

Jack sighs and looks at Maya. "Today."

"Bullshit!"

Jack crosses his heart with an almost exaggerated solemnity. "It's true, bruv, on Mum's grave."

Hook slumps back down in his seat. "But she's left me with nothing! No flat, no money, no Shelley... how could she do this to me?"

Maya looks at Jack, who rolls his eyes, produces a key and slides it across the table. "She left you this. Monica said you can stay there till you sell it – *if* you sell it."

"Well that's nice of her! Who bought the bloody flat in the first place?"

"I thought Monica paid most of it," says Maya, "from the proceeds of her place." Hook looks at her resentfully and she smiles apologetically. "Sorry."

Deep down, he knows Monica is being fair. He'd always had an obsession with owning a property, but Karen bought the first flat with her father's help and Monica owned the place in the Cally. When they moved into the Towers he'd been so determined to buy that he lied to the mortgage company and had been making up shortfalls ever since.

"I think you got off lightly," says Jack. "You fuck some barmaid and your wife says you can keep the flat."

"Fuck the flat. I need to find Ulrike. For all I know she's in real danger. Anyway, without her none of this makes sense."

To his disgust Hook wells up and his voice breaks. Maya comes around the table and holds him to her breast; Jack looks despondently down at the table. When he looks up again he seems angry, but not at Hook.

When Maya releases him all the air leaves him and Jack leads him upstairs. Apart from his sore jaw the only real impact of Hook's beating is that he now has a limp in his other leg: his weak leg takes the strain.

In the spare room Jack makes up a small camp bed between the desk and the bookshelves groaning with worthy tomes. Hook pulls himself between crisp white sheets and despite the fact it's the first time in days he's gone without booze he sleeps, and this time he doesn't dream, even of monsters.

A window smashes: Hook sits upright, every muscle tensing horribly. Paralysed by cowardice he listens, a sickening feeling in his stomach. Jack's shouting at somebody who shouts back; the front door thuds as if hammered by a SWAT team. Maya screams in her South London dialect and the commotion is altogether fearful.

Hook checks his watch, just after 10pm, and hobbling to the door of his room he listens intently. The noise has quietened down but there are dark murmurs, the occasional sound of hand slaps on flesh. Drawing up something deep he opens his door and walks downstairs.

To Hook's surprise Jack and Maya seem to be in reasonable conversation with an elderly white woman in her dressing gown; he dimly recognises her as the one carrying recycling a few aeons back. She looks sourly at Hook as he tenderly descends, clutching the banister.

"That's the nutter who was making all that noise last time!"

"That," smiles Jack, "is my brother. And yeah, it's a long story. But don't blame Chris for this. He's innocent – for once."

"What happened?" asks Hook shakily.

"Just a spot of trouble with the neighbours."

Hook looks at the elderly lady in astonishment.

"Not Mrs Marlow – she's a good girl, aren't you love?" Preening with delight the old woman waves goodbye to Jack and slams her door, "Just some yobbos from over the way who don't seem to like us much."

"BNP?"

"Only if it stands for Bloody Nazi Polaks. You'd think immigrants would be more understanding, wouldn't you? Especially in Soho for God's sake."

Hook isn't so sure. So far as the papers make out the Kurds hate the Turks hate the Greeks hate the Serbs; everyone hates the Nigerians and the Somalis are worse: a merry-go-round of ancient hatreds festering in the pot. But maybe he shouldn't believe everything he reads.

Maya goes to the kitchen muttering something about tea. Peeking over his brother's shoulder Hook sees Jack's car has been trashed – windshield smashed, tyres slashed – and the plant pots on the top step are broken. He shivers, but he's not sure why – Jack seems to know who's to blame.

His brother points at a dark window across the street. "I'm sure I just saw the curtain move. I'm getting a bit sick of those fuckers. I reckon Clyde Collins was right: send 'em all back."

"You don't know for sure it was the Poles, do you?"

"I've had enough nasty experiences with those boys. There's about twelve of them in there. Two-room flat. The place stinks with their cooking. Always playing music loud, drunk, shouting racist abuse; they're a nightmare."

Hook's about to remark on this paradox when a car slowly drives past. Its windows are down but that isn't unusual in this heatwave. Hook hears a flat crack.

Jack falls sideways. Hook holds out his arms but his body is heavy; Jack half falls down the stone steps to the shattered pots and Hook goes down with him. He looks down in horror, ears ringing, and sees a small red mark high up on his brother's chest. The car speeds up, screeches round a corner and all is quiet. Hook sits on the bottom step, brother in arms, shaking. Behind him he hears Maya coming with a tray full of cups and wills her to go away.

"Here we are," says Maya jauntily, "nothing a good cup of tea won't put –"

As she reaches the front door Maya looks down and sees Hook's white face. She looks at him, confused, then sees her husband.

Dimly, Hook registers the fact Maya doesn't drop the tray; she gently puts it down on the telephone table then walks down the steps. On seeing the hole she throws back her head and roars. Hook has never heard a noise so terrible in his life.

There's a strange moment in the ambulance. Maya's on the bucket seat next to Jack, holding his hand; next to her a paramedic administers god knows what as the screaming vehicle makes its way through the cluttered streets. It's almost eleven, still muggy, and Hook looks up from inspecting Jack's impassive face – his ghastly white skin and reddish beard dappled by liquescent neon – and catches Maya's eye.

It seems – though maybe it's some unconscious racist projection – that even as Hook looks at her, Maya's face loses the sophistication, the dinner parties and conferences, and she glowers with the embers of some primeval rage. Hook shivers despite the inescapable heat.

They rush Jack's stretcher off through some doors, Maya running alongside, and Hook's left alone in a cube of light, unattended, unnoticed. He knows he must wait for news, but every fibre of his instinct urges him to flee, though not from the would-be assassins so much as from Maya's wrath. When she finally walks through the door he tries to read her face, fails.

"He'll live," says Maya, her broad, deep voice making

Hook feel warmer and happier than he has in weeks. "In below the shoulder and out again; one broken bone, no permanent damage. They're keeping him under for now."

To divert her thoughts Hook asks, "Aren't you going to stay with him?"

"I need to get some things. The police have sealed off the house. They said if I need anything, to take it now."

"Where will you go?"

"Oh, back to my mum's: you know Chris, *home*."

The emphasis Maya's eyes place on the word gives Hook a pang of jealousy: is she having a dig at he who has demolished so many homes, first that of his mother and father, then his first wife, then a second? A home-wrecker, that's what they call women who split up a marriage: a rusty metal ball swinging into the brickwork, pulling out debris and strewing it all down the whispering street. Strangely Hook doesn't feel like a wrecker; he just feels wrecked.

Maya's subdued; Hook inspects her speech patterns for iotas of blame, scintillas of doubt, but finds nothing that might make her his latest and most terrible foe. He has no doubt that he was the intended target of that bullet, the only problem being there are so many suspects who might wish him dead he barely knows where to start.

They're walking towards the exit when Hook feels a hand on his shoulder. He turns, half-expecting to stare down the barrel of a gun, to find himself instead looking into the patient, bemused face of DI Schneider.

"Hello Chris, me again. I think it's time we had that chat, don't you?"

"Susan Cohen," says Schneider. "When did you last see her?"

Hook sighs and looks round the tiny room. There's a window in the door through which he sees the casualty ward bustle reassuringly – if he was under arrest they'd be at the station by now.

"Last Friday morning," says Hook. "I left her about... seven, went back half-an-hour later and she was gone. I haven't heard from her since."

"Did Miss Cohen speak to you about the murder of her uncle?"

"Of course." Hook hesitates, Schneider lifts his bushy eyebrows. "She told me they'd been having a lot of trouble with local yobs. She said Sid confronted them and they killed him."

"And you believe her?"

"Of course I believe her!"

"Supposing I told you Miss Cohen has a colourful past. That she's been in trouble with the police, had mental health issues, married a violent criminal –"

"I know all of that."

"Did you know that with her uncle's death she stands to inherit the pub?"

"Yes. And she didn't exactly seem overjoyed."

Schneider sighs again and rubs his face with his hands. "Look Chris, I need to know what's going on. Whoever shot your brother was probably aiming for you. Doesn't that worry you at all?"

"Of course it does!"

"And you've been beaten up, I see. Did you report this to the police?"

"No."

"Why not?"

"I haven't had... time." Hook knows it sounds lame. "Look, my marriage is falling apart. My wife's just flown off to America with my daughter."

"That must be very stressful."

"It is, yes."

"Have you ever heard of an organisation called the Five Rings?"

"Those nutters? Yes."

"In reality we believe there are only a few people actually involved in terrorist activities. They may be nutters but they're dangerous nutters."

"What the hell's that got to do with anything?"

Schneider looks at Hook as if debating whether to confide.

"I believe Susan Cohen's deeply involved. Up to her neck – and quite possibly out of her depth. We need to find her fast."

"I'd like to help, I really would. But I have no idea where she is."

"This isn't a case of protecting sources Chris, not this time," says Schneider. "This could be a case of national security."

"I'm not protecting any sources," says Hook, "I'm not protecting anyone."

Schneider lets him go, but he'll be back. Hook knows time's running out.

Maya waits on a bench outside the main entrance, staring into space. That raw, angry look has been replaced by a great sadness, a powerlessness that is if anything worse. Hook sits next to her and they look out onto the busy drive where ambulances, cars, doctors, patients and lunatics make random patterns.

"So," says Maya quietly. "What did *he* want?"

"Oh, you know, I was the only witness to the shooting."

"Bullshit," says Maya.

"Look, Maya –"

"What did he mean then, 'time we had that chat'? Sounds like you know each other pretty well. What's going on Chris?"

"Nothing," says Hook. "I swear. Can we go now?"

In the taxi Hook tries to think what to say to appease Maya's fury, but instead looks out at the darkened shops. Even in Islington the shops don't light up at night: too expensive, adverts for burglars. Hook remembers visiting some Northern shit-hole with Mullen as a junior hack: the boarded up shops, the gloomy exteriors. If Upper Street's going the same way, what are those places like now?

There's a police line and TV crew outside Jack's house, but his brother's neither famous nor dead. The cops take some convincing to let them through but finally they're inside. Under the watchful eye of a frowsy WPC they sit on the campbed, where for that brief fraction of time Hook had felt safe.

"Where will you go?" asks Maya, with what seems genuine compassion.

"I don't know."

"I'd invite you to my mum's but she hates honkies."

They both smile at the shared joke. Hook has long argued black people can be as racist as whites; Maya insists that's impossible as whites have all the power. The same argument as Monica's, pretty much, but better argued because Maya has her heart in it, invests in it a lifetime's experience.

"Maya, I'm... sorry I slapped your butt."

Despite the humidity the temperature drops; Maya frowns, bewildered. "Why bring that up now?"

"I don't know... I just feel everything bad started that night."

Sighing, Maya rubs his back reassuringly. Hook feels an erection stirring and thinks about Andy Gray. "You're troubled, Chris. Get your head down. Stay calm."

"Thanks, I'll try."

They part under the watchful glare of the camera lights. A young, pretty reporter tries to speak to Maya but she bats the poor girl off like a fly, so instead the girl comes after Hook, her burly cameraman in breathless pursuit, and sticks a mike under his nose.

"Are you a friend of the victim?"

"Family."

The reporter looks confused, checks her scribbled notes. "Family?"

Hook doesn't feel like explaining. He doesn't like the thought of being seen on TV either, not after what Schneider told him, so he pushes the camera.

"Oi! Mind the fucking lens!"

The cameraman's incredibly aggressive; Hook flinches. "Then leave me alone."

"No, you leave *me* alone. Who the fuck are *you*? Cost me six grand this camera, now fuck off! Go on, do one!"

Hook backs away then turns and walks as fast as he can, cursing his limp, hoping it makes the man feel bad but doubting it. On Goodge Street he waves down a lonely black taxi and hops aboard, not relaxing fully until he sees the red light.

The driver half-turns as he pulls into the traffic. "Where to guv?"

"Just drive around for a while."

"Anywhere specific?"

"I'll tell you when I know."

Hook pulls out his old mobile. "Mullen? I need to meet you. Now. No, not your place. Somewhere neutral. Somewhere safe."

Wednesday 30th June

There's a discreet hotel off Piccadilly where guests check in and out by card, never meet the staff and carry their own bags – except few people carry bags. Each room opens and locks via credit card and the charge is equally discreet on the bill. Most guests are politicians, businessmen with sleazy habits and prostitutes of all persuasions and peccadilloes; they arrive via an underground car park with a concealed entrance in window-tinted cars owned by the hotel and changed regularly.

Hook buzzes Mullen's room, hears a CCTV camera assess him and the door swings open. Inside he enters a lift and on the third floor walks along a carpeted corridor. When he knocks on Mullen's door it opens immediately.

Mullen's in slacks and a polo shirt and looks relaxed, if not exactly pleased to see him. Hook follows him into the room, with its bare blank walls, mirrored ceiling, and a plasma screen where the window should be – windows make things too easy for the paparazzi. Hook sits on the bed; Mullen opens the drinks cabinet, pours himself a juice and hands Hook a bottled beer, only then noticing Hook's battered face.

"What happened to you?"

"I was jumped."

Mullen allows himself a smile. "Oh, really? Past catching up with you Scarf Lad?"

"Doesn't it always?"

Mullen raises his eyebrows knowingly and lights a cig.

"Hmm. So, what do you want at this hour? Cost me a fortune to get this room."

"I need to find Ulrike now. I think she's in big trouble."

"I thought that was why *I* was paying *you*."

"I can't do it – not alone. Fuck the money."

Mullen shrugs. "What makes you think I can help?"

"You have contacts, Mullen. You could find her."

"Haven't you gone to the police?"

"They came to me. They're useless."

Hook sucks on his beer but it isn't working, so pulling out some coke he chops it up on the dressing table. Taking out a note he snorts two lines; Mullen doesn't flinch, but Hook knows he's taking everything in.

"This ex of hers," says Hook, looking up, head buzzing, fatigue blunted. "His dad runs a building firm, right?"

Mullen shrugs and sits on the bed. "Vic Cooper. That's right."

"What do you know about him?"

Mullen shrugs once more. "Not much. I think he brings in drugs from the continent. Maybe guns too. Small beer, really, but nasty with it."

"I think he's trying to kill me. Jack got shot."

Mullen's eyes widen. "When?"

"Just now. He'll live, he's okay. I think it was meant for me."

Mullen locks his eyes on Hook's and in this artificial light they're tiny black holes, devoid of reflection, devoid of life. "What can *I* do? My editor's gone off the idea. You know what it's like."

"Look, Mullen, I know we don't get on. But I'm Shelley's father. If anything happens to me, how will that make your niece feel?"

"I see your point – though of course as she's in Boston right now maybe she isn't as reliant on you as you think."

"Oh, you know about that."

"Of course I know about that. Monica's my little sister, remember?"

"Is that why you emailed her about my little fling with Ulrike?"

Mullen shakes his head, frowning. "No. That wasn't me."

"Oh. It's just you never were any good at keeping secrets, were you?"

"What do you mean?"

"You went to my dad, didn't you? Told him Karen and me were on drugs when she was pregnant."

Mullen sighs and looked up at the ceiling. "No. I didn't."

"Bull. Dad told me, before he died. He said a hack, Mullen..."

Mullen looks at him sympathetically. Hook replays the conversation he had with his father just before he died. His heart lurches.

Mullen stands and slaps him on the shoulder. "I'm sorry Chris. Monica said she'd told him. I think she was trying to find out about Karen and it slipped out."

Hook feels raw, dead inside, but just for a moment. Forcing himself to focus he shakes his head. "It doesn't matter now. Anyway, I don't have time for this. Come on Mullen, there must be something. Anything."

Mullen sits on the little chair by the dressing table. It was in sterile places like this that Hook took Monica when they were having an affair, when it all seemed fresh and new. Now he recalls it was almost as much a thrill keeping it from Mullen as it was from Karen. He sucks on the bottle until it's dry.

Mullen stands again and walks round.

"Well," he says finally, "I guess you could always check out Ulrike's stepfather. He might know something."

Again Hook's heart lurches: why didn't he think of that? Then he remembers: because he isn't a journalist. At least not a good one.

"Do you know where I can find him?"

"Well, I do know he had an office in East London, but you don't just go there. You go to a cab office, give an address and they take you somewhere different. All a bit smoke and dagger, if you ask me –"

"Can I have the address? And name?"

Mullen blinks with surprise. "Why Chris, I believe you've already met. Her stepfather is Iqbal Ahmed."

"*What*?"

"You didn't even know that? Blimey. The cab office is just by his restaurant."

Hook sighs. "I never was a good journalist, was I?"

"No, not really. You tried, Chris, you tried."

"It's a tough game. Too tough for me. I don't know how you stuck it but I have to admit Mullen, you're good."

Mullen sighs, shrugging languidly. "Well, if you recall, I never was any good at anything else. Except the long jump."

They smile and shake hands.

"Bye, Chris. Take care."

"Bye, Mullen. I mean – Mike."

The cab office is a bunker beneath a viaduct, the windows barred, the staff suspicious and the light outside flickering like a waning candle. Hook raps on the glass and one of the beleaguered men inside leans forward, stooping so his mouth kisses the gap at the bottom of the hatch, like the cubicle is full of water and he needs to get a breath.

"Where going?"

"Sentinel Street."

The man's face doesn't change. "Number?"

"Fourteen."

Still the man's face remains devoid of expression.

Hook nods meaningfully. "Ahmed sent me."

"Who?"

Hook smiles. "Fine, I'll tell him you were uncooperative."

"Take it easy. You want cab, you got cab."

An unmarked cab pulls up behind him driven by a young Bengali; Hook gets in the back. Without a word the driver sets off. As Hook expects they're on a main road out of town.

After a few minutes the car turns off the main road and into a suburban-looking cul-de-sac. The driver pulls up outside a nondescript house, a typical newbuild box of the type popping up on every green surface.

"How much?"

"Pay inside."

Shrugging, Hook gets out of the car and slams the door.

The driver rolls the passenger window down. "I come back two hours."

"What if I'm not ready in two hours?"

"Two hours long enough for anybody."

The car roars off; Hook turns and looks at the house. Either all the lights are out or there's a blackout. He walks up the path but just as he presses his ear to the mock-Georgian panel the door opens and a huge black face glares down at him – a man's head perched on a plinth encased in a dark bomber jacket.

"May I help you?"

The bouncer's speech is exaggerated politeness, the tone of someone utterly in control.

"I'm here to see Mister Ahmed."

The doorman looks him up and down with what looks like amusement. "And you are..?"

"Chris Hook. I'm a colleague."

"'A colleague'? From which line of business, sir?"

The word *sir* is almost shanked into him; Hook flinches from the impact. He holds up his council ID. "I work with Karen Greening in communications. Just tell him I'm here, he's expecting me."

The bouncer keeps chewing gum with a bovine quality. Then he shrugs and looks back over his shoulder. "Get Mister Ahmed."

Ahmed comes to the door, still in his suit, looking flustered; when he sees Hook, more so.

"It's 3am! What the hell are you doing here?"

"It's about Susan, sir. Your stepdaughter."

"I know the name of my stepdaughter, what the hell's the matter with you? Come in. Come." He gestures with extended fingers and the bouncer stands aside – but only a little, so that Hook is forced to brush past his chest and crotch to enter the house. Inside, several businessmen sit around eating. All appear to be of Bengali background.

The men crane to get a look at Hook but Ahmed leads the way to a quiet back room that appears to be a home cinema. There are a few lines of seats facing a large wall on which is mounted a blank TV even larger than the one at the Towers.

For one crazy moment Hook thinks he's stumbled on an Al Qaeda control room, Ahmed and his cohorts busily plotting the death of the decadent West; but in reality the bloke looks more like a shambling university lecturer stuck with a malfunctioning Power Point. Ahmed stands before the screen and gestures at the front row; Hook sits.

Ahmed appears to be trying to collect his thoughts.

"Okay, now listen to me. I do not appreciate this. You coming here, embarrassing me in front of my colleagues. Things are very tense for my community and you make it worse."

"How do I 'make it worse'?"

"You make outrageous allegations. You insinuate. You write crazy things in your newspaper. No wonder Karen got rid of you. No way did she send you here. I know her very well; she would not do this. So you tell me what the hell's going on or you leave right now."

"And I suppose your bouncer up front takes me somewhere quiet."

"What the hell are you talking about? More craziness! I am no gangster Mister Hook; I am respectable businessman. I know you speak to my stepdaughter, but she is crazy like her mother. She says I kill her uncle. She says I run brothel, vice den, bloody... Libdems. Disgusting lies."

"And why would she say all those things about you?"

"How the hell do I know? I am not Derren Brown. She wants money for her crazy causes, I don't care. I give Susan a good private education, cost me a leg. And how does she repay me? By stealing my things, spreading filthy lies, blabbing to bloody journalists."

Hook shifts uncomfortably. If Ahmed's bluffing, he's good – but why bother? He has all the cards, all the power. How much does he know about his fling with Ulrike?

"Do you know where she is, sir?"

"I wish I did, maybe I get my bloody van back. So. I don't care. You get nothing from me. Karen says you drink too much, maybe you're in it together and you need money for beer. Well you won't get it from me. Get a job."

"Thank you for your concern. I'm working at the moment."

"Oh really? For newspapers?"

"Freelance."

"Freelance. Oh God." Ahmed laughs. "Freelance. Now I am quaking. Sniff away mister. You will find no shit on me. Be off with you, mister, leave me alone. And if you repeat these outrageous allegations you'll see me in court."

Hook stands to leave and blood rushes to his head with a roar. He suddenly feels very tired.

"I'm sorry to have bothered you, Mister Ahmed. You won't be hearing from me again."

"Glad to hear it. Goodbye. And if you speak to Karen

before I do, tell her I am bloody not chuffed."

Hook's reaching for the door handle when something strikes him and he turns back. Ahmed's still by the screen, wiping his forehead with a hankie. "One last thing, Mister Ahmed. Did you say Susan stole your van?"

"Yes yes! A few days ago. Took my wallet, bloody keys and my van."

"Did you report this to the police, sir?"

Ahmed sighs. "I did not."

"Why not, may I ask?"

"Look," says Ahmed, eyes darting, "I do not want Susan getting in trouble. She was always in trouble. Thrown out of school, out of college. Blew her mother's business on God knows what. She came to see me a few days ago and we... talked, and then I find my things missing. Van, pass, wallet, whole shebang."

"I don't know any Liddle Towers, mate," says the cabbie as he drives up Holloway Road. "Do you mean them flats by the Lidl?"

"Yes," sighs Hook, too tired to argue, "the flats by the Lidl."

The cab drops him round the back and he looks cautiously around the car park where he was jumped. To his amazement the jeep's still there, so either his attackers weren't after the car or they didn't have time to take it. The damn thing's like the truck in *Duel*, following him around, except he's the ghostly driver.

Hook walks up the back stairs through choice rather than necessity. Some conservative part of him wishes he could put back the clock a few days, erase Ulrike and all the related problems, go back to what until recently was a life of stultifying boredom, frustration and despair, admittedly, but little in the way of danger.

On reaching the ninth floor Hook walks slowly to his door and listens: silence. When he goes inside it looks like the place has been ransacked by shopaholics. Monica and Shelley must have packed in a hurry.

Seeing fish flicker he thinks for a moment Ken and Deirdre have been resurrected but it's only the two dimensional screensaver of his laptop on the desk beneath Van Gogh. The fish tank has gone; so has all the life from the house, all the energy.

At least the vast TV is there on the wall, too big for the Jumbo. Hook switches on the rolling news: the service of peace is tonight and religious leaders of all the main persuasions are invited. The attempted bombing of a hostel for refugees in Hastings is being put down to a BNP splinter cell. Bored by it all he waits for news of the monster.

Now experts are saying there may have been some sort of colossal mistake. What they had taken for the cell tissue of a single living creature might in fact belong to some previously undiscovered coral, or weird bacteria. Even the missing ship of scientists has been found adrift, knocked out by a freak wave. The sense of disappointment in the announcer's voice is palpable.

The house phone rings. Switching off the TV Hook jumps up and waits for the answerphone but by now it'll be half way over the monsterless ocean. The phone sounds odd, ringing in the echoing flat. Van Gogh stares quietly. Finally, quite calm, resigned, Hook picks up the phone.

"It's me," says a female voice. "It's Ulrike."

"Are you okay?" asks Hook, voice now shaking.

"I'm in a lot of trouble," sobs Ulrike. "I need your help, Chris."

"I know. I know you do. And I want to."

As Ulrike tells him what he has to do, Hook closes his eyes. This is what he's feared all along, yet now the moment is upon him he feels calm, relieved. In the bathroom he switches on the brutal strip light and runs fingers through his beard, looks into his yellowing eyes and smiles.

Hook goes to the kitchen and takes a small, sharp knife from the drawer, then slips the blade through the gaffer tape and cardboard that block off the eastern wall. Hook tears it all down so that the living room wall is the night. Pre-dawn air rushes in. The sun's glow is beginning to light up the horizon; Hook puts a foot gingerly on the balcony and it holds his weight.

As he waits for morning, the city is dimming, lights off all over the place and shops closing down, Canary Wharf's towers in semi-darkness. How proud they seemed, how strong, these corporate obelisks – NatWest, Barclays, Credit Suisse – yet in reality they're nothing but empty boxes. London's a city of glass, a high-optic bank without nerve-endings or cause; an insubstantial dream haunted by soulless ghosts.

For some years, when bored and unable to concentrate on modern distractions, Hook had put his mind to inventing a perfect suicide attempt, one which seems 100% genuine but is 100% guaranteed to fail. He'd never discovered it and now it occurs to him that if he'd invested as much energy into success as he has into failure he might not have made such a mess of his life.

Death is the price you pay for life, did Bill Hicks say that? Part of Hook doesn't want to die because as well as missing the countless ways in which his children will change the world unrecognisably for the better, and then their children do the same, he'll miss the end of the cricket season, and all those books he's supposed to read, and the next *Private Eye*.

But another part, smaller but more insistent, has had

enough. That part of him will be glad when it's over, except of course he won't know. *That* seems a price worth paying.

Plenty have already paid that unimaginable price, great minds among them – he wouldn't be going alone, there's a crowd at the other end which for the first time in history is slightly smaller than the crowd he'd be leaving behind; he'd be getting away from the crowds, getting some *space*...

Hook takes his laptop and writes his article for Karen, one he hopes might make some sort of sense, a story his children might be proud of. Then he turns on his 'out of office assistant' and waits to commune with the sun.

A short, black middle-aged nurse leads Hook along a long white corridor, doors both sides full of glass to add to the illusion of transparency. There are all those nighttime hours when visitors aren't welcome, faceless medics mixing potions, friendly cops and sympathetic coroners to help out with a tricky case.

At the end of the corridor the nurse stops and reaches for her keys. When she opens the door a young man with long, wild blonde hair sits staring out of the window. The nurse turns and looks at Hook and he remembers the faces of other parents in cafes, in parks, judging him; though could *sh* know, all these years on, who he is and for what h responsible?

"He likes to sit," the nurse says neutrally, "all day."

Hook smiles coldly. "His options being?"

She says nothing. Hook goes in. He doesn't expec a reaction: it's been too long. The boy's grown, now, on the outside. Even from behind Hook strong arms, his thick neck. But when he tur Hook with those same scared eyes, lets out th Hook turns to jelly. All of his failings, as are in that howl.

"Don't be scared," he manages to whisper. "It's Daddy. See?"

Hook advances with a photograph of him holding young Byron in a park; Karen took it so wasn't in it. Byron howls again and looks round in panic for an escape.

Hook begins to sing: "*Half a pound of tuppenny rice, half a pound of treacle...*"

Byron starts to nod his head; he smiles, gurgles, all the years of medication have failed to dull the synapses of memory and possibly – and this is probably wishful thinking – of original love. Hook continues, not caring that the nurse will think him a fool and a hypocrite, as he walks towards his son.

"*That's the way the money goes... pop goes the weasel...*"

Over the phone Karen gives the centre permission for Hook to take Byron home. They edge south out of the suburbs in the ~~len~~ jeep, back to the safety of the city, Byron beside him with laughter at everything his dad says. The lorries ~~tle~~ though not the war and the roads are clear; the ~~quickly. Hook debates driving round the~~ ~~set,~~ but that's not his destiny now and

~~ves~~ a text:

~~ur~~ dead prof-dc

~~vasn't~~ about fish-boy and the jeep ~~ssage~~ to Maya; she'll deal with it ~~rapper's~~ god help him.

~~and~~ Hook walks up the garden ~~rings~~ the bell. When she opens ~~she's~~ wearing a dark Hijab with ~~roars~~ with delight and hugs his mother, then without a backward glance runs past her into the house: home.

Karen smiles at Hook's expression. "Don't worry, Chris. I haven't gone nuts."

"Karen, I... I don't know what to say."

"I know this must be a shock for you but it's something I've thought about for a long time."

"I mean I always knew you had a spiritual side, but..."

"Please don't judge me, Chris. I prayed with Iqbal a few times and it just seemed to make sense. Not much else does, at the moment."

Hook is nonplussed: Karen, this woman he married, betrayed, fucked and worked with – created a child with – has become someone he can't understand.

Karen looks down at the key he's holding out. "What's this?"

"Monica's taken Shelley and I'm going away too. I want you to have the flat."

"Don't be ridiculous!"

"Not a word. Byron's twenty-one soon, he'll have to leave the centre. I owe you, Karen. I owe you so much. If you sell this place you can make sure Byron gets all the care he needs for as long as he needs it. I'm so sorry I wasn't there for him."

"Chris, really there's –"

Hook raises a finger to his lips and Karen takes the key, blushing. He turns to leave.

"Oh, and Chris?"

He turns back.

"Yes?"

"I don't suppose you finished that article about Iqbal by any chance?"

Hook bursts out laughing and Karen smiles nervously. "I emailed it to you at work. Check your inbox. It's quite a story."

"Thank you."

"Don't mention it."

"Will you be at the ceremony this evening?"

"Ceremony?"

"The religious service – I mean I know you aren't religious, but..."

"You never know. I might drop in."

Karen smiles. "Good. I'll be taking Byron. Maybe we'll see you there."

Hook smiles and so does she, again, from within her Hijab. He sees, then, the unbridgeable chasms between them, but rather than feeling hatred he lowers his gaze, nods his head. Karen holds up her hand in a gesture of farewell and she looks truly happy, and that's it: that's all.

The builder's van with Cooper & Son on the side is where Ulrike said it would be in a multi-storey on the eastern edge of London. Hook parks the jeep and drops the keys down a drain. Two sets of keys are taped inside the van's exhaust pipe. Hook slides open the side door and carefully lifts a blanket from what looks like a pallet of building materials. The device is huge, wires going off in all directions, gas cylinders and bags of nails packed lovingly around it like a Christmas present.

Hook puts the blanket back over the device like over a sleeping baby and goes to the driver's seat. Holding his breath and closing his eyes he turns the key and the van starts first time. Ulrike has emailed him a map that shows the route to the stadium and a diagram of the underground car park. His instructions are clear: drive carefully, go slowly and you'll be fine. Not that he has a choice; not if he wants Ulrike to live.

The closer he gets to the stadium the worse his feelings of terror and exhaustion become. He's just pulling off the North

Circular when his mobile rings and he's so frazzled with fatigue and worry that he almost smashes into the side of a double-decker bus; his heart skips a few beats.

"Chris?"

"Who's asking?"

"It's Farzana."

"Farzana!"

"Chris – where are you?"

"I… think I'm lost."

"Chris, listen! I looked into your story. The gang that beat up the old man – one was arrested this morning. The lorry driver picked him out. He says he was paid to do it by Susan Cohen. DI Schneider says there's a warrant out for her –"

Hook smiles, foot caressing the brake pedal as a pedestrian skips over the road. He starts to sweat and winds down the window.

"Farzana, it doesn't matter now."

"Of course it matters, she –"

"No. It's okay. I'm on the case. Oh, and Farzana?"

"Yes?"

"Thank you. You'll go far."

Just lose the outfit, it'll drag you down, he feels like adding; but doesn't. Instead he concentrates on the road ahead, the road to Ulrike. As he enters the Olympic zone Hook shivers. He's stuck in a jam, crawling forwards slowly, wriggling impatiently in his seat. There are armed police and army trucks everywhere. The building's in sight when the news comes on the radio:

'*… faith service organised by the main political parties and leaders of the faiths in response to the communal violence engulfing the country. Leaders of the Christian, Jewish and Muslim religions will call for tolerance and understanding and lead prayers for victims of the troubles at eight tonight.*'

Atheists aren't invited then. Hook can see their point, the

point they're trying to make. Not that it will make much difference to what happens afterwards, the reprisals, counter-attacks, more bloodshed. But that now isn't his concern: all that concerns him is Ulrike.

At the barrier Hook nods as he presents his biometric ID to the guard, an unsmiling white guy: ex-services probably. The man scrutinises him closely, squints in the back at the covered pallets then passes back his card and nods.

Along with the other vehicles, mostly coaches and mini-buses containing religious nuts of every hue, Hook circles under the earth, lower and lower until he finds level nine, row 49. Spotting a white van with a cordoned off space next to it Hook stops; behind him someone hoots. Driving over the cones he pulls into the space next to the other van, which is identical in every respect, except it has '*Ahmed Balti*' written on it.

Hook turns off the ignition and breathes out. He looks round this subterranean space, this car-catacomb. Everywhere there are men, women, boys and girls in a variety of ethnic dresses, every shade under the sun, filing over to the stairs that lead up to the stadium. Most look happy, to Hook, some sing familiar songs.

Remembering his pressing deadline Hook gets out of the van, pulls at the sign on the side and it peels off easily. Beneath is another sign: '*Ahmed Balti*'. He feels a chill pass through him and rubs goosebumps off his arms. Then, remembering his instructions, Hook takes a photograph of the two vans side by side and texts the picture to the number Ulrike gave him.

A minibus pauses beside him as it waits for a space; Hook looks inside and sees it's full of handicapped kids rocking, laughing, staring; a child with Downs' Syndrome spots him and waves happily. Hook waves back, feeling sick. He looks at his watch: seven-thirty-eight. He has to get out. Time to go.

One Sunday afternoon Hook's father made the surprising announcement that he was taking him to the country, to catch fish and catch up. They piled into the old transit van and his father drove north up the M1 before pulling off and up into the High Peaks of Derbyshire.

Hook's father barely spoke: he just looked straight ahead through mirrored sunglasses, rolling up fags and passing them over to his already suspicious son, fifteen, still nursing the bruises from his last school beating.

As Hook choked and looked around at the barren fields and bleak moorland crushed by rain clouds, a great feeling of dread and loneliness enveloped him and he kept craning his neck to make sure the rods and fishing basket were still there among the toolboxes and sacks of grout.

A couple of miles down some empty B-road his dad led the way up a drive towards a huge, imposing house. The rain was coming down hard; around the back of the house two middle-aged men were playing tennis in the rain, their feet generating peacock-sprays of white.

"Is this where we're fishing, Dad?" asked Hook nervously.

His father flicked his fag out of the window.

"I just need to see someone about some work. Come on."

Hook's father parked up and led his son past the tennis court, where the two men were laughing and sliding around like big kids, ignoring them completely. He knocked at the back door and some cook or cleaner led them into a large library. Making some excuse about sizing up a job his father stepped out of the room.

Hook looked around and noticed a portrait on the wall: Van Gogh's self-portrait as a young man. Those brooding eyes, that shy, sulky expression, seemed to mirror Hook's own feeling of abandonment the day his father left him behind.

Years later Hook sought out a print of the picture and framed it for the living room. He wasn't sure why he wished to be reminded of such an unhappy period of his life; maybe he connected with the photograph because he knew someone else knew how it felt, to be lost and alone, potential untapped.

When he reaches the industrial estate in Canning Town Hook pulls in behind a stack of sea containers and waits, heart beating dully. Suddenly a young female figure runs round a corner towards the van and there she is, with dark shades over her eyes and a beret on her head – Ulrike.

She smiles, wide and deep, as he leans across, opens the passenger door and reaches out his hand. Ulrike takes it and he pulls her up; her radiant beauty is as great as he remembers. It's five days since he left her, sleeping in the Anne Boleyn; it seems a lifetime.

As Ulrike reaches for her seatbelt, she kisses his cheek then checks her watch. Hook's left the engine turning and lifts his foot off the clutch. The van moves forward, easing back onto the motorway and heading east, towards the coast. Both are silent: there's too much to say.

As he drives, Hook risks a few quick glances at this stranger. Ulrike's hair is tied back, she has no make-up and wears combat trousers and a black t-shirt. He's never seen anyone so beautiful.

Swiping at a fly in disgust she looks at her watch again.

"Late for a date?" asks Hook softly.

Ulrike turns to him and smiles a strained smile. "You're my date, sweetie."

"I missed you, Ulrike."

"I missed you, too. You have a beard!"

"Yes. What do you think?"

"It's nice. You look like... an artist. A painter."

"Hey, let's paint this town red, what do you say?"

Ulrike smiles wanly then looks straight ahead.

Hook nods at the road map on the dash. "Where to?"

"Why don't we check into a hotel tonight? A good one. I know a place near Ramsgate. We can get the ferry from there in the morning."

"Expensive?"

"Don't worry darling, it's on me." Ulrike laughs expansively, checks her watch.

"I'm glad you're safe," says Hook.

Ulrike frowns. "Yes, of course."

"I came looking for you."

"I saw you. You came to the pub, didn't you? I was inside. I wanted to shout to you but I was gagged, tied up."

Ulrike appears to be about to expand, changes her mind, looks down. Checking the time on the dashboard clock, Hook steers carefully through the busy traffic. By some fluke, all the lights change as he approaches so he doesn't even need to touch the brake. He's heard of this phenomenon before: surfing the green.

"You can tell me the truth now, Susan."

Out of the corner of his vision he sees the blur that is Ulrike's face turn to him.

"The truth?" Her voice, so delicate, so small.

"I know," says Hook. "I don't mind, Ulrike. I'm on your side, remember?"

Ulrike gives him a small, shy, scared look, then smiles timidly. "Yes, that's what I thought. I knew you'd understand."

"I do understand. Believe me."

They're on a raised section of motorway; in the rearview mirror Hook sees the Olympic site glowing in the evening, full of politicians, religious leaders, believers, praying for peace.

Hook points over his shoulder at the stadium. "You just wanted to shake things up a bit."

Ulrike laughs out loud. Finally, Hook understands why he's

been such a useless journalist: he's a crap judge of character, always has been.

"Something like that."

"They'll blame your stepdad, Susan. And by extension all Muslims. Is that what you wanted?"

"Well, if that happens, the Muslims will fight back. Rise up."

"That's what the IRA wanted too. But it never happened; most people didn't blame the Irish for the actions of a few nutters. Didn't your dad tell you that?"

Ulrike sighs. "Look... we needed to do *something*. To make people understand."

"They'll work out it was you eventually."

"And you, Chris. After all, you drove the van. But by then it won't really matter, will it?"

Hook has so many other questions, but time is short. No time to ask about her uncle's murder; why she lied about her father; above all why the urge to destroy within her is so much greater than the urge to create.

Seeing the great headless horse and spotting the sign for the Dartford Crossing he wheels over into the left-hand lane and off onto new tangents. There's something beautiful about driving on a motorway as night falls, slotting in with the stream of lights.

Ulrike sighs and looks in the mirror. Hook feels with his right hand for the knife in the van door.

"Actually," says Ulrike casually, "before we get to the hotel, I know a quiet little lay-by. Pull in and I'll make it worth your while."

"A lay-by?" asks Hook, sadly.

"Yes. Somewhere quiet where we can be alone."

"Will anyone be waiting for us there, Susan?"

The girl, whatever she's called, laughs. "Don't be silly! I just thought we could – you know. Catch up."

She puts her hand on his thigh; Hook keeps his eye on the road.

"And where do we go from there?"

Her hand moves up his thigh and strokes him through his trousers.

"Where do you want to go from there?"

Hook smiles, stiffening. "Away from all this. I've had enough. I want some peace and quiet."

"Me too, darling. What's this?"

They're on a long bridge over a river, the sun setting behind them. Susan holds up something she found in his pocket: a crenulated bottle top.

"Nothing. Maybe we should get married, what do you say?"

Susan looks surprised. "That sounds – fab! Yes, lets!"

"A real white wedding, all the works. Out in the country. Lots of flowers."

"Wonderful, darling. Fuck!"

Susan bites her lip and pores over her mobile.

"We could have lilies," says Hook.

"Yes, fabulous, darling."

She points nervously at the LED on the dashboard. "Is that clock right?"

"About a minute fast. Almost eight, my darling."

Hook puts his foot down to create some space. They're almost at the middle of the bridge.

He clicks his fingers, starts to laugh. "Oh – I just remembered, we can't have lilies."

"Lilies? Why not?"

"Because," says Hook, putting his foot down to clear more space from the cars behind, "lilies are for funerals."

Ulrike squints in the rearview mirror, then back at Hook. Then she turns again and looks in the back of the van – she's been looking so hard at the faraway stadium she hasn't seen what was right under her pretty nose. Pulling the blanket aside and seeing what's underneath she gives a little moan of horror. As he accelerates Hook leans over and places an arm hard around her shaking shoulders, vowing never to let her go again.

"*Please*," sobs Ulrike, "please. I'm carrying your baby..."

Hook's foot hovers between the brake and accelerator. Then he reminds himself that for the first time in his life he's doing something good, something that will make a difference. They're driving into the night; the sky shows no signs of breaking, no sign of rain or storms on the horizon. The dashboard display has been flashing 7:59 for longer than he can remember. He has 13,610 turns on the clock: more than enough. Ulrike's shoulders shake beneath his arm.

Softly, with a lump in his throat, Hook begins to sing:

"*Every night when I go out*
Monkey's on the table
Take a stick and knock it off
Pop –"

Bid to bomb ceremony fails
Terrorists killed when bomb explodes
By staff reporter Mike Mullen

An attempt by a terrorist cell to bomb the service for peace at the Olympic Stadium failed when the bomb went off prematurely last night.

The bombers were driving a van laden with explosives when it exploded. It is thought they were planning to detonate the device beneath the main stand, causing hundreds of casualties.

Although some witnesses reported that the van was driving away from the stadium, police have no doubt they were intent on causing mayhem. The two fanatics, believed to be a male and female, died instantly. There were no other casualties but the bridge remains closed to traffic.

Meanwhile, the ceremony at the Olympic stadium went ahead as planned. Thanks to a last-minute request by Home Secretary Clyde Collins the so-called 'service of peace' was extended to atheists.

Additional reporting: Farzana Rahman.

Book Group Questions

At Legend Press, we only publish books that are well worth talking about, that will generatate conversation, as well as being written by some of the world's top writers and being fantastic reads. After all, the reactions and conversations they generate are what makes books so unique, thought-provoking and so amazing.

A vital part of book conversations are book groups and to be of assistance we've listed a few questions in no particular order that may be worth considering. Whether you take them into account or not, we expect this book to generate debate and please feel free to send us any comments:

info@legend-paperbooks.co.uk

1. How do you feel towards the main protagonist, Hook, and how do your feelings change through the book?

2. How do you feel about the other characters in the novel and how do these perceptions change?

3. What do you believe are the main issues raised in the book and do you feel there is any resolution and/or development suggested of these issues as the novel progresses?

4. *Out of Office* features frank discussion of a number of taboo issues. How do you feel these hot topics were handled in the novel?

5. How do react to the vision of London and its description; how does it vary from your current/future perception of the city?

6. Mark Piggott wrote a national feature tackling the idea that very few modern authors are writing about the here and now, actually portraying contemporary life for the majority. Do you feel this novel achieves this?

7. *Out of Office* is fast-paced, action packed and full of twists and turns, but is also written with a strong literary voice by an author with a great deal to say. Where would you place the novel's genre?

8. Hook walks out of his job and willingly throws himself into freefall and out of the society that restrains him. Could you relate to this and what is your overall reaction?

9. The novel is packed with powerful images. Are there any that stood out to you and how did you feel about the overall style?

10. The novel takes a major twist at the end. Did you feel it was an effective end and one that provided resolution? How did you feel immediately after you finished *Out of Office?*

I hope you enjoyed this fantastic novel. Please come and visit us to see more of Mark Piggott's work and also other amazing books at Legend Press: **www.legendpress.co.uk**

About the author

Author of *Fire Horses*, Mark Piggott has had short stories and poems published in anthologies, magazines and websites including *Pulp Books*, *Aesthetica* and *3AM*, satirical websites and various blogs; and as a journalist has had dozens of features published in the *Times*, *Guardian*, *Telegraph*, *Independent*, and many more.

www.markpiggott.com

Make your mark by choosing independents

Out of Office
Mark Piggott

Legend Press
Independent Book Publisher
www.legendpress.co.uk